THE LAST DRAGON

SILVANA DE MARI

Translated from the Italian by
SHAUN WHITESIDE

MIRAMAX BOOKS

HYPERION BOOKS FOR CHILDREN

NEW YORK

For my father, who showed me the way,
even if he had lost his

For information address Hyperion Books for Children,

114 Fifth Avenue, New York, NY 10011-5690.

Originally published in Italy by Salani. Reprinted by permission.

First United States edition, 2006

3 5 7 9 10 8 6 4 2

Designed by Christine Kettner

Printed in the United States of America

Library of Congress Cataloging-in-Publication Data on file.

ISBN 0-7868-3636-9

This book is set in 12.5-point Deepdene.

Reinforced binding

Visit www.hyperionbooksforchildren.com

PART ONE

CHAPTER ONE

HE RAIN had been falling for days. The mud came up to his ankles. If it didn't stop raining, even the frogs would drown in this world that was now one enormous bog.

The little elf would certainly die if he didn't find a dry place to stay very soon. The world was cold. His grandmother's fireside had been a warm place. But that was a long time ago. The elf's heart ached with longing.

His grandmother said that if you dreamed hard enough, things came true. But his grandmother couldn't dream anymore. One day his mother had gone to the place from which you didn't come back, and from then on his grandmother hadn't been able to dream at all. And he was too little to dream. Or perhaps he wasn't.

The little elf shut his eyes for a few seconds and dreamed as hard as he could. He felt a sensation of dryness on his skin, the feeling of a blazing fire. He felt his feet warming up. He felt as though he'd had something to eat.

The little elf opened his eyes again. His feet felt even colder than before, and his stomach seemed even emptier. He hadn't dreamed hard enough.

He straightened his soaking cap on his soaking hair. He was wearing the yellow cap that elves wear. His coarse, woven yellow cape was heavy and rough, and it didn't keep anything out. More water ran down his neck and began trickling beneath his jacket to his trousers. All his clothes were yellow, rough, soaking, dirty, and worn.

One day he would have clothes soft as sparrows' wings and warm as duck down, the color of dawn, the color of the sea.

One day he would have dry feet.

One day the shadows would lift, the frost would retreat.

The sun would come back.

The stars would shine again.

One day.

The dream of food filled his thoughts once more. He imagined the flatbreads his grandmother had made, and again his heart ached from longing. His grandmother had made flatbreads only once in the little elf's life. It had been at the last feast of the new moon, when even the elves had been given half a sack of flour, when the moon had still shone.

Shading his eyes with one hand, the little elf tried to peer out beyond the rain. The light was fading. Soon it would be dark. He would have to find a place to stay before nightfall. A place to stay and something to eat. Another night sleeping in the mud, on an empty stomach, and he wouldn't make it through till morning.

His big eyes narrowed with the strain, and his gaze wandered among the gray shades of the trees. Then he closed in on a darker shadow, just visible in the distance. His heart leaped. Hope was reborn. He hurried as fast as he could, his tired legs sinking up to the knees, his eyes fixed on the shadow. For a moment, as the rain grew heavier, he was afraid it might be nothing but a darker patch of trees. Then he began to make out the roof and the walls. Submerged among the trees, choked by climbing plants, was a tiny building made of wood and stone.

It must have been a shepherd's shelter, or a charcoal burner's.

Grandmother was right. If you dream hard enough, for long enough, if you allow faith to fill you up, your hopes will become reality.

Once again the elf dreamed of a warming fire. Thoughts of smoke, heat, and the scent of pine resin filled his head and warmed him up for a few seconds. But the furious barking of a dog startled him awake, and he looked around. He had been mistaken. This was no dream. The smoke, the heat, and the smell of pinecones were really there. He had come close to a fire that belonged to some humans.

Daydreams can kill.

The barking of the dog exploded in his ears. The little elf started to run. He might be able to make it. Otherwise the humans would catch him, and a cold, hungry, peaceful death would become an impossible dream. One of his feet caught on a tree root, and he fell face-first into the mud. The dog was on top of him. It was over.

The little elf couldn't even breathe.

Moments passed.

The dog's breath was on his neck, it was holding him down, but its teeth still hadn't sunk into any part of him.

"Leave him," said a stern human voice.

The dog backed away. The little elf started breathing again. He looked up. The human was extremely tall. On its head it had yellowish hair coiled like a rope. It had no hair on its face. And yet his grandmother had been categorical about that. Humans have hair on their faces. It's called a beard. It's one of the many things that distinguish them from elves. The little elf concentrated, trying to remember, then it came to him.

"You must be a female man," he concluded trium-phantly.

"The word is *woman*, fool," said the human.

"Oh, sorry, sorry, woman-fool, I be more careful, I call right name, woman-fool," said the little elf eagerly. The lan-guage of the humans was a problem. He wasn't terribly good at it, and they were always so touchy, and touchiness made people fierce. On that point, too, his grandmother had been categorical.

"Boy, do you want to come to a bad end?" the human threatened.

The little elf was still puzzled. According to his grandmother, the absolute lack of any kind of logic, more concisely summed up by the term "stupidity," was the fundamental characteristic that differentiated the human from the elfish race; but, despite his grandmother's warnings, the stupidity of the question was so profound that he felt he had lost his bearings.

"No, I don't want, woman-fool," the little elf assured her. "I don't want come to bad end. That not on my agenda," he insisted.

"If you say 'fool' once more, I'm going to set the dog on you. It's an insult," the woman explained, exasperated.

"Oh, now I understand," lied the little elf, desperately trying to grasp the meaning of her words. Why had the human wanted to be insulted?

"Are you really an elf?"

The little elf nodded. Better to say as little as possible. He glanced anxiously at the dog, which snarled back at him.

"I don't like elves," said the human.

The little elf nodded again. Fear merged with cold. He started to shiver. No human liked elves. His grandmother had always said so.

"What do you want? Why are you here?" asked the woman.

"Cold." The little elf's voice was breaking. He started to tremble. "The shack . . ." His voice broke again.

"Don't try pretending that you're dying of cold. You're an elf, aren't you? You've got your powers. Elves don't suffer from cold or hunger. They can stop feeling cold or hunger whenever they want to."

The little elf took a long time to grasp what she meant, and then it sank in.

"Really?" he asked brightly. "I really can do those things? So how I do them?"

"How should I know?" snapped the woman. "You're the elf, not me. We wretched humans, stupid as we are, we're the ones who are made to suffer cold and hunger." The human's voice had developed an unpleasant edge.

Fear coursed through the little elf; it rose into his throat, dry as a desert, and up to his face. He started to cry, weeping without tears, sobbing in terror.

"What on earth have I done wrong?" the woman wondered aloud. The little elf went on crying. It was a heartrending sound that pierced the soul. It contained all the grief in the world.

"You're a child, aren't you?" she asked.

"Born lately," confirmed the little elf. "Your human lordship," he added, after searching for a phrase that would not sound offensive.

"Do you have any powers?" asked the woman. "Tell me the truth."

The elf went on looking at her. Nothing the woman said made any sense. "Powers?" he asked.

"All those things you can do."

"Oh, that. Well, there are many things, let me see. Breathe, walk, see. I also can run, talk . . . eat when something to eat. . . ." The little elf's tone became wistful.

The woman sat down in the doorway of the shack. She lowered her head and sat there for a moment. Then she drew herself up.

"I couldn't live with myself if I left you out here. You can come in. You can sit by the fire."

The little elf's eyes filled with horror, and he took a step backward.

"Please, your human lordship, no . . ."

"What's wrong with you now?"

"Not the fire. I been good. Please, your human lordship, don't eat me."

"Eat you? What are you talking about?"

"With rosemary, I think. My grandmother tell me that, when she is alive. If you not good, then human come and eat you with rosemary."

"Your grandmother told you that? Very nice!"

The little elf grew excited at the word "nice." He knew that one. He felt he was on safer ground now. His face brightened and he smiled.

"Yes, it's true, that's right. Grandmother say, 'Humans also cannibals, that the only nice thing you can say about them.'"

He had got it right this time. He had managed to say the right thing. The human didn't get angry. She looked at him for a long time, and then she started to laugh.

"I've got enough to eat for this evening," the woman reassured him. "You can come in."

The little elf slowly dragged himself inside. If he'd stayed outside, the cold would be the death of him. What did he have to lose?

A fire of pinecones blazed in the grate, giving off a smell of resin. For the first time in days he found himself in a dry place. On the fire was a real corncob, roasting away. The little elf stared at it as though in a trance.

Then the miracle happened.

The human took out a knife, and rather than using it to skin him and chop him up, she cut the corncob in two and handed the elf a piece.

The little elf still had some doubts about the human. Perhaps it wasn't as bad as all that, but then again, she might just be fattening him up until she got ahold of some rosemary. But he ate the corn anyway. He ate it kernel by kernel, making it last as long as possible.

Night had fallen by the time he finished. He nibbled at the husk as well, then wrapped himself up in his rough, damp cape and went to sleep, curled up like a baby dormouse next to the dancing flames.

CHAPTER TWO

DAWN WAS gray, as dawns always are. Thin strips of light filtered in between the logs of the shack, and through the coils of smoke that still rose from the embers of the fire.

The little elf awoke with a curious sensation. For a moment he didn't understand it, and then it came to him: he wasn't cold, he wasn't starving, and his feet weren't wet.

Life *could* be wonderful.

And the human hadn't eaten him yet, either.

The little elf cheerfully got up. He was wrapped in a shawl made of real wool. It was coarse, grayish wool, more holes than wool, really, but wool nonetheless. The human had covered him up. That was why he wasn't cold. He wondered why the human had bothered. Perhaps if he caught a cold he wouldn't be as good to eat.

The human was already awake. She was tinkering with the embers, using a kind of tiny pole to put some of them into a perforated iron ball that held straw and a big piece of seasoned wood.

The entire operation struck the little elf as hugely idiotic, which is to say, exquisitely human.

He said nothing, but just handed back the shawl.

"You can keep it," the human muttered. "You were shivering last night."

The human hung the ball of smoking iron on a pole, covered it with treated leather, and slung it over her shoulder.

"I'm going to the county of Daligar," she said curtly. "It's up in the hills, on the high plain. They say that the water drains down from the plain, and that there are still fields and cultivated land up there."

Silence. The little elf was pondering the meaning of this information. Perhaps it was a form of politeness; maybe he was supposed to reply by saying where he was going.

A shame, then, that he wasn't going anywhere. All he was doing was leaving the place where he had been before, which simply no longer existed, or rather, it did still exist, but under about ten feet of water, mud, and rotten leaves.

"What is it? Cat got your tongue?" the human asked.

"No cats here, Excellency," said the little elf. He had finally managed to remember the respectful term of address for humans. "These things are called dogs, Excellency . . . and if he eat my tongue, now there would be blood all over the . . ." he started explaining, patiently and politely, but the human interrupted him.

"Fine, fine. Forget it."

The human looked at him and gave a longer breath than usual, shaking her head. "Maybe the intelligence and the magic arrive later on. Like wisdom teeth."

"Like what, Your Highness?" asked the little elf, alarmed by the word "teeth." If only he could have been sure which polite address was the correct one!

"These teeth here at the back, the ones that come after all the others."

The human showed him. It was a terrible idea. The little elf started crying again.

"You said you not eating me, Your Majesty," he sobbed.

The human gave that long breath again. "You're right, I did say that," she replied. "So there's nothing to be done, I can't eat you now."

She snapped her fingers at the dog and set off for the door. The little elf felt sad. Crazy and unpredictable though she might have been, the human was at least someone. It was better than being alone. The little elf's heart tightened, and he felt sadness filling everything up, as darkness does when night falls.

The door was big and made of ill-fitting, badly connected pinewood planks, but it had sound bronze hinges.

"This shack must have belonged to some hunters, or furriers," said the human. "Not simple charcoal burners."

The dog ran off happily into the rain.

Meanwhile the human remained in the doorway, studying the shack. She raised her eyes to the stone tiles, which were in good condition, and studied the pieces of wood jammed in among the stones in the lower part to keep the drafts out. They were very dry and free of mold, and were splintered around the edges.

"This shack hasn't been abandoned," commented the human. "The owners could come back at any moment."

The little elf began to grasp the meaning of her words. "Do they eat elves?"

"They certainly don't like them. If I were you I wouldn't stick around to ask them," said the human.

The little elf darted outside even faster than the dog.

As they set off, the human asked, "Do you have a name?"

"Yes," the little elf said stoutly.

The human snorted. "And what would that name be?"

Grandmother's lessons in human grammar started to return to him. "No, not *would be*. 'Would be' is for uncertain things, and a name is a certain thing. So you must ask not what it would be, Excellency, but what it be. . . ."

"And what is that name?" yelled the woman, making the little elf start. "Fine, fine, I won't shout anymore, I promise. Don't start crying again. I won't shout, and I won't eat you. What's your name?"

"Yorshkrunsquarkljolnerstrink."

"Can you repeat that?" asked the human.

"Yes, of course I can," confirmed the little elf smugly.

The human sighed. "Repeat," she said.

"Yorshkrunsquarkljolnerstrink."

"And do you have a short form of that?"

"I certainly do."

A pause, and the human breathed in that funny way again. Conversation with them really was torture: Grandma had said so.

"And what is that short form?"

"Yorshkrunsquarkljolnerstri."

"Of course," said the human, who suddenly seemed awfully tired. "I'll call you Yorsh," she concluded. "I must have done something terrible in an earlier life, and I'm paying for it now," she muttered.

At least that meant something, the little elf thought. That was why the human was so mad and stupid: it had taken her eight questions just to find out his name.

"My name's Sajra," said the woman.

Yorsh hurried after her, happy with this introduction.

"What's the dog's name?" he asked.

"It hasn't got a name," the woman replied. "It's called 'dog' and that's that. It's a short sound and I didn't have to look very far to find it."

It struck the little elf as impossibly sad that a creature should remain unnamed, identified only by a common noun, like a tree or a chair. But he had experienced the woman's unpredictable rage, so he decided to keep his observations to himself.

Anyway, he wouldn't leave the creature without a name. He would give it a name in his head. But he would have to be careful: you don't just choose names at random. A name is a name. A major responsibility.

The rain went on falling.

They made slow progress because of the mud.

The woman's legs were longer than his. Yorshkruns-quarkljolnerstrink had to run to keep up with her, and he was terribly tired. By now he was hardly afraid of the dog at all, and a couple of times he had even dared to touch it, to lean his body against it. The dog had not objected.

"You have another them things with yellow kernels?" the little elf asked discreetly.

"I have one more corncob, but I was planning on saving it for tonight."

"If we dying in the mud before tonight, who eat the corncob?"

"Are you hungry now?"

"Yes, I hung . . . no, not hungry now."

"Well done, you learn fast. So learn this. If we eat the corncob now, then tonight we'll have nothing, and that would be terrible."

"Perhaps the world come to an end before tonight. Perhaps we come to an end before tonight."

"Shut up and walk. Use your breath to keep moving."

"I managed, no, I managing . . . mmmh, no I *manage* to do both together, walk and talk about the corncob. In fact, less tiring if we talk."

"Shut up," said the woman. Her tone had changed.

"But—"

"Shut up," hissed the woman. She knelt by the little elf

to make herself less tall, less visible. The dog snarled. The woman's eyes explored the cane thickets and the bogs surrounding the path.

"Fine if we eat tonight. You not get angry—"

"Run," yelled the woman. She got to her feet, took the little elf by the arm, and ran.

"Come on," she shouted to the dog, who started running along with them. The little elf fell, got back to his feet, then fell again. He started crying.

"Not get angry, not get angry, we eat tonight!"

"They're following us," explained the woman, still running, with the last breath left in her. "You see that hill down there? My legs are longer than yours. I'll head down there and draw them after me. You slip into the brambles and bring the fire to safety. Take it. I'll see you on the hill."

The woman gave him the stick with the metal ball and ran for it, breaking branches and uttering hoarse cries. The little elf squatted in the brambles and stayed there, his heart racing.

He wondered who was following them. Maybe the owners of the shack where they had spent the night. Maybe they had taken offense at the intrusion. Maybe they had found some rosemary, and needed an elf to go with it.

Fear seized him.

His eyes swept the cane thickets beneath the light rain, but he couldn't see anyone.

The fear started to fade slowly away, and turned into sadness.

Again he was alone. Again, all the way to the horizon, there was no one but him.

Yorsh thought once more of his grandmother, holding him in her arms as chestnuts boiled in the pot.

Sadness filled the whole of his being, and started to make way for despair.

He thought once again of the human woman. She terrified him, and yet she had given him the corncob, and that was something. Better than being all on his own again, like this. Just him, on his own, all the way to the horizon. He started crying again, very gently, without making a sound, just inside his head, as the rain fell softly around him.

He thought that if he ever saw the dog again, he would call him "The one who breathes close by," but the woman had said that a dog needs a short name, and that wasn't one of those.

CHAPTER THREE

B Y THE TIME the woman reached the hill, the light was fading.

Yorsh's heart swelled as soon as he spotted her.

Breathless, the woman dropped into the mud. The dog was with her.

"It was a hunter," she said, panting. "With a bow. I managed to give him the slip."

"Ohhhhhhhhh," said the little one, genuinely impressed. "And what will he do with a slip?"

"No," the exasperated woman explained, "it just means I left him behind."

"Ahhhhhhh! I understand," lied the elf. "What's a bow?" he asked.

The dog started barking.

"Call off your dog," said a voice.

Suddenly, the little elf understood what a bow was: a curved piece of wood with a piece of string attached to it so tightly that it could fire an iron-tipped stick at the woman's heart.

The hunter was even taller than the woman, with dark hair that fell all over the place, above and around his face and—yes—he did have a beard. His clothes looked warm, warmer than clothes made of cloth, and from his belt there hung an impressive collection of daggers and a hatchet. He had appeared from behind the little elf. While the woman thought she had given him the slip, he had crept around the wood from the back.

He and the woman stood staring at one another, and then the woman whistled to the dog.

The hunter lowered his bow. "I just want a bit of fire. Mine's gone out. I just want to relight my fuse. I saw you had some."

The woman studied him. "Nothing else?"

"Nothing else."

Another long look passed between them, and then the woman nodded.

"Give him the fire," she said. "Hey, I'm talking to you. Give him the fire. Where have you put it?"

"I hid it over there," the little elf said.

"Really?" said the woman. "Okay, good idea. Where exactly did you hide it?"

"There, in the pond, under the water, so that no one can see it," the elf said proudly.

It was so nice to win approval. He remembered the times when his grandmother held him in her arms and told him he was the best little elf in the world. He was filled with the happiness you felt when the spring wind blew away the clouds, when spring had still existed.

He trotted cheerfully down the hill toward the pond. The rain had stopped. A pale strip of blue appeared between the clouds and was mirrored in the water, where the little one bent down to pull out the stick with its iron ball. Little streams of water trickled out of it.

The man and the woman had followed him, watching him in silence. The woman sat down on a tree trunk and put her head in her hands.

"You've put it out," she said in a strangled voice.

"Yes, of course, it makes it easier to hide!" He gestured with his arm to indicate the act of hiding something, and the shawl fell from him, revealing his yellow clothes.

"He's an elf," said the hunter in astonishment.

"Yes, that's right, he's an elf," the woman confirmed in a toneless voice.

"Are you trying to make life difficult for yourself?" asked the man.

"No, that happens all of its own accord," the woman replied.

"Has he got powers?"

"No, he's just a child."

"One born lately," the little one agreed.

The man had no intention of giving up. He turned back to the little elf. "Do you know how to light a fire?"

"Yeeeesss, I think so. I've never done it, but everyone knows how to light a fire."

The woman raised her head and looked at him, aghast.

"Then light it," the hunter said.

The little elf put his hand to the dry iron ball that the hunter had taken from his knapsack. He closed his eyes. The image of fire filled his mind, warmed his nostrils, its heat glowed in his memory.

When he opened his eyes again, fire was flickering inside the ball.

The woman was breathless. "You can light a fire without tinder?"

"Yeeeeeeessss."

"Why didn't you tell me?"

"You hadn't asked me."

"I asked you if you had powers!"

"Yes. I replied: big powers—breathing, eating, being alive. Fire-lighting is a little power. You have to raise the temperature and fire is born. Everyone knowing how to do that."

"I don't," said the woman.

"Noooo?" The little one was flabbergasted. "That's impossible. Everyone knowing . . ."

"And if we know how to light a fire, why do we carry tinder around with us?"

"Because you're humans," the little one explained serenely. "You're stupid."

"Are you being punished for something you did in another life, or do you have some other reason for dragging an elf around with you?" The man seemed to be growing more and more perplexed. "Despite the joy of your company, I'll leave the two of you at the first village we come to. People don't like it when you light fires with your thoughts."

"Why not? It's easier than carrying a ball full of fire."

"You could burn a person or a house. A house with a person in it, or two, or fifteen."

The idea was so appalling that the little elf closed his eyes and groaned with pain. Inside his head he could see the burned bodies, and smell the charred flesh. He shuddered with horror, then began to cry. Not the usual string of whimpers and squeals, but a long howl, full of high-pitched groans and heartrending wails.

"Make him stop!" shouted the man. "Make him stop. It's unbearable!"

"See what you've done?" the woman snapped back. "Please, little one, everything's fine, nothing has happened. It's just a figure of speech."

"Figuring speech!" The little one was indignant. And yet it worked. He stopped crying. "Figuring speech. How dare you, how can you, how can you dare to say something with all that pain in it just for figuring speech!" He started crying again.

The man sat down on a tree trunk, taking those long breaths, just like the woman. The sky opened up. The first stars they had seen in weeks began to appear.

"I've got a rabbit," said the man. "I caught it this morning. You've given me the fire, I've got a rabbit, and it's stopped raining. So let's pitch camp and eat something. My name is Monser."

Silence fell for a moment, just a short moment.

"Sajra," said the woman.

The little elf stopped wailing. "Do robbets have little kernels like corncobs?" Yorsh inquired quickly, brightening at the word "eat."

The man started laughing.

"No," he said, "rabbits have beautiful fur, so you can keep your feet warm afterward, look!" He opened his bag so that the little elf could take a look.

Yorsh put his hands on the rim of the bag and cheer-fully peered inside. The idea of something that would warm his stomach and his feet as well was simply heaven. Not even his grandmother, who knew everything, had ever men-tioned such a treasure. So perhaps humans weren't so . . . A long scream pierced the moors.

A long, terrible scream, filled with all the grief in the world.

"It's a corpse," cried the little elf. "Look. He's been hit with the pointed stick. And now he's dead. Are you going to eat a corpse?"

"Why, elves eat rabbits alive?" The man was exasperated.

"Elves never eat anything that has thought, that has run, that has been hungry and has feared death. Grand-mother said that humans eat what's been alive. With rosemary. Is there any rosemary here? I don't want to be eaten." And the little elf plunged once again into his moan-ing, heartrending wail.

The woman put her head in her hands.

"Exactly what dreadful thing did you do in that former life of yours? Did you sell your mother?" asked the man.

"I think it's better if you go. Thanks for the offer of the rabbit. It doesn't matter. You've got fire. So, see you."

"You're not going to give up a piece of rabbit for *him*?"

"I know, it's madness, but I can't bear to hear him crying. Please, go."

"I can't," said the man uncertainly.

"Why?"

"I can't abandon a young woman in the moors. It would be dangerous enough if you were on your own, let alone with him tagging after you!"

"Thank you, noble sir, I've managed this far on my own. I don't need any help. Take your—"

"Hang on, what's he doing?"

The woman turned to look. The little elf had picked up the rabbit and was stroking it gently. His fingers slowed where the fur was drenched in blood. His eyes were closed and he seemed to be dreaming. He had stopped crying.

"What on earth are you doing?" the hunter asked.

"I'm thinking," the little elf replied.

"Thinking? What about?"

"About him, about the robbet."

"*Rabbit*." The hunter corrected.

"Rabbit. I'm thinking about how he breathed. How he ran. He . . . yes, he felt smells tickling his nose. The last thing he smelled was wet leaves and mushrooms. He didn't smell the hunter. There was a smell of wet grass and mushrooms, yes, a good smell. I'm thinking about how he breathed . . . the blood flowing inside him. . . ."

The rabbit quivered, opened its eyes and held them open with terror for a few quick intakes of breath, then shook itself, leaped to the ground, and started running. It avoided the hunter's feet, hurtled between the dog's paws, leaped over the tree trunk the woman was sitting on, and then, after one final swerve, disappeared forever into the cane thicket.

The little elf wondered if "Rabbit" might be a good name for the dog. Perhaps not. They were a bit similar, but the shapes of their tails were completely different.

The man and the woman stood for a long time staring at the spot where the rabbit's white tail had disappeared. The little elf looked exhausted. He crouched trembling on the ground, then slowly began to get his strength back. The dog came and lay next to him, and the elf hugged it.

It was now completely dark, except for the stars that began to shine on the pond.

"Apart from your mother, did you sell some of your little brothers?" the man inquired.

Rather than replying, the woman turned to the elf.

"Can you do that with people, too?"

"Humans, elves, or trolls? Certainly not. You can only do it with little creatures that don't have much in their heads: the smell of water, the color of the sky. What's really easy is flies, mosquitoes, and gnats; you just have to touch them and dream of flying for a moment, and they start buzzing again."

"Really?" said the man. "How wonderful! In the summer, someone who can save mosquitoes is valuable company. Someone who can revive mosquitoes and bring my dinner back to life, the one time I had any. You're a dream come true. How did I manage to live without you?"

"Can you do anything else?" asked the woman. "Can you multiply corncobs? We've got one. Can you turn it into three? Or five?"

They really were stupid. "Of course not; you can't multiply matter."

"And what about bringing a dead rabbit back to life?" the woman asked.

"That you can do. A creature dies when it loses its energy. Its strength. Fire goes out too, when it loses its strength. Bringing a creature back to life is like lighting a fire—just a little transfer of energy, from inside my head to outside my head."

The hunter turned toward the woman. "Come away," he said. "Come away, it's dangerous. Leave him here and come away."

"I can't. He's . . . well, yes, he's a child."

"A pup," corrected the man.

"One born lately," the little elf clarified.

There was a silence. The woman shook her head.

"Right then, ladies and gentlemen," the man said, "it's been a real pleasure to meet you. I would even say it's been genuinely fun. I wouldn't like all this happiness to hurt me, so I'm setting off again on my way as a horrible hunter who squashes mosquitoes, lives by eating rabbits, and prospers by selling their skins. And should our paths ever cross again, I hope I'll have time to run away before you see me."

The little elf seemed interested in this discovery.

"Oh, really? Don't humans like being happy? So that's why you spend so much time trying to make yourselves miserable! Not just because you're stupid!"

"No," the hunter replied. "Human beings as a rule try to be happy. What I said is called 'irony.' I'm going because your company prevents me from being happy, or even from eating my rabbit. But rather than saying one thing, I say its opposite. Humans sometimes do that. Do you understand?"

"Yes, of course," the little elf lied. They really were stupid. Crazy and stupid. Hopeless.

"Wait," said the woman. "I'll give you my corncob. It was our fault that you lost your rabbit." She pulled the last corncob out of her knapsack and held it out. The little one watched the yellow kernels changing ownership. His eyes lost their sparkle, and sadness swept across his face, but he didn't dare breathe.

"Is that the only one you've got?"

"Yes," the woman replied. She too looked as though she had just buried her mother. Her mother and her little brothers.

The hunter thought for a moment, then slung his quiver and bow over his shoulder and sat down on the only flat rock on the hill.

"Well, the rabbit's gone. I'll stay here tonight, and we'll share it."

The sky clouded over, but the rain didn't start up again.

They pitched camp on a dry rock. The corncob roasted. The hunter cut it into three and they ate it slowly, one kernel at a time, and then the little elf nodded off and slept like a log. For a few moments, before he fell asleep, he thought of a name for the dog. "He who runs in the wind" seemed nice, but he knew that it was a little too long to be acceptable.

Once sleep had enveloped the little elf, the hunter covered him with his fur jacket to keep him warm. He also pulled the elf's jerkin up over his head: over his eyes, his ears, and his nose. Then he took a smaller knapsack out from beneath his quiver, and from it he pulled a quail. He plucked it in furtive silence. The woman helped him as best she could. They put the bird on the fire, downwind from the little elf, and when it was cooked, or at least not too raw to be edible, they finally ate it. This time they ate it in silence and in a hurry, like two thieves, always glancing at the bundle that consisted of the little sleeping elf. When they finished, they gave the bones to the dog, who made them disappear into his stomach, and gathered up all the feathers. Then the hunter crept off to dig a little hole and hide them.

Then, at last, they all fell asleep.

CHAPTER FOUR

AYBREAK WAS a little less leaden than usual. Once again it wasn't raining, and the occasional thin strip of pale blue appeared in the sky.

The man got up first. He stretched and took a deep breath. Wet leaves and mushrooms. A good smell. He looked at the woman and the little elf as they slept. He gathered his things together, slung them over his shoulder along with the stick carrying the tinder, recovered the fur jerkin that he had wrapped around the little elf, and went on his way. As he was climbing down the hill, he turned and looked at them again, the woman and the little elf, two bundles around the remains of the fire. The little elf was shivering with cold. You could see that even from so far away. The man turned back and put the jerkin around the little one again, and then poked the fire. Finally he went on his way. Halfway down the hill he turned once more and looked at the two bundles by the fire. He walked another half mile, then turned again. The light of the flames melted into the light of the rising sun, which had appeared for a few minutes on the horizon for the first time in months. Even at that distance, the woman and the little elf were still visible. The man stopped and looked at them for a long time, then slowly, one step after another, he turned back.

He sat down on a rock and waited.

The first to wake was the little elf.

A long scream swept across the moor. Full of all the grief in the world.

The little elf screamed for a long time about the horrible blanket made from the skin of corpses. The scream continued, and then scattered among other screams that mingled with the echo of their predecessors, while the sun appeared, then disappeared, then reappeared until it started raining again.

Finally, they all set off together. Utterly disconsolate, the little elf failed to see a tree root, and tripped over it, whimpering quietly until midday. At that point, the hunter threatened to run him through like a kebab if he didn't shut up, prompting a series of terrified wails that persisted until the evening.

Darkness was beginning to fall when the little elf realized that he was unusually hungry. His hunger came from deep within his belly and reached his head via his cold feet and also, somehow, his freezing ears. He described to the others, in great detail, the feeling he had inside, but could not establish whether it was simply a void, a lack, or a real negative entity.

He then moved on to speak of suffering in general, and the fact that it was unclear whether it, too, was a separate negative entity, or simply a lack of joy, or even, to be more precise, of well-being, because . . . No, the lack of well-being in general is a greater suffering than the simple lack of joy—which may, in fact, constitute a stable and almost normal situation. Generally speaking. And with regards to suffering, had he ever told them of the time he had got a splinter under the nail of his big toe on the right? Or was it on the left? No, it was on the right . . . Yes, now that he'd thought about it he was sure, the thorn had slipped in and his grandmother had pulled it out with a needle—A NEEDLE. And then there was that time he had fallen and cut himself on the elbow. The blood had come from inside him and spilled outside. A horrible, HORRIBLE thing. His left elbow. While the nail had been on his right toe, he was sure of that now. He'd even been left with a scar . . . on his elbow, he meant. Did they want to see it? The scar. Were they sure they didn't want to see it?

While the little elf was carrying on about the third time he had had a cold, and about the amount of mucus, not to mention its color and density, that had emerged from his nose at various moments in the development of the illness, they came upon some green bushes that both the woman and the hunter identified as rosemary. From that moment, for the first time since dawn, the little elf fell silent.

Then, as they passed through a grove of chestnuts and larches on the side of a hill, they turned a corner and Daligar suddenly appeared. It was at the bottom of a little valley, on the bank of a little river that was full to bursting. It looked like a place out of a fairy tale. There were lots of houses, all with lights in their windows, as though to illuminate the sharp and pointed wooden stakes that protected their external walls. All the windows were reflected in the dark water and, as though that were not enough, there were other fires as well, one on each of the towers that punctuated the city walls, where the archers stood. And on the walls there were yet more torches, one every six yards, corresponding to the pairs of halberdiers, and all those lights were reflected in the water of the moat. The drawbridge was raised, and it too, like the walls and the towers, was equipped with sharpened poles aimed outward, giving the whole city the appearance of a mammoth hedgehog.

The hunter stopped to contemplate the view.

"They don't look very friendly," he observed.

"Yes, they do!" the little elf objected. "People turn lights on when they're waiting for their friends. When there are as many candles as that, there are corncobs as well. It'll be lovely there. There will be tables with corncobs on them, and chestnuts too, and candles! And they might have plates as well. And even a real bed. And big fireplaces. Shall we go?"

"No, let's sleep now, and then tomorrow we'll slip away, giving the place a wide berth."

"Why?"

"Because of their friendly drawbridge, lit up like a birthday cake and closed like a seashell. Because it looks like the kind of place that's hard to get into and even harder to get out of," the hunter replied.

"What's a seashell?" the little elf asked.

"It's a thing in the sea, the water that lies beyond the mountains of darkness," the woman explained.

"Can you eat it?"

"Absolutely not!" the hunter explained, pretending to be outraged by such a suggestion. "Shells are alive, they are born, they die, they think, and they're even quite good at writing poems. Drawbridge and palisades aside, you're an elf and elves are only allowed to stay in 'Elf Camps,' and this isn't one of those. If we show up with you, we'll end up hanging from one of those big towers before dawn tomorrow. Don't even ask what would happen to you. People like you who show their faces outside of an Elf Camp come to horrible ends, you know? Really horrible."

They put down their bundles and set about collecting wood and pinecones for the fire. The hunter cut down two big branches and arranged them one against the other to form a tiny shack, a kind of lair, to give them some shelter during the night. The woman looked for moss, ferns, and dry grass to fill it, so that they would have something soft to sleep on.

"By the way," said the woman. "Elves have been put in

Elf Camps since the beginning of time. I've heard that the punishments, if one of you strays out of the camps, are no laughing matter. What are you doing traveling around?"

"The Elf Camp I was in was drowned," replied the little elf. The memory gripped his soul. His eyes faded with sadness, turning a vague grayish color into which the blue vanished. "Yes, it was all under water. And then my grandmother told me to go."

"Go where?"

"I don't know. Just go."

"But didn't your grandmother know how to do any magic? I don't know—heat up the water and make it disappear the way summer puddles do, something like that?"

"You can do that with a small water. A bowl of water. Not if there's enough water to drown the world. And Mama had gone to the place you don't come back from. For me, she was my mama, and for Grandmother she was her daughter. And Grandmother stopped doing magic. When you have too much sadness, the magic drowns in it, like people in water. If you think things hard enough, they become true. But if you have sadness inside, all that comes out of your head is sadness. You are sad, and you don't even light the fire. We had a fire because there was always some in the grate. If it had gone out, we would have been left without it, because Grandmother no longer had the strength and I was too small. Then the water came and even the fire in the grate went out, and then more water came and then more, and Grandmother said to me, 'Go away.'

"'Away where?' I asked. 'Anywhere but here,' she said.

'The water has flooded even the sentry posts. They won't stop you. Away. I'm too old, but you can do it. Go away and don't turn back.'

"And I went away. One step after another, in the mud and in the water. But I turned back. In the Elf Camps, the cabins have no doors and not even windows, just big open holes, so I could see Grandma sitting on her chair and the water rising, and she was there and the water was rising, and then all you could see was water."

The little elf started crying again, a series of faint, almost imperceptible moans.

The man and the woman lit the fire using the hunter's tinder. Then, searching in the undergrowth, they found a handful of sweet chestnuts. They roasted them and gave almost all of them to the little elf because, strangely, they both noticed that they weren't hungry.

The little elf ate them slowly, one crumb at a time, to make them last longer, and his sadness dissolved in the pale pulp of the chestnuts.

Before he went to sleep he thought of a name for the dog, which was the same color as the chestnuts. But the dog ran and barked, while the chestnuts stayed silently where they were and never came to lick your face and couldn't even wag their tails. "Chestnut" wouldn't work either. He would have to come up with something better. But before he could, he fell asleep near the fire, in between the man and the woman, wrapped up in his woolen shawl.

CHAPTER FIVE

HEY WERE WOKEN by the halberdiers.

The halberdiers were on patrol.

Not just the city of Daligar, but its surrounding area was forbidden to anyone who was not a resident, a relative of a resident, a guest of a resident, or in some way welcome to the residents, and they did not fall under any of those categories.

The patrol questioned them about the existence and quantity of such possessions that they might have about them, and in general, their means of support; and the reply the patrol received, that "they didn't have a damned thing except the clothes on their backs and three penny coins," made the halberdiers even less cordial than they were already.

The patrol made detailed inquiries into the state of their health. Did they have ticks, lice, fleas? Had they had contact with people suffering from cholera, leprosy, pestilence, scrofula, plague, vomiting attacks, dysentery, fever, spots of any kind, ulcers, rheumy eyes, intestinal worms? Because in that case they would be killed on the spot to avoid any form of contagion. And was their child in good health as well? Why was the mother holding him tightly in her arms in that shawl if he was well? Because he was tired, small, and tearful? No, small, tired, and tearful children were not forbidden.

Then they moved on to weaponry. Did they have any sharp weapons, anything that threw or fired projectiles, anything incendiary, bruising, penetrating, cutting, burning, any weapons that could be used for hunting, for hand-to-hand combat, for battle on horseback, on muleback, on all fours, for duels, for gang warfare, trench warfare, siege, counter-siege, target-shooting, or hobbies? Yeeeesss? A bow, a dagger, a hatchet, a little billhook, a knife for cutting bread. All confiscated. And the two iron balls for carrying fire: incendiary weapon.

They had been the ones who had cut two whole branches, property of the county of Daligar, and uprooted four fern plants to have a shelter? That fell under the definition of "crimes against the state," for which there were appropriate proceedings. Would they mind keeping the dog under control while it was put in a cage? All kinds of animals, whether domestic or wild, were prohibited, and their animal fell under both categories.

They entered Daligar under the escort of the halberdiers. It was the strangest and most incredible place the little elf had ever seen. There were humans everywhere: big, small, male, female, armed, unarmed, with clothes of every imaginable color.

There were voices. Everybody seemed to be selling everything. Loaves of bread, corncobs, big apples, cooking pots, firewood, wood for making chairs. There were funny birds everywhere, walking among the people. They were strange birds, big and fat, with wings too small to fly, and with a strange cry in which they constantly repeated the sound *coco*.

The halberdiers escorted them to the middle of the square, where there was a kind of baldachin covered by a series of red and gold fabrics, which looked strangely like a gigantic cradle, and in it was a man all wrapped up in a long, embroidered white garment that even covered his head, giving him the appearance of an enormous newborn baby.

The enormous baby announced that he went by the curious name of JUDGEADMINISTRATOROFDALIGARANDSURROUNDINGDISTRICT, which wasn't exactly a pretty name like Yorshkrunsquarkljolnerstrink, but a nice name nonetheless.

The JUDGEADMINISTRATOROFDALIGARANDSURROUNDINGDISTRICT asked their names, ages, jobs or skills, and more important, what they had come to do in Daligar without being residents, relations of residents, guests of residents, or at least welcomed by the same.

The hunter replied that he didn't care at all about Daligar and its residents, relations of residents, guests of residents, and sympathizers, or whatever they were, and that all they wanted was to leave Daligar and its neighboring district as soon as possible and get back on the road.

The JUDGEADMINISTRATOROFDALIGARANDSURROUNDINGDISTRICT observed that if they did not love Daligar, its neighboring district, and its residents, including relatives, guests, and sympathizers, they need only have stayed at home, wherever such a place might have been located, so as to spare the halberdiers the trouble of having to discover, interrogate, and arrest them, and him, the JUDGEADMINISTRATOROFDALIGARANDSURROUNDINGDISTRICT, the inconvenience of meeting, judging, sentencing, and expelling them, not to mention the crime against the state, the chopping down of two whole tree branches, and the uprooting of four fern plants, which they had been so barbaric as to inflict upon the community.

The crowd murmured its agreement. At that point it began to rain again, and moods did not improve.

The sentence was a fine of three pennies, which was precisely what they had (talk about a coincidence!), the confiscation of all their weapons, and their tinder. They were left the dog.

"Well," murmured the woman as they started to leave, "that could have been worse."

"How?" asked the hunter.

At that moment the JUDGEADMINISTRATOROF-DALIGARANDSURROUNDINGDISTRICT's second case of the day began.

It was a woman whose cart had just killed one of the funny birds that went *coco* and which went by the name of "chickens." The woman held it in her arms, and it was clearly visible that its neck was broken. As she passed by Sajra, a tiny finger attached to a little hand, poking from a sleeve of an unmistakable yellow color, emerged from under the gray woolen shawl to settle on the soft feathers around the break, and stopped there. The chicken's neck resumed its normal curvature, and then slowly its eyes opened wide.

After which all hell broke loose: the chicken running off, the word "elf" echoing through the crowd, everyone shouting and crashing into each other, and then the three of them standing in the middle of the halberdiers, who held the tips of their lances straight at their throats.

"So," replied the woman. "Now it is worse."

After the chicken's resurrection, the atmosphere had become truly incandescent. This time the attention of the JUDGE-ADMINISTRATOROFDALIGARANDSURROUNDINGDIS-TRICT was focused on Yorshkrunsquarkljolnerstrink.

"You are an elf," the judge said severely. His tone was solemn and unchanging. His tongue had slowed on the word "elf," articulating each letter very clearly. They fell like stones on the dumbstruck crowd.

"He's just a puppy," said the hunter.

"A little one," said the woman.

"One born lately," explained the little elf contentedly. "Yorshkrunsquarkljolnerstrink," he said, introducing himself with a little bow.

"It's forbidden to belch before the court," said the judge darkly, "and I, JUDGEADMINISTRATOROFDALI-GARANDSURROUNDINGDISTRICT, also forbid you to lie." As he pronounced these last words, the judge rose to his feet with an increasingly solemn air.

The little elf was perplexed. Elves can't say anything except what they have in their heads. Well, yes, one can be polite every now and again—say that one understands when the words are incomprehensible—because treating stupid people as stupid shows a lack of good manners, but that's all.

"And I demand that you address me with the respect that I deserve," the judge continued.

What was the polite form of address? The little elf struggled to remember.

"Fool!" the little one shouted.

No, perhaps that wasn't it.

"Foolency, no, Excellidiot." What was it again?

"Silence!" the judge bellowed at the sniggering crowd. "And you, call me JUDGEADMINISTRATOROF-DALIGARANDSURROUNDINGDISTRICT!"

"Certainly! Certainly!" the little elf replied enthusiastically, a huge smile brightening his face: "JUDGEADMIN-STRATOROFDALIGARANDSURROUNDINGDISTRICT is a most beautiful name. We could give it to the dog!" he added triumphantly.

At this the crowd really ran amok. An old man nearly exploded with laughter, and a halberdier dropped his halberd on his foot. This provoked general hilarity, and the elf couldn't help joining in: when human beings laughed, they looked really lovely.

The only one who didn't laugh was the judge. "Answer me," he said, turning back to the little elf. "Do you know this man and this woman?"

"Yes," the little elf said firmly.

"Apart from the most grave accusation of bringing an elf with them, and the yet even graver accusation of having employed deception to bring him inside our beloved city, have they done anything else?"

"Yeeeeeesssss. The male human eats corpses, with rosemary, I think, and then he makes money by selling their skins, and that woman has sold her mother and her big brothers, no, the little ones . . . mmmm . . . yes, first the little ones, I don't remember."

Total silence had now fallen again. Then an infernal clamor broke out: one really couldn't make anything out anymore.

"I told you I tended to get into trouble," the woman said to the hunter. "Why didn't you go your own way?"

"I must have sold my father in a former life," he replied.

As he was being dragged away, the little elf saw the chicken again: it was perched on a window ledge, where it had a kind of nest with two eggs in it. Elf and chicken looked at one another for a moment and greeted each other, because for that one moment they had had the same mind, and that united them forever.

The little elf wondered if "Chicken" or "Hen" might be a good name for the dog. They weren't the same shape, but the color of the chicken's tail feathers was like that of the dog's tail and back paws. Then he reflected that the dog didn't lay eggs, and the chicken didn't lick your face if it thought you looked sad, so that name didn't fit either.

CHAPTER SIX

HEY HAD BEEN put in a place called "prison."

It was really lovely.

It was all made of solid stone with some big columns that held the vaults up into arches. That kind of architecture was from the Third Runic Dynasty. You could tell because the arches weren't round, but made of two semi-arches that crossed at an acute angle, while round arches are from the First Runic Dynasty, and elongated ones are from the peak of the Second.

And there was real straw to sleep on. And they'd even given them a bowlful of corn and peas that was really good.

{ 45 }

Really good, and so much of it. The little elf had given a few kernels of corn and some peas to a delightful swarm of shiny fat rats that had appeared from every corner of the room once the smell of the food had begun to spread, and which were now running about in all directions on the stone floor.

This place really was paradise.

And there wasn't rain everywhere, except on the face of the woman who was, strangely, raining all by herself.

"Why are you dripping?" the little elf asked the woman.

"They're called 'tears,'" the man replied. "It's our way of crying."

"Really? And what about that stuff that's running out of her nose, which she's wiping away with her sleeve?"

"That's always part of crying."

"When we elves are sad we lament, so that the others can hear our sadness and do something to reduce the torment," said the little elf with ill-concealed pride. "But sitting on the ground and dripping from your nose and eyes, so that your eyes go red and you have to breathe through your mouth, is like giving yourself a cold on purpose."

"You could say that," the man remarked curtly.

"Why are you crying?" the little elf asked the woman.

Once again it was the man who replied.

"Because they're going to hang us tomorrow morning."

"Really? And what does that mean?"

"No," said the woman. "Please, no, or you'll start him off, too, and I don't want to hear him crying."

"Fine. Listen, little one, tomorrow they're going to

hang us. It'll be lovely. They'll hang us up and we'll be able to look down on the whole crowd and the roofs of the houses. It'll be like being a bird and flying."

"Ohhhhhhhh. Really? So why is she dripping?"

"She's crying because she gets vertigo. When she's up high she feels very ill and sometimes throws up. Tomorrow's going to be horrible for her. A real nightmare."

"Ohhhhhhhh. Really?" The little elf was speechless. You never stop learning. "No, then. No, no, no, no, no, no, no, no. If it makes her feel sick, then no hanging," the little one said stoutly. That thing about flying around above the roofs must be wonderful, but to make someone feel sick . . .

"No?" the huunter asked.

"No."

"So what are we going to do? They've decided to hang us."

"We could leave."

"Great, good idea." The hunter seemed truly impressed. "A really good idea. You're a good thinker. Do you have a solution for the locks?"

"We'll open them!" explained the little elf enthusiastically.

"Of course. Absolutely brilliant! And what about the keys?"

"Those long things that turn around and go *clank* and the doors open?"

"Precisely, those long things that turn around and go *clank* and the doors open."

"See this corner here? They're about five yards past that. You can see the corner if you look through the bars."

The hunter, who had been lying down, suddenly sat up.

The woman, who had been huddled with her arms around her knees, wiped her face and got to her feet.

"How do you know that?" she asked.

"It's in their heads," said the little elf, pointing at the rats. "They walk past them lots of times a day. They don't know what keys are, but they have the image of them in their heads."

"Can you do anything to get the keys? I don't know— make them fly to us?"

"Nooooo, certainly not. Such things aren't possible. Gravity is inviolable."

"What is?"

"The principle by which everything goes downward," explained the little elf. "You see!" He dropped his last two peas, and the rats scurried toward them.

The man and the woman sat down again.

"It's the principle by which our bodies will go down tomorrow, while our necks stay up in the rope," explained the woman, beginning to cry again.

"I can send the pretty little animals for the keys. The keys are just above the bench against the wall. It's an easy place for a pretty little animal to get to."

The man and the woman were both on their feet.

"Really?" the woman asked.

"Of course," the little elf confirmed. "What's the

problem? They're our friends now," he added happily, pointing at the rats. "If I think hard about a pretty little animal taking the keys and bringing them here, that thought is an image that passes from inside my head into the head of the pretty little animal, and then it does just that."

The little elf leaned forward, and his tiny fingers brushed the rats' heads. The animals swarmed merrily away through the bars that closed off their cell, and after a loud *clank* and a series of fainter rattling noises, they reappeared dragging a big bunch of keys. The little elf picked them up, chose one from the big bunch, and *clank*, the heavy lock opened.

"There we go," said the little elf.

The man and the woman dashed out.

"Now where do we go?" the woman asked.

"From here, it's all in the heads of the pretty little animals. Ten yards to the left, then left again until you get to the stairs. Then there's a gate"—once again the little elf chose the right key straight away—"more stairs, another gate, hoopla, down again, stairs, gate, key. *Clank.*

"There we go." The little elf continued to lead the way. "Now we pass along the underground passages till we get to the river. It's so lovely here. Look, these are round arches, First Runic Dynasty."

"Really splendid. We'll come back some other time to look at them properly. Now, let's get going. You know, they might be offended that we've refused to be hanged," the woman suggested.

"Ohhhhhh, look!" the elf exclaimed.

"Those marks?" the woman asked.

"They aren't marks, they're letters," the elf declared.

"They're marks, they're for decoration," the hunter insisted.

"No. They're letters. Runes from the First Dynasty. I know how to read them. Grandma taught me. She knew how to read them. 'This . . . was . . . built . . . *This was built beneath the place where the river runs . . .*' A good thing I read it. If we go this way we'll drown. Up and round. Here we are, look, the last gate, the last key, and we're out." *Clank*. "What a lovely sound: those are bells, aren't they? Isn't that the sound of bells?"

"It's the soldiers' armor. I think they're really irritated. They must be truly offended," the hunter said.

"Hey, look!" The little elf pointed toward a column. "These ones on the pontico—"

"*Portico*," the woman corrected him.

"On the *portico* are elongated arches; Second Runic Dynasty. They're the first I've seen."

"I'm genuinely impressed. Could we try to get a move on?" the hunter insisted.

"And these are runes from the Second Runic Dynasty. . . . You can tell them because the top parts of the letters have those circular spirals."

"Fascinating! Is that the best you can do with those legs of yours, or can you go faster?" the hunter asked.

"This kind of spiral is a symbol of infinity . . . no, of time coming round again. It's a prophecy!" the elf exclaimed.

"Really, truly amazing. Do you want me to pick you up so that we can run faster?" the hunter asked.

"'When . . . the . . . water . . . covers . . . the earth . . . When *the water covers the earth* . . .'" the little elf read.

"But now let's get a move on. They're after us. They're really offended. I'll pick you up so that you can read more comfortably while we're running," the hunter said.

"Hey, it's about elves! *'When the water covers the earth, the sun will vanish, the darkness and the ice will come. When the last dragon and the last elf break the circle, the past and the future will meet, the sun of a new summer will shine in the sky'* . . . Hey, wait, slow down. There was something else, but I didn't manage to read it. It said something about somebody great and . . . powerful . . . *'great and powerful will marry . . . must marry a girl bearing a name like the dawning light who sees in the dark and is the daughter of'* . . . I didn't read whose daughter she was!"

"As if we cared!" said the man, with the last breath in his throat. "She certainly won't be our daughter. She'll be the daughter of some king or some wizard. People like us are never mentioned in writings on the wall."

They were out of the building. The hunter was running with the elf in his arms and the woman beside him. The streets were narrow and full of twists and turns, and fortunately, almost deserted, apart from the man, the woman, and the elf—and the soldiers chasing after them.

The soldiers really were offended about the hanging business and had started firing little pointed sticks at them, and that's not nice, no, no, no, no, no, that can hurt.

The little elf was starting to think he'd had enough.

They were so touchy: all they'd done was refuse to be hanged!

One of the soldiers appeared in front of them and aimed his bow. The little elf wished with all his might that this wasn't happening. The image formed in his head and flew into the heads of the creatures who had been one with him. The rabbit, which was running through the reeds at that moment, came to a baffled standstill. The chicken, which was crouching in a niche among the high columns just above the soldier, jumped from its straw and flew as hard as its wings would let it into the face of the soldier, who stumbled and fell, freeing their path.

At the end of the square were the cages of confiscated animals. The woman's dog was barking as loudly as he could. Luckily, there were no locks here—just a big hook that the woman undid.

A street, a corner, another street, the town walls, the drawbridge: safe.

No, not yet. The drawbridge had closed right in their faces. The hunter, holding the little elf in his arms, dashed up the stairs along the walls. The dog, running ahead of them, tripped up a soldier who had appeared. Once they had reached the top, the man took the woman by one wrist and, still holding the little elf in his arms, mounted the parapet and hurled himself toward the freezing water of the river below. The dog followed after.

"Maybe a bit of hanging wouldn't have been so dreadful!" the little elf objected. But it was too late—there is nothing to be done about the law of gravity.

They all plunged into the dark water.

The little elf wondered if "Law of Gravity" might be a good name for the dog, but, thinking about it, it wasn't short, and it didn't capture the idea of something soft that knew how to play.

CHAPTER SEVEN

THE WATER got into their mouths and ears. The little elf felt the cold and desperation filling everything. Desperation and fear can fill your head, and magic drowns in it.

Then, all of a sudden, he had the idea of being a fish. He thought . . . how to phrase it . . . about fishiness, about the pure essence of an aquatic animal.

He thought about the sensation of having gills, the pleasure of cold water, the joy of feeling yourself slipping, flying under the waves as a bird flies under the clouds.

Breath filled his lungs, and the coldness of the water became a delight.

He let himself slip beneath the surface to avoid the pointed sticks that were raining down on the water, fired by all the archers in the Daligar garrison. He swam over to the others. The dog was managing quite well, but the man and the woman were doing stupid things, as usual; she kept putting her head under the water, and he was trying to hold it up. The little elf tried to say that this wasn't the time to play at fighting, and then he explained the correct method: allow the image of the fish to form in your head, focus your attention on gills, but the hunter wouldn't listen to him and was actually incredibly rude.

Luckily, the current was going in the right direction— far, far, even farther, far from Daligar, from its halberdiers and its hangings, toward the high plain and the hills.

The landscape was getting gentler. There were stones along the banks, and more reeds. The water wasn't so high, the current less impetuous. Finally, they managed to reach the shore and drag themselves out.

The woman wasn't breathing well. The air coming out of her made a sound like water, a kind of gurgle that sounded like a boiling pot of beans.

The hunter looked desperate. Water and mud were dripping down from his hair and into his face, and the little elf wasn't sure, but he could have sworn that the man's eyes and nose were dripping as well.

"Do something," yelled the man. "If you can, do something, please. You can do something, can't you? She's dying."

The little elf was stunned. He stretched out his hand and put it on the woman's face.

The little elf felt water gurgling, and the woman's throat was burning as though one of those pointed sticks had got into it. But the most horrible thing was what was in her head: a sensation that these were the last minutes, that everything was about to end.

The little elf concentrated on breathing with all his might—air going in and air coming out, the smell of wet grass, of cane thickets, of mushrooms.

The air goes in, it smells good. Your lungs expand. The air goes out. Your head is filled with the scent of the air, and we know that this breath is not the last one, but afterward there will be another and then another and then yet another.

The woman coughed up a lot of muddy water, then opened her eyes and breathed. The little elf coughed, too. They were both shivering and extremely pale. The hunter smiled happily, then ran to fetch reeds and dry branches. When the pile was big enough, the little elf touched it with his fingers and the fire cheerfully began to blaze. They were cold and drenched, but the hunter went on collecting wood and the fire continued to grow, and gradually, the icy cold and wetness began to ease. The woman fell asleep. The hunter found some nuts in a squirrel's nest and shared them with the little elf.

"We have no weapons now, but we haven't been hanged," the man said.

"What a shame. We had to give up the chance to swing about in the air on the end of a rope! It would have been so nice!"

The man started laughing.

"We can do it if you really want to. They haven't confiscated my rope. Now I'll show you. This branch is strong enough. I tie it here, then here. I'll tie the rope double like this. There we are. Do you want to try? Hold on tight. Now I'll push you."

It was wonderful. Up and down. Down and up. Canes, river, sky—then again—sky, river, canes.

There were hills in the distance, and beyond them the light of the setting sun. The little elf had never seen a sunset. There had always been clouds. Now everything was pink, and a few little long, thin clouds shone like a gold necklace. The last rays lit groves of chestnut trees that alternated with small cultivated fields.

The most wonderful thing you could imagine. As wonderful as flying. The little elf was filled with happiness.

The woman woke with a smile.

The little elf laughed like a mad thing.

"Look, I'm being hanged!" he said delightedly to the female human.

"No," she replied. "This is called a 'swing.'"

She stopped smiling.

"Being hanged is a horrible thing," she went on. "They put a rope around your neck and pull it by using the weight of your own body. The rope tightens, the air can't get through, and you die, just as I was doing with the water a little while ago."

The little elf froze in astonishment.

Then he slipped down from his improvised swing.

His eyes were wide with horror.

He turned gray.

He gasped for breath.

He crouched on the ground and began a long series of broken lamentations. The man and the woman felt ice beneath their skin.

"Why did you tell him?" The man was furious. "He was happy. For once in his life he was happy."

"Because he will meet other men, and because the next humans he meets will want to hang him too, for being an elf. And I don't want him to go along with it happily, convinced that the gallows is a swing. Better to be unhappy but alive."

The woman picked up the little elf and hugged him. The lamentations gradually ceased. The first stars began to shine. The gentle profile of the hills stood out against the sapphire sky.

She put the little elf on the swing and started gently pushing him once again.

"You can start being happy again, if you like. You've just got to remember that if men catch you, they'll hang you."

"And then will they eat me with rosemary?"

"No."

"Without rosemary?"

"Men don't eat elves. Never."

"So why would they want to hang me if they weren't even going to eat me? That's not nice, no, no, no, no, and why would they bother?"

The swing rocked gently.

"Because all men hate elves."

"Why?"

A long silence followed. The swing swayed gently. The dog yawned.

"Because it's your fault."

"What's our fault?"

"Everything."

"Everything?"

"Well, all the things that go wrong. The shadow. The rain, the water covering the earth. The famine. Our children are dying of hunger, and it's your fault. Villages have been swept away by the water."

"We make it rain? How?" The little elf was indignant. "How?"

"How should I know? Maybe by thinking about rain."

"If I could cause rain by thinking about it, I could think about a blazing sun to dry my feet. And then," the little elf said urgently, "we would really be stupid, because water and misery overwhelm us as they overwhelm you, or more so. Why did Grandma not think about the sun while the water was rising and rising? Why did Mama not think of staying with me when she was going to the place from which you don't come back?"

The little elf started crying again. A quiet whimper.

"Well." The hunter seemed perplexed. "Everyone says it's your fault. . . ."

He turned toward the woman, in search of help.

The woman was standing near the swing. She was frowning slightly, but not angry or sad. "We despise elves because you're cleverer than we are. You're unbearable, but clever," she concluded. "You've got magic. You know more things. Where we see drawings, you see words. . . . I think we're afraid of you. And because we don't know exactly when you can show your powers, we think you must be terribly powerful. Our powerlessness is so . . . complete . . . that anyone . . ."

The little elf had stopped crying.

"While we're on the subject of knowing how to do things," the woman went on, "how did you always manage to work out the right key to slip into the lock?"

The little elf looked puzzled.

"The right key in what sense?" he asked with interest.

Now it was the woman's turn to be puzzled.

"Well, the one that fit perfectly with the machinery of the lock in question, and therefore opened it."

"To slip into the lock?" The little elf was startled. "Ahhhhhhh, really? You have to put it in?"

"And it . . ."

"*Fits.* That means it sits snugly. Am I right?"

The little elf was thinking so intensely that his forehead wrinkled. Then his face brightened. "I get it!" he cried. "There is a key for every lock: you slip it in, and if it's the right one, it sits snugly in the mechanism, and when you turn it, it slides the horizontal piece of iron that blocks the door. It's ingenious. Truly ingenious! Incredibly intelligent for humans, really! Grandma always said that the most you'd ever manage was putting a capital on a column, but in fact, you can also be ingenious! It's brilliant!"

"Thanks," the hunter said curtly.

The little elf rocked happily back and forth on his

swing, proud of the new knowledge he had just acquired.

"But how did you manage to open it if you didn't know about the keys fitting?" asked the woman.

"I put the key to the lock, and then in my head there was the door opening, and then . . . *clank*, the door opened."

"Does that mean you knew how to open locks? Without keys, without rats. Without anything?" the woman asked.

The little elf went on swinging lazily back and forth, still frowning: "Yes!" He burst out laughing. "How funny! We risked being hanged, and I knew how to open locks all the time!"

"Terribly amusing," observed the hunter. "I'm clutching my sides."

His tone was that of someone who has choked on a piece of corn.

Still swinging, the little elf went on thinking about their escape. All of the sudden he remembered something: "The prophecy!"

"The curlicues on the portico?"

"Yes, the spiral letters. Second Runic Dynasty. Now I remember:

"*WHEN THE WATER COVERS THE EARTH,*
  THE SUN WILL VANISH.
THE DARKNESS AND THE COLD WILL COME.
WHEN THE LAST DRAGON AND THE LAST ELF
  BREAK THE CIRCLE, THE PAST AND THE
FUTURE WILL MEET.

THE SUN OF A NEW SUMMER WILL SHINE IN
THE SKY.'

"And then there was something about the last elf having to marry somebody. . . ."

CHAPTER EIGHT

HAT DOES it mean?" the woman asked.

"I don't know. I think it might mean . . ."

The little elf broke off. The dog had jumped to his feet and was snarling at something in the distance.

"Ohhhh, look, a moving tree!" said the little elf.

"It isn't a tree. It's a troll," the woman whispered.

"Really? That's a troll? I've never seen one before!" The little elf looked overjoyed. "What are the two bushes behind the troll? Are they baby trolls? Do trolls have babies as well?"

"Those things behind him are the two biggest and most heavily armed humans I have ever seen," the hunter replied, backing away.

But it was too late to run. The two giant "bushes" had them cornered.

These giants looked a bit like the hunter. They had the same clothes, made of rags and animal skins, and some daggers; but the really striking thing about them was their axes: little dark ones the size of a hand, huge great wood axes that would have cut off a head with a single blow, two-bladed hatchets of various sizes with wooden handles, and all of them keenly honed.

But as tall as the giants stood, the troll was even more enormous. It towered over them, and in the fading light its cyclopean shadow engulfed the tree and the swing and the little elf who was rocking back and forth on it. The dog's growls made way for a whimper of terror.

"Stay where you are," ordered the hunter menacingly. "He's an elf, a real elf," he went on, pointing to the little one. "His magic can burn you like a flame, topple you like a hurricane. He can close your throats so that you can't breathe any better than a hanged man can."

"It's not true, it's not true, it's not true, it's not true, it's not true, it's not true, no, no, no, no, no, no, no, no," the little elf protested.

Why did the hunter go on saying such horrifying, horrible, horrendous things?

"It isn't true that we do those things! We don't hurt anybody! We've never hurt anybody! We can't hurt anybody, because if we hurt somebody, the hurt we have done, which is outside our heads, goes into our heads, because everything that is outside our heads is inside our heads, and everything that is inside our heads is outside our heads!"

The little elf had had enough of being run down by everybody, he had had enough of everyone speaking ill of him and his race! And this was the last straw.

The hunter, for once, was speechless.

The two giants were speechless as well.

They looked at the hunter, then at the little elf, then again at the hunter, then the little elf, then the hunter.

"Funny sort of weapon," the bigger of the two giants said to the hunter. "Are you paying for something you did in a former life, or do you have another reason for dragging an elf around with you?" The two new human arrivals seemed genuinely baffled.

"I must have sold my father," the hunter agreed.

"Troll eat elfs," spluttered the troll, drawing closer.

The dog whimpered, increasingly terrified, but bravely added a growl to his whimper.

"You can't eat him. He's just a puppy," said the hunter.

"A little one," said the woman.

"Born lately," the little one explained.

"Troll eat elfs," the troll repeated.

The little elf began to laugh. "Yes, of course, with rosemary. That's called 'irony'!" He beamed.

The troll was dumbstruck. He went on staring at the little elf's face with the smile stamped upon it, as he might have watched a donkey flying, or the moon coming down to play football.

The little elf approached the troll. Its huge face was completely expressionless, like the mask of a stone idol. The little elf was so used to finding himself confronted by frowning, angry, or worried faces, that he felt reassured by this granite blankness.

The troll's skin was scaly, like that of lizards, which are pretty animals, and of which the little elf was particularly fond, because lizards live in the sunlight, and sunlight is beautiful. The troll's face, too, was very like a lizard's, and like a lizard's skin, the troll's skin was covered with iridescent patches of green and purple, which were the little elf's favorite colors, because they were the colors of his grandmother's curtains, when elves were still allowed to have curtains.

The great fangs that emerged from the troll's jaw and pointed upward gleamed like crescent moons and didn't worry the little elf in the slightest because, convinced as he was that anything you used for biting was inside your mouth rather than outside it, he took them for decorative elements—unless they were for holding doughnuts, either as a kind of mobile dispenser or, in more festive fashion, as a pole in some kind of game, in which you had to throw doughnuts over the poles.

That thought filled his mind with joy. The joy gurgled like water boiling in a pot, and then, also like water boiling in a pot, it bubbled over so that everyone could enjoy it.

"How handsome you are," the little elf said to the troll. The sound of his voice, full of tenderness and cheerfulness, resonated in the minds of his listeners.

Everyone picked up on this moment of joy and belief in life, produced by such a beautiful creature as the troll.

"How big you are! You're the first troll I've ever seen, you know! You're . . . impressive. Yes, impressive. Grandma didn't tell me that a troll could be so handsome. . . ."

"Ha . . . ha . . . handsome?" The troll began to recover from its initial shock.

It had almost stopped breathing. For a few moments it seemed that it was changing its expression, or perhaps it would be more correct to say that it was assuming one.

"Handsome. Yes. Even Grandma said she'd never seen one. A troll, I mean. What was it Grandma used to say? That the first troll you meet is also the last one. Who knows what that means? Doubtless that there aren't many trolls, so that if you see one in your life you're not doing too badly! Which means it's good luck to see a troll! I'm so happy. HAPPY. I haven't met just any troll, I've met one who's so handsome. HANDSOME."

"Ha . . . ha . . . handsome?" bleated the troll.

"Is it true that you're always traveling and you never stop?" the little elf went on. "Is it true that you've seen the world? The whole world, even beyond the hills? Is it true that you've seen the sea? Is it true that the sea exists? You know, the big water, water everywhere like a field, except instead of grass there's water. It must be lovely to be a troll. It must be really lovely, and on top of everything else to be so handsome."

"Ha . . . ha . . . handsome?" spluttered the troll.

"Yes, so handsome. And it's an honor to make your acquaintance. My name is Yorshkrunsquarkljolnerstrink."

"I sorry you have cough. You say again me handsome."

"You're very handsome. VERY HANDSOME. VE-RY HAND-SOME." The little elf was truly enchanted. His voice was growing dreamier and dreamier. "It must be nice to be so handsome."

"Elf good dinner, but this elf say me ha . . . ha . . . ha . . . handsome."

"Anyway, I don't believe those stories. I know you'd never eat me! You're just doing irony."

The woman was white in the face. The hunter, too, who normally never lost his composure, was extremely pale.

"We'd have been better off staying in Daligar," he said. "At least we'd have had one last meal before they hanged us."

"How much did you get for your father?" asked the bigger of the two giants.

"Lousy deal," the hunter replied gloomily.

The little elf approached the two giants.

Anyone who went about with somebody equipped for the transportation of doughnuts, or for target-throwing, could only be infinitely peaceful and kind, not like this hunter, who went around with a bow and arrows and daggers, and who was always so irritable.

"Are you lumberjacks, really?" the elf asked.

"Lumberwhat?"

"Who, us?" The two giants grew more and more alarmed.

"Lumberjack carpenters!" The little elf happily ran his little hand along the sharp blades of the axes, hatchets, and choppers. "You turn the branches of dead trees into things for living people. Cradles and rocking chairs. My grandma had a rocking chair. It was a rocking chair with my cradle attached to it, so when she rocked, she rocked me as well. Do you make rocking chairs?"

As he thought about rocking chairs and toys, the little elf's mind filled with tenderness. He felt a boundless need for normality, for the everyday, for home. Once more he felt a longing for the mother he had never known, and the grandmother who had left him.

And all of that boundless tenderness overflowed from his mind and into his voice.

The others all felt as though honey were flowing through their veins. They wanted it to go on like that, for the honey to keep on flowing through their veins; they wanted that sudden good feeling of being loved to go on forever.

"Well . . ." The two giant humans were still hazy. "More or less."

"And toys? Do you make toys? Dolls, rocking horses?" the little elf asked.

"T . . . toys?" Giant Number One asked.

"What, us? Dolls?" Giant Number Two chimed in.

"Have you never made a rocking chair, or a cradle to go with it?" the little elf asked.

"Mmmmmmno, no, no, not yet, it's never occurred to me," Giant Number Two added.

"You could, it's a good idea, a kind idea," the elf suggested.

"Mmmmmyes, a kind idea," Giant Number One agreed.

{ 69 }

"And you never carve trees that aren't dead yet?"

"Mmmmmmmno, no, never," said Giant Number Two.

"We kill them first," confirmed Giant Number One, "so they don't get hurt."

"It must be nice to be a woodcutter. And being a farmer must be a lovely job as well. Where first you have land, and then there's grain. It's been nice meeting you. He's so hand-some, and you are kind."

"Kind?" Giant Number One asked.

"Ha . . . ha . . . handsome?" the troll asked.

The two giants looked at one another, then shrugged.

The darkness was becoming blacker and blacker. A very light rain set in.

For that night they all stayed together, around the little fire that the little elf had lit, beneath a kind of impro-vised roof made of branches that the two giant "woodcut-ters" had cut with their axe blades.

The dog and the little elf slept cuddled up together, like two interlocking commas, and after them came, in sequence, the three mountains: the smaller of the two giants, the bigger of the two giants, and finally, twice the size of the other two sleeping figures, the troll.

The hunter and the woman were on the other side of the fire.

The two giants were snoring. The troll muttered in his sleep: "Ha . . . ha . . . ha . . . ha . . . ha . . . ha . . . ha . . . ha . . ."

"Is he going to go on making that laughing noise all night?" the hunter asked in exasperation.

"The minute he stops bleating, he'll skin us," replied Sajra. "If I were you I wouldn't complain."

The hunter stopped complaining.

The laughing noise of the troll merged with the quiet snoring of the other two.

The woman turned over in her sleep and almost brushed against the hunter, who remained motionless until dawn, for fear of waking her and making her move away.

Curled up between the dog's paws, the little elf wondered whether "Little Troll" might be a good name for a dog. It seemed pretty, but the dog didn't have doughnut holders on either side of his mouth.

Then he fell asleep and dreamed of the sea.

CHAPTER NINE

AWN CAME, all pink and gold, and the darkness and the last stars faded away. The sky was clear. A landscape of green hills shone brightly under the sun, dotted with little valleys still filled with fog.

A few birds sang.

The first to wake was the troll, followed by the little elf, who didn't stop commenting even for a moment on the troll's handsomeness, power, and enormous size.

The little elf commented on the splendor of the purple crests that the troll had beneath his neck, which were now covered with drops of dew that glittered in the light. Then he praised his limbs, which looked like half-moons on a midsummer night, and his round, reddish nose that looked like a full moon on a midwinter night. Then he spoke profusely of the kindness of the two giant humans, now awake, who transformed dead trees, and trees in their death throes, into cradles and tables and toys. Tears of emotion shone in the eyes of the troll and the woodcutters.

One of the two giants brought out his knapsack to offer everyone breakfast.

Startled, the hunter looked at him with puzzlement, as though he had just met the ghost of his own father. The knapsack contained six corncobs, or the astronomical figure of a whole one each, and a piece of smoked ham.

Yorshkrunsquarkljolnerstrink looked sorrowfully at the piece of ham, and uttered a little groan. It was quite restrained compared with his laments over the rabbit, because the creature's death was too far in the past now to evoke the pain and fear of death.

"So, can we eat it?" the hunter asked hopefully.

"Never!" replied the little elf. He turned to the troll and the giants. "You're not going to eat a creature that used to be alive? You? You who are so handsome and kind?"

"Mmmmmmmmmm who, us?"

"Mmmmmmmmmmno, not us."

"Who knows how it ended up in the knapsack."

"We handsome and kind, not eat this thing you not want."

The hunter was growing more and more puzzled and alarmed: the whole conversation—which seemed entirely normal to the little elf—struck him as strange for some reason.

As the corncobs roasted on the fire, the little elf dug a tiny hole and buried the piece of ham. He covered it over and decorated it, for want of flowers, with a bunch of red berries. Throughout the whole operation, the hunter had not for so much as a moment stopped staring at the ham, with the face of someone watching the burial of a close relative. Perhaps he had recognized the pig, and was growing emotional over the memory.

The idea of one corncob each had been an illusion. The troll ate three, the giants one each, and the man, the woman, and the little elf divided the sixth between them; but even that was a feast.

Finally, when the sun was high, a real sun shining in a real blue sky, the two groups said good-bye.

The man, the woman, and the little elf walked along, followed by the dog, in the bright sunlight. In a little glade they found a piece of parchment nailed to a tree. It marked the passage of two dangerous bandits traveling in the company of one of the ugliest trolls ever seen in living memory. A reward was offered. The little elf thought it was a stroke of luck they hadn't met them! Instead, they'd met the two woodcutters and the handsomest troll ever seen in the universe! Curious how many trolls there were hereabouts.

"Can anyone tell me what's happened, and why we're still alive and in good health?" asked the hunter.

Sajra smiled. "Whatever is inside the little elf comes

out and enters the head of the person listening to him," she explained. "When Yorsh is desperate, it's unbearable to us, and when he's frightened, we start to panic; even so, we go on thinking our own thoughts as well. But to . . . to *simple* minds, what the little elf says is a kind of flood: it fills their heads. He said 'handsome' and 'kind' and they . . . how can I put it . . . adapted to the definition."

"Simple minds?" asked the hunter.

"Simple minds," she confirmed.

"Simple minds," the hunter repeated. Then he stopped and struck his forehead with his hand: "We forgot the rope; it was tied to the tree as a swing. You wait for me here. I'll run and get it."

The woman, the little elf, and the dog sat down in the glade. The sun was a real joy.

The hunter ran like the wind. He reached the spot where they had set up their camp, but the ham's grave had already been opened up and emptied. Even the simplicity of simple minds had its limits. He hadn't been alone in thinking of recovering the corpse.

He took down his rope, rolled it up, stowed it in his knapsack, and then set off back along the road.

As he walked, he thought of the conversation that had been left in midair. What was that about a prophecy?

He rejoined the others in the glade and asked them.

Yorshkrunsquarkljolnerstrink searched his memory and recited: "'When the water covers the earth, the sun will vanish, the darkness and the cold will come. When the last dragon and the last elf break the circle, the past and the future will meet, the sun of a new summer will shine in the sky.'"

"What does that mean?"

"I don't know."

"Didn't your grandmother ever talk to you about the rain?"

"Of course she talked to me about the rain."

"And what did she say?"

"She said, 'It's raining again today,' or, 'Cover yourself up, it's raining,' or, 'The blankets are going moldy. . . .' Once she said, 'The roof's leaking. . . .' Another time she said, 'Frogs will come and live here.' Then the third time I caught a cold, did I ever tell you about the third time I caught a cold? It was when the mucus blocking my nose turned into—"

"No, I mean, didn't your grandmother ever tell you anything about why it has been so cold and has rained so much over the past few years? Didn't she ever tell you whether it would stop sooner or later, or whether there was anything we could do to make it stop? Anything like that."

"Oh, that! No, she never said a word."

"Are you sure?"

"Yes."

"All right, then," said the woman. "What do you know about dragons?"

"They're big, they've got wings, they fly, they are difficult by nature, specially since men massacred them, and they are the keepers of the ancient secrets of the world, and they can read the runic scripts. Not like some people I know, naming no names, who think they're just scribbles—"

"We've got to find the last dragon and the last . . ." the man broke off, as though something had suddenly occurred to him. He looked at the little elf and didn't dare continue.

"The last elf," the little elf said, finishing his sentence. "Poor thing! The last elf. It must be terrible to be the last elf. To be always on your own. Aside from the fact that there won't be any more elves. It's appalling. APPALLING. It hurts me even to think about it. Hey, it means I might meet another elf. And when I meet that elf, he won't be the last one, because there will be two of us, and it'll be love . . . ly. . . ." The little elf stopped. A shadow crossed his face: "But if I exist, he can't be the last one. . . ."

There was a silence. A long silence.

"*I'm* the last elf."

Silence. A long silence. Suddenly the sun disappeared and the fog rose up. A bird cried hoarsely. The woman bent down and wrapped the little elf in her arms and held him tightly, as she had never done before.

"It's a prophecy. We don't know what era it refers to. Perhaps it'll happen in a thousand years. . . . Perhaps it isn't even true. Prophecies aren't always true, in fact . . ."

The little elf turned ashen. All the light fled his greenish-blue eyes.

"Maybe *two* thousand years," the man agreed. "Maybe it'll never happen."

He too had bent down and put his arms around the little elf.

They stood there like that, a single block in the fog. Soft rain began to fall. Not even then did they move.

The dog joined them, bringing their number to four, all clustered together in the rain.

The first to move was the woman. "We can take shelter under the trees."

"There's a tower somewhere near here," the little elf said. He seemed exhausted. There was no light in his eyes. "I hear the sound of water. We're close to a stream, not far from the city of Daligar, with the river behind us. I know where we are. There should be an abandoned tower around here, with a tree on top of it."

"How do you know?"

"I can hear the sound of the stream, and I've seen the drawing. I know where we are."

"What drawing? What are you talking about?"

"I'll tell you. But first, let's find shelter."

They struggled over spiky bramble bushes. There was the stream. The water was clear and the banks were covered with soft green grass. Not far from the spot where they had emerged from the brambles, a little clearing opened up, with a half-dilapidated tower rising from it. At the top of the tower grew an enormous oak tree.

They took refuge inside. The central room of the tower was intact, and there was even a bundle of wood, almost dry, which the little elf managed to light.

The hunter had filled his water bottle from the stream,

and there was enough for everyone. He had even managed to catch a trout, and explained to the little elf that there was no choice: either the fish died, or they—elf, woman, dog—would die of hunger.

The little elf nodded. The dog stayed close by him, warm and silent.

He distracted himself from his despair by trying to find a name for the dog. "Faithful" might not be a bad name. The one who never abandons you, never leaves you, is always there to fight for you. Perhaps it needed shortening a bit. Faithful . . . Fidelity—wasn't there an old word his grandmother had taught him? That was it: FIDO. At last, the perfect name. FIDO, the faithful one. That was the right name. My faithful companion, my faithful dog, Fido.

Having found a name for the dog, the little one returned to his despair. He was the only one left. The others—hunted, chased, deported, mocked, sometimes hanged, sometimes, more simply, left to die of hunger—were all dead, expelled from the realm of the living. There was no one left but him. He was the last one.

CHAPTER TEN

T HE MAN and the woman each ate their half trout, feeling like a pair of torturers, huddled in a corner, while the little elf suffered in the corner opposite. The hunter had brought him a few mushrooms that he had found, but the little elf wanted nothing to do with them. He asked only that the two humans go out and bury the remains of the little trout, far away and in a decorous fashion. Feeling like the worst kind of idiots and the worst kind of criminals that had ever existed, they obeyed.

Upon their return, the little elf got up from his corner and pulled out a worn embroidered bag from beneath his yellow clothes. He turned it upside down, and out came, in order: a spinning top made of wood and painted sky and midnight blue, a tiny book bound in threadbare blue velvet with silver embroidery that formed Elfish characters, and a piece of rolled-up parchment tied with a pale blue string.

"Blue is the color of elves," the little elf explained, "but it's forbidden us now. We hate yellow."

The humans nodded.

The little elf untied the lace and opened up the parchment.

"Do you know what this is?" he asked.

"A piece of parchment," the hunter answered.

"Yes, fine, but do you know what these marks are?"

"Drawings?" suggested the man.

"Letters?" guessed the woman.

"It's a map! When she told me to go away, Grandma made me take the poetry book, and the map as well. The poetry book was my mother's, and the map was my father's. He was a traveler. That was why he died. Elves weren't allowed to go anywhere outside the Elf Camps. When he tried to come home, to the Elf Camp where we were staying, the sentries patrolling it caught him and he was condemned to death. That's why I never met my father. This is his map. What he's drawn shows the journey we've just taken, as well as the one we still have to take. But . . . don't you know how to read a map? It's easy. The names are written both in Elfish and human language."

Silence. A terrible doubt ran through the little elf's mind.

"You can't read! You can't read at all! Not just the ancient runes, but not even the human language we speak now!"

Silence. The man shrugged. The woman nodded.

It was terrible.

The little elf felt sorry for these two poor things, lost in a world where written words had been forgotten.

The little elf explained the map: on one side there were the Dark Mountains and, beyond the Dark Mountains, the sea. In the bottom left corner was a big group of houses next to a river and surrounded by walls—that was Daligar. The river was called Dogon, and that was written, too. The river they were on at the moment was a nameless stream, and near it was drawn a tower topped by an oak tree, the same tower they were currently in. Not far away, the stream met the Dogon—the river of Daligar—and then, beyond Arstrid—the last village shown—it carried on toward the Dark Mountains. The Dogon ran through the mountains along a deep valley, marked so clearly on the map that you could even make out the rock overhanging the pass. It was a rock with a pillar of smoke above it, and a caption that read *Hic Sunt Dracos*, in the language of the Third Runic Dynasty: "Here Be Dragons."

You had to follow the stream to get to the river. You had to follow the river to reach the dragon.

He was the last elf.

He had to do it.

"How can you be sure?" asked the woman.

"My name, my name's in it. My name is Yorshkrun-squarkljolnerstrink. *Nerstrink* means 'the last' in Elfish."

"Perhaps it doesn't mean anything. Perhaps it's a sound like any other, without a real meaning. My name is Sajra, which is the name they give to a flower that grows on the walls of my village, but I'm not a flower."

"What does the rest of your name mean?" the man asked the elf.

"Big and powerful," the little elf replied.

"Then it must just be a collection of sounds," the man agreed.

"*Shk* is an absolute intensifier."

"A what?"

"It means 'most.' *Runsq* means 'big,' and *uarkljol* means 'powerful.' The biggest, the most powerful, and the last, the one after which there will be no more."

The little elf seemed different now. His big eyes shone with green and blue, the colors of the elves lighting up his face as though from within. He actually looked taller.

"Let's set off tomorrow," the elf said calmly. "Let's go in search of the last dragon. He and I must break a circle. I don't know which circle. I don't know what it means. But afterward, the sun will come back."

Then the little elf raised his eyes and looked around. They were surrounded by the walls of the ancient tower. "My father has been here," he said, his voice filled with emotion. His eyes lingered on the ancient stones; he brushed them with his hand. "My father touched these stones," he added. He looked at the map once again. "There's a strange drawing on the map here, as though it's pointing to some-thing underneath us."

He looked to the ground, and there, beneath bundles of firewood, was a trapdoor.

Together, the three lifted the heavy door and climbed down the stairs to a tiny cellar, where they found a sword, an axe, and a bow. They were encrusted with silver, and the silver formed unmistakeable Elfish letters. Along with the bow there were three arrows, which were also en-crusted with silver and covered with the spirals of mysteri-ous words.

"What was your father's name?" asked the man, when he managed to get his voice back.

"Gornonbenmayerguld."

"What does that mean?"

"'He who finds the way and shows it to others.'"

In the case holding the arrows, there was also a blue velvet bag containing three gold coins.

"Your father left you a proper inheritance," the man concluded.

The little elf felt he had become less of an orphan. It was a curious feeling. As though loneliness were a glass wall that had, for the first time, shown cracks and fissures.

He was the last member of a tribe that had been destroyed, but a little of the affection that the present denied him now reached him from the past.

He ran his fingers over and over the collection of objects. They had been made for him; they had been left to him.

Someone had loved him as he made them.

He hoped that Death was a place from which his father could see him.

CHAPTER ELEVEN

T DAWN, the mist rose up. They set off at a fair pace, following the torrent. After a few hours, a light rain began, which did nothing to slow them down.

At the end of the morning, they came in sight of the river. The brambles had made way for tall sweet-chestnut trees, which meant that they would walk quickly, and on a full belly. They ate the chestnuts raw, so as not to waste time cooking them.

The river widened. The sky brightened. The rain stopped. In a loop of the river they came across three houses that stood next to a field of corn and a vineyard. It could only be Arstrid, the last village marked on the map. There were meadows and a grove of chestnut trees, with foothills rising up behind it. The Dark Mountains were not far off. Between the houses were trestles, on which a dozen trout stood smoking over a huge copper pot. There was an orchard of trees overflowing with apples. In the middle of the river's loop, tied with big cables and poles, three boats bobbed in the current. Scattered among the vines, the meadows, and the chestnut trees stood ten or so fine-looking sheep and a few goats. Each of the houses had a chimney pot with smoke emerging from it.

"Before the endless rain, the whole world must have been as rich and beautiful as this," said the woman.

The inhabitants, about a dozen men and women, plus an indefinite number of children, gathered to meet them. They wore clothes made of thick wool, either untreated or dyed with indigo. They looked at the little elf's yellow tunic, and the Elfish bow that the hunter carried, but showed neither fear nor malevolence.

The hunter spoke first. He greeted them politely, said his own name, and asked if it was possible to buy food, one of the boats, and clothes.

The group did not reply immediately. There was a long whispered discussion, and then the one who appeared to be the oldest, a tall man with a short white beard, asked what they had to pay with.

"A piece of real gold," suggested the hunter.

Interminable haggling followed. There was nothing to be done: the old man wanted three coins. The hunter had to give in.

Finally, the deal was done. The boat they chose was small but solid. The hunter loaded on a wineskin of goat's milk, a big sack of apples, a smaller one of corncobs, and two even smaller ones of smoked trout and raisins. Then he bought a tunic, a pair of breeches, and an indigo-colored cloak for Yorsh, so that he could free himself of his rough and tattered yellow rags.

Yorsh's face lit up at the sight of them.

"The other elf wore blue as well," said the old man. "The one who passed by a few years ago. The one who sold us, for these three pieces of gold, the pot of concord and abundance."

"The what?"

"The pot of concord and abundance," explained the old man, indicating the big smoking pot. It was a strange pot, with a kind of double bottom that held charcoal and logs from which the smoke was rising. "While that pot still works, we are protected against poverty and disharmony. The rain now falls only as it should, and since the elf passed this way, the brawling has stopped. Before, there were at least three brawls every day. And they didn't always end well—we're all handy with knives in these parts. The three gold pieces were these very same ones. One of them some-what oval and another slightly dented on one side. The little elf is his son, isn't he? Well, it's been a pleasure doing business with you. Not only have we recovered the village's gold, but if you, too, spread harmony and abundance, it's nice to have helped you."

"You don't think that having one of the three pieces

of gold might help us later on?" ventured the hunter.

"I'm sure you're clever enough to take care of your-selves," the old man replied. "The other elf taught us the lesson of commerce and negotiation before he left. He really was an extraordinary creature."

Sailing in the boat was wonderful. They just lay on their backs while the current did all the work, carrying them in the right direction. The boat was deliciously comfortable. There was a wooden roof to shelter them from the rain, and an iron brazier where they could keep a fire to warm their feet and roast their corncobs. The riverbanks were rocky in some places, and in others were lined with slender beaches, but always deserted. For the first time in their lives, their constant companion, hunger, had abandoned them. The lit-tle elf even allowed the three carnivores a few mouthfuls of smoked trout.

The mountains grew closer every day. By now, more of their time was spent in the shadow of the peaks. The little elf stayed silent, close to the brazier, clutching his poetry book.

"Your father must have had some extremely powerful magic," the hunter said one morning.

"Grandma said he didn't. Magic isn't the same for everyone: some have more, some have less. Grandma said that Papa was, all things considered, the least magical elf she had ever met. She said the only thing he could do with his magic was light a fire—when he was in good health and the wind was blowing in the right direction. While

Grandma even knew how to boil water without fire and cure veruccas with herbs."

"So how did your father manage to make that village rich and peaceful? How did he get the rain to ease?"

"I don't know. None of it makes any sense!"

Now the shadow surrounded them on all sides. The river continued on peacefully through the middle of an enormous gorge.

Above them, the sky had become a corridor parallel with the river, between two high rocky walls that flanked it on either side. The walls ran steeply down to the river from great heights.

Up above them, on the higher of the two walls, a pile of rocks could now be seen. It might have been a peak, but it might also have been a building. But there was no doubt about the huge plume of smoke that hung above it, and the legend engraved beneath it in vast letters:

HIC SUNT DRACOS

Here Be Dragons. Letters from the Second Runic Dynasty.

The current was fast, but the little boat was equipped with an oar, and the man had managed to draw closer to the shore and moor the boat by throwing a rope around a jagged projection of rock. The rope tensed, the little boat abruptly veered into the corner, and its prow settled in a bush. Hidden by the bush was a tiny beach, about a yard or two long. It was the only landing area in the whole gorge, and it opened onto a very narrow, steep flight of steps dug into the pale rock.

The little elf pulled out his map and looked at it.

"I've worked out what this sign means: a waterfall. I can hear it. We can't go back, and there's a waterfall ahead. We may as well take the steps!"

They set off. The steps were narrow and steep. In some places they had collapsed. In others, the moss had made them treacherous and slippery. After they had walked for a few hours, the sun appeared. They were now high enough to see the waterfall—a big vertical wall of water that formed all the colors of the rainbow.

The exertion was beginning to take its toll, and they were stopping more and more frequently. By the time they reached the top of the steps, it was already early afternoon. Beyond the Dark Mountains lay a vast plain, and past the plain, a long strip of blue that stood out against the sky. The sea! They were seeing the sea! The little elf perked up again. His exhaustion vanished, too. He had seen the sea, like his father had. Above him towered the words:

HIC SUNT DRACOS

Then the road curved around and reached a great stone shape, which they could now see was an enormous rock hollowed out inside to form a building. The summit of the rock was lost in the dense layer of low cloud that surrounded the peak. He had done it. He had arrived.

The man held his bow with the arrow at the ready. The woman clutched the little axe. Even the dog seemed rather uneasy, sniffing around nervously.

The little elf reached the pinnacle. There was an enormous entrance flanked by writing. They were letters from the First Runic Dynasty.

"What's written on it?" asked the man.

The little elf began to decipher the writing, feeling both scared and excited. His destiny was about to unfold. His fate was staring him right in the face.

"'Proi . . . betur proibetur spu . . . tare, proibetur sputare.' No spitting."

"No spitting? That's not possible. Are you sure?" the hunter asked.

"Yes." Yorsh was baffled, too.

"Wait a minute. We traveled across half the world, wore our lungs out on that damned flight of steps—"

"The steps weren't that bad!" the elf protested.

"They weren't that bad because I was carrying you! I've climbed as many steps as there are drops in the ocean, to come and read a sign telling us that we're not allowed to spit? Wasn't there supposed to be a circle, the future, the sun of the new spring? Have a look and see if there's anything else; there are more scribbles there."

"No spitting, running, making crumbs, or talking in a loud voice," confirmed the little elf. "Wash your hands before entering," he added.

At that moment the door opened and the dragon appeared.

CHAPTER TWELVE

HE DRAGON looked annoyed.

He was very old, and it isn't easy to decipher the expression of a dragon, particularly if it's a very old dragon and it's the first time you've met one, but it was obvious how annoyed he was.

The wooden door was gigantic, as high as a half dozen trolls standing on each other's shoulders. It had opened with an impressive noise, to reveal a huge hall in which clusters of stalactites and stalagmites stretched out and met one another, creating intricate networks of light and shade. The dragon lay at the center. Light came from above, filtered by dozens of little windows, sealed by thin sheets of amber that bathed everything in a gilded glow.

"What evil, ill-starred strangers, has befallen you? Why trouble ye my calm with foul uproar?" The dragon's voice took them somewhat by surprise. They gave a start, then they looked at each other, trying to establish which of the three was the best placed to reply.

The hunter was the first one to pluck up the courage. "Well, my noble lord, I am a man and he is an elf. . . ."

"Not everything is perfect in this world," the dragon commented, apparently unimpressed by this information. "Not all creatures can be born dragons, the best of nature's forms," he concluded.

For a moment the hunter was perplexed by this interruption. He took a few deep breaths, and then began again: "He, the little elf, I mean, is called Yorshkrunsquarkljolnerstrink."

This information didn't seem to impress the dragon, either. "The sign clearly states that spitting is forbidden," the dragon replied.

"I wasn't spitting. That's his name. His father's name was Gornonbenmayerguld."

"Everyone has his own name," returned the dragon, less and less impressed.

There was an embarrassed silence. Destiny seemed uncertain, and fate had clearly been lost along the way.

Yorshkrunsquarkljolnerstrink tried to get the conversation going again: "We've read a prophecy that spoke of you, foo . . . no, Excellency."

"Who was it framed this prophecy?" the dragon asked.

"The humans of the Second Runic Dynasty, in the city of Daligar."

"Toilsome, indeed, is the art of saying sooth, and never have the humans got it right. They who gave credence to scribbles on a wall have always been thought doltish. Now, *messires*, pray trouble me no longer, by which I mean that I wish you to depart."

The big door closed again. The din was so deafening that a few little stones rolled from the top of the pinnacle, and the four had to dart quickly aside.

"What on earth's he talking about?" the hunter asked.

"He said the prophecy was stupid, and that we have to go," the little elf said wearily.

He dropped onto a large stone. The dog approached and licked his face.

The man was stunned, too. He squatted on the ground, with his head between his hands.

"Why was the dragon so sure that the prophecy was written on the wall?" the woman asked finally. She was the only one still standing. "It would be much more likely to be on a parchment, a wooden panel, a shield, an icon—the places people normally write."

The woman bent down, picked up a stone, and hurled it with all her strength at the door.

"Hey, you," she yelled with all the breath she could muster, "open up, unless you want us to break it down!"

"Have you gone mad? Do you want to die?" the hunter asked.

"No, quite the contrary. I don't want to die. We're at

the top of a mountain that you can only reach by a river that is too fast to travel back against its current, and which leads to the most deadly waterfall anyone's ever imagined. If there is a way out, it leads from the lair of that what's-its-name in there, so it's worth trying, or else we'll be up here for all eternity, and the crows will pick our bones. And at this point there's no turning back. We're here, and in some way we will confront the dragon."

She turned toward the door once more, and this time she struck it with the little Elfish hatchet. Splinters flew in all directions. "Hey," she shouted again, "I'm talking to you!"

The door opened once more, this time only by a few inches.

"How durst ye . . ." the dragon began.

"You know about the prophecy as well, don't you?"

"I did hear something," the dragon admitted, "but that has no significance."

"Are you afraid?" the woman asked. "Is there something in our coming that frightens you, that might put you in danger? Something that we don't know about. It's strange that you're not curiouser. . . ."

"More curious," the little elf corrected.

The woman glared at him.

"It's strange that you're not *more curious*. And what about the mythical hospitality of dragons? You haven't even invited us in!"

"My venerable age," the dragon began by way of self-justification, "and the pain caused me by the bones of my feet . . ."

"Don't be afraid," said the woman.

"Don't be afraid?" snorted the hunter. "Who of? Us? He'd just have to sneeze and we'd be like charred corncobs."

"Don't you understand? He's old, tired, and alone, and he has no powers now. It's the dragon that's afraid of us. Don't you understand anything?" The woman was truly irritated. "Don't be afraid," she repeated to the old dragon.

There was a long silence. The only sound, far in the distance, was the waterfall.

Then the dragon started to cry. It was a series of convulsive sobs, which turned into the whimpering of a frightened puppy.

"I'm beginning to understand how the dragons died out," snorted the hunter. He narrowly missed a kick in the shins, and finally the door reopened, fully, this time.

The hall was enormous. Among the stalactites and stalagmites, veils and veils of cobwebs caught the amber light that filtered through the windows, giving everything a magical appearance. The room was filled with dense smoke, the heat was stifling, and a luxuriant vegetation of golden beans stretched across the floor and climbed up the walls. At the far end were myriad openings leading into other halls that were just as full of veils and veils of soft cobwebs, on which spirals of smoke swirled, amid full, round bean pods.

"Where does this smoke come from?" asked the little elf.

The dragon's lamentations grew in both intensity and volume, and the stalactites began to tremble with the vibrations of its shriller cries. The hunter began to look anxiously around him; and for the first time since she had entered the grotto, the woman, too, seemed frightened. The dog resolved the problem: he approached the dragon and licked it, whimpering gently, as dogs do when they are comforting someone. The dragon stopped crying. He slowly raised his big head and looked the dog in the eyes for a long time. The dog wagged his tail. The dragon calmed down. His breathing returned to normal. The stalactites stopped trembling.

Trustworthy. Faithful. Whenever he needed him, there he was. Fido: it was quite definitely a perfect name for the dog.

The little elf began to stroll about and look around him. Everything was quite extraordinary. The dragon was huge; his scales formed complicated and sumptuous spirals of pink and gold, although some of them were worn, and in places turning gray. Many of them were missing, knocked out by ancient wounds that had healed into trench-like scars in which one's hand could have disappeared. His feet had claws that must have been sharp at one time, but which now were worn and blunt. The dragon's head rested on his front paws, and when he moved, a slight shiver ran through his body.

He was an old one.

A poor creature whose strength was gone.

The woman was right.

Yorsh went on strolling about. He had come close to the deepest part of the gilded cavern.

What he saw here took his breath away. At the bottom, there was a mammoth crater from which intense jets of steam escaped, fast as lightning, toward the equally mammoth hole at the very top of the cave, and hurtled outside to form the plume of smoke. It was a volcano! A steam volcano! Grandma had told him about it.

The little elf remembered the afternoon when his grandmother had told him about the hot heart of the world, about volcanoes and earthquakes. She had drawn pictures on the beaten-earth floor of the shack, because there had been no parchment for some time, and she had shown him how the hot heart of the world gives heat to volcanoes. She had also heated, over a candle flame, a bottle half full of water, and had shown him how the heat made the cork come out with a little *plop* and a puff of steam. He had split his sides laughing, and his grandmother had laughed, too, and then she had brought out three nuts that she had been saving for a special occasion, saying that it was always a special occasion when people laughed. It had been a good idea, too, because afterward they hadn't had any more nuts, but also his grandmother had never laughed again, so there had been nothing to celebrate.

The little elf woke from his memories and looked at the column of vapor rising up in front of him. He knew what it was—a long well that communicated with the hot heart of the world, the center of the earth where the fire from which the vapor was born still burns. Ancient underground rivers come into contact with heat and turn into steam that rises and rises until it emerges from the earth as a plume of cloud. That was why an enormous cloud always hung above the mountain! It was born out of the mountain. In fact, it came from the center of the earth, and it just passed through the mountain. Then the steam reached the sky, where it was freed, and spread out until it blocked the stars from view. Clouds. And then more clouds, and more and more and more. Blocking out the stars for years. Clouds and more clouds. Rain and more rain.

"This is a volcano, isn't it?" The little elf seemed suddenly to have regained the power of speech. "A steam volcano. The steam comes from the center of the earth, it comes out here, rises up and obscures the sky, and becomes a cloud that turns into rain."

He looked at the others. His face had brightened—now he knew.

"That's why everything's so dark and it rains!" he explained delightedly. "You just need to move that huge stone there and block the hole, and everything will return to the way it was before. No more mud. Apart from anything else, this stone seems to fit neatly into the crater. Its shape matches the hole exactly."

The little elf continued to observe, walking around the enormous crater and the enormous rock.

"Yes, they really do match. Even the ridges in the rock line up!"

The little elf turned to face the dragon. "That rock there blocked up the crater, and you moved it! You opened the volcano!" The little elf's tone was filled with fury. "How could you do something so stupid? It's caused years of mud and rain! It's *causing* years of mud and rain!"

"Stay away from his jaws," the hunter said to the others. "You do know that if he spits we'll be burned to a crisp?"

But the dragon didn't seem to have any intention of killing them. Clearly dragons are only terrible when they're young, and this one seemed to be very, very old. Very old, very tired, and in despair. He started whimpering and crying once again, and several of the stalactites trembled. The dog whimpered, too, in an attempt to provide comfort.

The woman stayed calm. She went over to the dragon and even dared to stroke one of its paws: "It doesn't matter, it doesn't matter, we'll sort everything out now. Don't be afraid. But you've got to explain to us, or we won't understand. Tell us everything from the beginning."

The sobs began to subside. The stalactites stopped wobbling. The dragon sniffed a few more times, then began his story.

CHAPTER THIRTEEN

"I KNEW THIS place a long time ago, when I was still a child," the dragon began.

"A puppy," corrected the hunter.

"One born lately," said the little elf.

"It was at the time when I still had a name. Now it has slipped from my memory, since for centuries upon centuries no one has uttered it. I came here, because here lies the most precious treasure in the whole world," the dragon went on.

"Really?" the hunter asked. "A treasure? Where is it?"

"All around us."

The hunter looked around. He could see nothing but stalactites and cobwebs.

"Were the spiders of the Second Runic Dynasty

thought to be valuable?" he asked disappointedly.

"Admire," said the dragon. He filled his cheeks and blew gently. Centuries of dust and cobwebs flew away, revealing millions of books. "This was the great library of the Second Runic Dynasty. It was a time of knowledge, and people treated this place as though it were a temple: in silence, and no spitting, with clean hands, and the dust wiped from their shoes. And to be quite certain that nobody misbehaved, dragons have always been here, and that's why there are signs that say 'Here Be Dragons.' This was the biggest collection of knowledge that had ever existed. Then men lost writing. They forgot how to read. Barbarism flooded the world. The very memory of this place faded away. Many people never believed in its existence, but with my wings, I finally found it. And when I reached this place, great was my joy. All the books in the world were for me. Tears still come to my eyes when I remember.

"When old age arrived and snatched my strength from me so that my fire no longer lit, and my wings no longer spread—when I could not even remember my name—then here I settled.

"I was too tired, too aged to fly.

"All that I had to keep me from succumbing to hunger was a handful of golden beans. I had gathered them far hence, in places where the sun shines brightly and enough rain falls. To stave off death, I had to grow more beans, which need more heat and more water than could be found at the top of this mountain.

"But this mountain is a volcano. I moved the rock, and

good warmth and good steam came to warm my bones and my beans, so that my bones would cease to hurt and the beans would grow full well.

"And soon I grew afraid that all the steam, which rose into the sky, would darken the sky and make the earth cold, but too hard it was to cover the crater and leave it closed, to die of cold and hunger, frozen and with nothing to chew upon."

"But it's your fault that there is hunger and misery!" cried the little elf, as the hunter tried to lift him out of the trajectory of the dragon's nostrils.

The dragon recommenced its lamentations, quietly and faintly. The stalactites stayed where they were.

"Does everyone we meet spend all their time crying?" asked the hunter.

"Not everyone," the woman replied. "Only the ones who don't spend all their time trying to hang us."

"Can you put that big rock back?" the little elf asked, firmly but politely.

"To die of cold, enfeeblement, and famine?"

"No," the little elf said bravely. He became more res-olute. "I won't let you die. I swear I will always be with you and will feed you. I will heat this place by burning bun-dles of twigs, and I will collect the twigs from the wood. If no more beans grow, I will plant corncobs. I will ease your hunger. I swear on my elf's honor."

There was a long silence. Yorshkrunsquarkljolnerstrink was calm and serious. He almost gave the impression of being slightly taller.

The dragon spoke first: "Old I am, and quite weak. I can no longer fly now, I can no longer burn. If you deceive me, there is nothing left for me but to die of cold, with my belly empty."

The dragon stretched out with his big muzzle on the ground.

He closed his eyes.

There was a long silence.

Yorshkrunsquarkljolnerstrink approached the dragon and put a hand on his forehead: big, rough scales passed beneath his fingertips. Infinite tiredness. The little elf felt it in his head, through his fingers. Total and absolute exhaustion.

"I'll protect you," said the little elf, "but for the time being, put the stone back in the right place."

The dragon nodded. He pressed his muzzle to the center of the rock and pushed with all his might.

It was slow work: one step at a time, but by evening, the crater was blocked.

The hunter and the little elf pushed as well. The woman roasted the beans along with corncobs. A smell of warmth and good things wafted all around them. The dog had settled on a carpet of bean leaves as soft as velvet, and was dozing peacefully.

Yorsh started talking again. For the first time in his life he felt strong; he knew what to do, why to do it, how to do it.

"I will stay with you and find you things to eat," he promised. "Do you like corncobs? Yes? Good. I have some in my pocket. While we eat the remaining beans we will plant the kernels from the corncobs and make a field of them just outside. They grow even without heat and without steam. And then we'll read. You'll see, it'll be lovely.

"I think this is the circle we must break: the water becomes steam, which becomes a cloud, which becomes rain, which becomes water. Now the circle is broken. I will stay with you, and I won't let you die of hunger."

The dragon looked enchanted.

He nodded his head happily.

He asked to see the corncobs once more, and to hear the story of their cultivation. Then he wept a little, but this time with joy, and finally he came out with the strangest speech he had delivered all day. He said that the other elf, the tall one, the one that had passed this way some time ago, had told the dragon to keep the crater closed because he feared that was the cause of the darkness and the rains; and he, too, had offered to help ease the dragon's hunger. But after a day, the elf had changed his mind, telling the dragon that he could leave the crater open if he felt like it, because it would be good for the beans. And that with the plume of steam rising up, the route would be easier for his son to find, who would have to pass this way too, sooner or later, to fulfill his destiny.

The little elf couldn't breathe.

His father had been here.

His father had been here, had had the chance to stop the darkness, to give the right level of rain—the right level of sunshine—back to the world, to stop the world's famine and misery, and he hadn't done it.

It was appalling, horrendous, atrocious, unimaginable, unspeakable. . . .

"Terrifying," said the woman.

"Chilling," agreed the man.

The little elf was experiencing one of the most wretched emotions of creation: being ashamed of one's own forebears.

His face crumpled.

The light in his eyes went out, his mind was filled with pain, and his magic was drowned in it. He wouldn't be able to bring even a midge back to life.

"Why?" asked the woman.

"How do you sell a pot of good weather for three gold pieces in a world where the sun shines? His father had profited from the rain. The elves have always had an eye for a deal, haven't they?" replied the hunter. An icy rage filled his voice. He paced up and down the cave, taking great strides. He gave the fire a kick, sending corncobs and beans flying in all directions. The dog stopped wagging his tail and whimpered with fear.

"Years of misery, years of famine, of darkness, of despair, all because of a stupid dragon and an elf who . . . who . . ." The hunter searched his brain for an insult that was sufficiently harsh. Finally he found the worst one of all: "All because of an elf who behaved like an elf."

Yorshkrunsquarkljolnerstrink gave a faint sigh. But this time only the dog came to comfort him.

"Is there any way out of here?" the man asked the dragon in a tone both abrupt and tired. "I mean, without getting killed in the waterfall, for people without wings?" he added.

There was. At the end of the clearing, there was an old road that snaked through the Dark Mountains toward the southern side, away from the river and the waterfall, to lose itself in the dense forest to the north of the Dark Mountains. The woman and the hunter prepared to go. The dog would come with them, but the little elf would be left behind.

By the time they went outside, night had already fallen, but it was so clear and bright, full of the most brilliant stars, and with a luminous moon, that they decided to leave anyway.

The road began exactly opposite the spot from which they had arrived. It was not at first easy to see, hidden as it was among the cedars, and in places invaded by clumps of daisies, but was still recognizable because it had once been paved, and some of the old paving remained.

The slabs were small and hexagonal, and fitted into each other like the cells of bees in a hive. Hidden among the daisies were little columns that must, in the past, have supported railings to help walkers up and down. From time to time, the road opened up into little terraces, giving them a place to rest. As they made their way down, cedars made way for larches, and then enormous chestnuts, and a few oaks.

The night was so clear that even at that late hour, Sajra stopped to pick chestnuts. She put them in her knapsack, one after another, trying not to hurt her hands on the spines. She collected them by the dozens, filling her hands with spines despite her precautions, and then burst into tears.

"Well, it's still better than being hanged!" muttered the hunter.

Sajra didn't weep for long. She got back to her feet. She turned around and set off for the slope.

"I'm going to the little one," she said resolutely. Gently, calmly, but resolutely. The tone of someone who isn't coming back. "It wasn't his fault," she went on. "He hasn't done anything. In fact he's sacrificing his life with the dragon so that the sun can shine again. He's saving the world. And we haven't even thanked him! Perhaps his father was a swine, but so what? It doesn't mean the little elf isn't decent. And anyway, his father wasn't responsible for the age of mud. He just didn't stop it from happening. It's not the same thing. He didn't want to sacrifice his life to be with the dragon and save the weather. Maybe he couldn't. Maybe he was sick. Maybe there were other things he had to do. Get back to his son, perhaps, try to warn him about something. What do we know? And how dare we judge him? People blame elves for everything, and it doesn't seem right for us to join in the chorus. He didn't cause the darkness. He just didn't save us. . . ."

The hunter followed her in silence. At intervals he emitted a grunt of disapproval, but not only did he not slow down his pace, he actually quickened it as best he could, despite his exhaustion. By the time the moon sank, they were back among the cedar trees. The clouds were covering the stars, and the darkness was complete. Climbing was impossible. The two squatted down together, along with the dog, on one of the terraces, and the rest of the night passed like that.

At the first light of dawn, they rose to their feet and

climbed as fast as they could, with the urgency of those who have caused an injustice, who have failed to control their rage and have to put it right, because they have hurt a little one, a puppy—one born lately.

When they finally reached the library, the sun was shining brightly, and the waterfall in the distance gleamed with all the colors of the rainbow. The door to the grotto was open, and the dragon was sleeping in the golden light of his cave. The library had been carefully cleaned: all the parchments were gleaming, neat and tidy.

The little elf was sitting in one of the inner rooms. He was surrounded by parchments covered with silvery Elfish characters, with strange drawings of balls and circles. He was as happy as an eaglet who had just learned to fly, and was sitting in the middle of a series of balls that spun in unequal circles, oblique and elongated, around a central ball, which, in turn, rotated on its own axis.

"My father wrote them," said the little elf, showing the writings and drawings. "But I made this!" he added euphorically, pointing to the balls rotating in midair. "I used an old dragon skin—you know, they change them like snakes—to make the globes, and now I'm making them imitate the planets. As long as they're small things and as long as they rotate, I can make them stay in the air, even in defiance of gravity."

A long and complicated explanation followed. There were parchments and parchments about the movements of the stars, in the rooms off to the side. But the dragon had

never reached them. Given the dimensions of the openings between one room and another, everything that was
not in the central room was as inaccessible to the dragon
as the fresh air outside. The dragon had never been able
to study the astral movements, but the little elf's father,
He Who Finds the Road and Shows It to the Others—
Gornonbenmayerguld—had been able to show them to the
dragon, and the dragon had understood. Yorsh's father had
left such clear explanations that Yorsh had been able to
grasp everything in the course of a single night.

The conclusion was that the variation in the climate
had happened because it had happened, and nobody was to
blame. Now it was going away again because the moment
had come for everything to return to normal, and nobody
could claim the credit for it. The volcano had nothing to do
with it. Its plume of white steam wasn't powerful enough
to turn the region into a muddy bog! The little elf used a
large number of meaningless words: meteorites, variation in
the terrestrial axis. Once again he mentioned the law of
gravity, even though nothing here was falling to the ground
and no one was going to be hanged.

The gist of the whole business was that the years of
rain and mud had come by chance because of an enormous
rock that had passed in the sky, where no one could see it,
and now the rain and mud were going because the rock
was moving away, and this brought something called the
"angle of the earth's axis" back to a position where the
climate was optimal. Or at least not too vile. In short,
the usual: a bit of sun, a bit of rain, every now and again a

lovely day with a light breeze for flying kites or sowing grain.

The hunter and the woman didn't understand very much. But they didn't interrupt to ask what a planet was and whether "globe" meant the same thing as "ball." They listened politely to the elf's explanation and agreed with him that, since they had begun traveling together, the weather had, for the first time in years, started to improve. The blue of the sky, the sun, the stars had all reappeared. Pieces of sunset. Fragments of dawn had shown up, after years, in the middle of the clouds and the downpours.

The clearest thing about the astronomic explanation, it seemed to them, was the linguistic aspect. The language of the Second Runic Dynasty was extremely precise. The prophecy said:

> WHEN THE LAST DRAGON AND THE LAST ELF
> BREAK THE CIRCLE,
> THE PAST AND THE FUTURE WILL MEET,
> AND THE SUN OF A NEW SUMMER WILL
> SHINE IN THE SKY

When. Not *quhen.* In the Second Runic Dynasty, *when* means *at the same time, simultaneously.* Whereas *quhen* means *in consequence of,* an event happening as a direct result of another event taking place. But this prophecy read *when,* indicating it would simply happen during the same period of time. Not as a consequence of. And the circle that the little elf and the dragon were to break was not the cycle of water, steam, cloud, rain, and water, but the other circle, the horizon that closes around you, and you're the only one inside it. The circle of loneliness. The little elf had to meet the last dragon to join the past and the future: to recover the knowledge of the glorious past of humankind, when science and knowledge had filled people's lives, and recover them for the future. It was so clear . . . so lovely . . . and his father had understood everything and left a trail for his son to follow, like a trail of stones gleaming in the moonlight.

"And what about the pot of good weather?"

"It's an ordinary smoking pot. The improvement in the rain would start in the lands closest to the Dark Mountains, which are protected from the winds that come from the west. My father foresaw it."

"In human language, selling a smoking pot for three gold pieces is called a 'swindle,'" the man said, narrowly escaping a kick in the shins.

"In Elfish language it's called 'genius,'" the little elf replied cheerfully, "not just because my father left me the way of getting here, but also because, by selling it dearly, he brought them harmony. They, the inhabitants of the village, convinced of superior magic that would bring them peace as well as good weather, stopped fighting among themselves, and that's worth much more than a bit of gold. The key rule in business is that when you pay a lot of money for something that isn't valuable, you've still done a deal. I think the head of the village understood that, too!"

There was a long silence, then the man started laughing. It was a long, liberating laugh. The woman burst into tears and hugged the little elf for a long time, holding him tightly so that she would remember him always.

"Maybe we'll meet again," the little elf said, hoping with all his heart. Maybe they would meet again, but now they had to part. They had to live their lives, which consisted of fields, meadows, and geese to tend, maybe children to raise, certainly not books and golden beans. He had sworn to stay with the dragon. Sadness filled him, and the spheres that were spinning in midair rolled softly to the ground.

"Sooner or later, it will happen," said the woman.

They stayed there hugging for a long time, while the sun rose higher and higher and the library was flooded with gilded light. The beans shone like jewels in the middle of the ancient shelves.

"I'd like to give the dog a name," said Yorshkruns-quarkljolnerstrink.

Sajra hugged him even tighter.

"Of course."

Yorshkrunsquarkljolnerstrink was filled with emotion. His chest swelled with pride.

"FIDO," he said triumphantly.

"Fido?" asked the hunter. "Fido? Dogs are called Tail, or Patch, or Paw, or simply Dog. Fido's a silly name for a dog; it's peculiar. He'll be the first and last dog called—"

He wasn't able to finish his sentence. The usual kick in the shins pulled him up short.

"It's a lovely name," said Sajra. "It'll be fine."

They hugged for a bit longer, then a bit longer, and another bit longer.

Meanwhile, the dragon had woken. He yawned half a dozen times, after which he was informed that he could reopen his volcano and keep his aching old bones warm amidst the golden beans for all the time to come.

The old dragon was so delighted, he wagged his tail, knocking down three stalagmites and a piece of shelf. The joy also stirred up the dragon's memory, like a ladle in soup, and something surfaced. Not his name, which was now lost forever, but something else. He remembered that beneath the big portal was a casket containing something that looked like the beans, but which broke your teeth if you tried to eat it. What was it called again . . . that thing that's used to make scepters and crowns. Did they know what to do with it? the dragon wondered. They did? Oh good, well then, perhaps they could do the dragon the favor of taking it. It was a nuisance where it was.

The hunter and the woman looked at the little elf one last time and waved good-bye forever.

As they were going down the very long road, followed by the dog, the hunter often helped the woman over the more difficult points, giving her his hand. Then he went on holding her hand, even when there was nothing to slip on, nothing to clamber over. She didn't withdraw it. The dog followed them contentedly.

"If you like, with the pieces of gold the dragon has given us, we can buy ourselves a bit of land and live happily," said the man.

The woman didn't reply.

"With a vine, a little grain, a few corncobs," he added.

The woman stopped.

"Some chickens," she suggested.

The man smiled and squeezed her hand.

They went on in silence.

They had almost reached the bottom of the road when the man spoke again.

"You know, this morning, when the first light came and shone on you, well, that is . . . ehmmmmm, we . . . we could . . . I thought . . . You know how lovely it is when the sky turns pink, at dawn, I mean, if we had a daughter, we could call her Rosalba, the pink light of dawn."

The woman didn't withdraw her hand.

"It's a pretty name," she agreed with a slightly shy smile. Then she thought about it: "If we *have* a daughter *we can call her* Rosalba," she corrected.

She dodged a kick that nearly caught her on the shin.

She started laughing.

Then they hugged. And stayed for a long time in each other's arms. Each feeling the warmth of the other's body.

They hugged for a long time beneath the bright sky that lit them up, not least because they had wanted to do just that from the first moment they had set eyes on each other.

PART TWO

CHAPTER FOURTEEN

ROBI SAT DOWN on a tree trunk. She looked at the clear sky, then at the trees at the bottom of the valley. The leaves were starting to turn yellow. In the meadow, the last flowers of early autumn shined in the light of the rising sun. They were the little yellow flowers that Robi's mother had called the "king's buttons," and those blue flowers that look like bells, and the ones that are a kind of little ball, and if you blow on them, all the bits fly away and the flower disappears.

Autumn was coming. That meant winter would not be far behind. First autumn, then winter. That was the rule.

Autumn: few chestnuts, hardly any maize porridge, a few apples, cold feet, and a snotty nose.

Winter: no chestnuts, hardly any maize porridge, no apples, frozen feet, nose so snotty that the snot runs down to where you breathe and turns into coughs; you could warm yourself up with firewood. Not in the sense that you could burn it. No, that was forbidden, but in the sense that you cut it with an axe: after one trunk, another trunk, and then another trunk, and in the end, your back and arms ache and you had blisters on your hands, but for a while at least you weren't dying of cold. Then the cold came back, and you were left with the blisters on your hands.

If you survived, spring came, and then you had to go around the farms, feeding the animals, repairing the fences, and taking the cows to graze, and that was a good thing, because sometimes you could pinch an egg or a bit of milk, but you had to be clever. The farms were all in the county of Daligar, and a theft from the county of Daligar, even just an egg, meant twenty blows with the cudgel. They couldn't count, but twenty meant a blow of the cudgel for each of the child's fingers and toes. Cala was missing a finger because she had aimed badly when chopping wood with the axe. When they beat her, they added an extra blow.

In the summer you had to compete with lice and mosquitoes for your blood. But there was so much food to steal that everyone managed to polish something off without being caught, even the dopiest ones, the ones who had just arrived, the ones who still cried.

Robi was clever. She had never been caught. Not last

year, at least. Two years before, when she had just arrived at the orphanage, she had been caught three times, but she had been little at the time. Dopey, like all little children. And she had always had her father and mother in her head. To be a good thief you have to concentrate. When you have your father and your mother and the house that was your home in your head, concentration isn't enough. Even when you tried to keep your father and mother out of your head, you just had to think of your little green-and-pink wooden boat or your rag doll for tears to come to your eyes. Now it was fine. Now she concentrated. No one caught her any-more.

All of a sudden, the memory of her mother's apples filled her so quickly that she could almost smell them. Her mother cut the apples into slices and left them to dry in the woodshed. She pretended to be angry when Robi stole some of them, and then she chased her all around the wood-shed, and when she caught her she covered her with kisses, and they both laughed like mad. She ate the dry apples with warm milk by the fire in the hearth, while she held her doll in her arms, and outside the snow fell in thick layers, and the world turned white like the wings of the wild geese when the sun passes through them. Then, in the evening, her father came with something really good to eat. Her father was a hunter as well as a farmer, a shepherd, an apple-planter, a pig-breeder, cowhand, carpenter, roofer, shed-builder, and fisherman, and he always brought good things home for dinner. In winter it was trout, because they were easy to catch. You made a hole in the ice that covered the river and you waited for a while. The memory of trout roasted with rosemary also filled her head and her stomach with a spasm. Robi dismissed the memory. If she were caught now, there would be no kisses. She dismissed her tears. Tears are for children. She wasn't a child anymore.

The sun appeared and lit her up. The air grew warmer. At the bottom of the clearing there were two big walnut trees. Walnuts are wonderful at the start of autumn, when they are on the trees, because they are fresh: you take off the bitter skin with your nails, and under it is the nut. But the walnut trees could be seen from the windows of the little wood-and-stone house that towered over the crooked building of the orphanage. Too risky. Beyond the walnut trees, there were brambles, which were nothing like walnuts, but were something, nonetheless. But the blackberries were within the view of the archers who stood guard in the sentry boxes. True enough, at that time of day, the guards were probably still asleep, but it wasn't worth the risk to steal watery things that didn't fill your stomach even long enough for the scratches from the bramble bushes to stop hurting.

Robi closed her eyes, and behind her eyelids a dream was born, the one she always dreamed every time she was able to sit in peace with her eyes closed. She dreamed of a dragon with a prince riding on its back; a prince with hair so fair it looked like silver. It was a huge dragon, with two enormous green wings that filled the sky. The prince wore a white jacket that flew across the sky. The prince was smiling. The dragon was flying toward her. They were coming to get her, to take her away from here, forever. It was a dream that had formed all by itself. At first it had been indistinct: something pale on something green. With each passing day, the dream became more clear. It was as though the prince and the dragon were flying through fog and getting closer to her every day.

Robi dismissed the dream. It was stupid. Dragons didn't exist anymore. They had been cruel and wicked animals, and they had all been wiped out centuries ago. And kind princes must be extinct as well, or perhaps they had gone to other countries, because all memory of them was lost.

Robi opened her eyes. A flock of partridges rose up in front of her in the golden light of early autumn. There was a flutter of wings, which, for a moment, filled the sky with dark turquoise. The flock had emerged from the whitethorn bushes in the lower part of the clearing, the side that was invisible both from the orphanage and from the sentry boxes. Her father had been a hunter. If he were still alive, he would have taken out his bow, and she and her mother would have eaten roast partridge with rosemary. Her father's name had been Monser. He'd had black hair like hers, and had been big and tall like an oak. His mother would have plucked the partridge and used the feathers to sew them one by one to her jacket, to make it both splendid and as warm as toast. Her mother's name had been Sajra. Robi tried to pull the filthy cape of coarse grayish hemp cloth over her ankles to warm them up a little, but it was too short. Her mother had had dark blond hair, and made the best apple fritters in the whole valley.

Robi got to her feet. She didn't have her father's bow

and arrows, but still the turquoise partridges meant food—
they laid eggs in early autumn, when they were nice and fat,
after spending the summer gobbling butterflies, worms, and
beetles. You can even eat butterflies, beetles, and worms,
but only when there's nothing better, while eggs are one of
the best things that exist in the world. When you have an
egg in your stomach, it's not just hunger that fades away for
a while, but cold and fear, too.

Robi glanced around nervously. She had woken up
first—everyone else was still asleep. She heard the restless
slumber of the other children in the dormitory. There were
groans and coughs as usual, and from the little house she heard
the regular snores of the two guardians, Slump and Phlesh,
husband and wife, affectionately known as "the Hyenas," who
slept in a real house with a real fire. Before her the valley
opened up beneath the sun, and the mountains looked blue in
the distance. The first snow gleamed on their peaks. The soldiers' sentry boxes were far away, and the lower part of the
clearing was out of their sight. The soldiers, according to the
Hyenas, were there to protect the children of the House of
Orphans, just in case some evildoer came to do who knows
what, perhaps to steal their lice, the only things that were in
any abundance. In reality, without the soldiers in the sentry
boxes, not one of the children, not even the smallest and stupidest, would have stayed in that horrible hovel, along with
the two Hyenas and their cudgel, vying with worms for maize
porridge, working until they couldn't stand, until they were
soundly thrashed, until they died of cold or were eaten alive
by mosquitoes, depending on the season.

Robi didn't move until she was sure that everyone was asleep and no one was watching her. Even if you found it in a partridge's nest on the moor, in a walnut tree that didn't belong to anyone, or among the thorns of a blackberry bush, all food had to be handed over. If you ate it yourself, it was seen as theft. Theft and selfishness. Selfishness was a serious crime. The parents of Iomir, who was Robi's best friend, had been selfish, SELFISH, sel-fish, as Phlesh spat out every time he said it. Selfish meant that they had tried to pay less tax than they were supposed to, with the laughable excuse that otherwise their children would die of hunger, and the ridiculous pretext that the beans and grain they had pulled from their land, by their own backbreaking work, by the sweat of their own brows, belonged to them and not to the county of Daligar.

Where her own parents were concerned . . . Robi preferred not to think about her own parents. She dismissed the thought. Not this morning. Not after discovering where the partridges had their nests.

She crept over slowly, not going in a straight line, so that if someone spotted her she could give the impression that she was taking a perfectly innocent stroll. She wasn't sure that it would be believable that a little girl half dead with hunger would set off for a stroll on the moor at dawn, but Slump and Phlesh were not the brightest creatures in the world, and she could always say she had been woken by a bad dream and wanted to forget it. Bad dreams came frequently.

The grass grew taller. Robi went down on all fours to

disappear into it. She crept as far as the bushes. The nest was at the height of her nose: she almost bumped into it. Inside were two eggs: two moments without hunger. They were small eggs, their shells speckled with a delicate brown color that turned to gold at its palest points. Robi took one egg between her hands and felt its warm smoothness against her skin. She closed her eyes for a moment. When her mother had pressed her close, she had told her that when we're happy, the people who have loved us and who no longer exist, come back from the realm of the dead to be near us. Now perhaps her father and mother were with her.

Robi opened her eyes again. She took another look at her incomparable treasure of two partridge eggs, and then set about devouring them. The egg she had in her hand she ate immediately: she made a little hole in it by striking it against a branch, and sucked it with fierce joy—first the white part and then the best part, the yolk, which she sipped up slowly, drop by drop, with a pleasure bordering upon the joy of life itself.

The problem was the other one: her first idea was to eat it immediately. What you have in your stomach you can't lose, and no one can steal it from you. But two eggs is such a lot: sometimes your stomach, when it is very used to being half empty, can't hold things. It begins to hurt and you throw up. And also, however much you put in it, half a day later your belly is gripped with hunger again. It's better to eat a small amount at a time. Robi wrapped the second egg in a big clump of earth, wrapped that in turn in a handful of grass, and hid it not in the big pocket under her cape, which was used for tools, but in the other one, the hidden one. Under the filthy, grayish jute jacket she had made—using big thorns as needles and a piece of string stolen from the bags where they kept the maize porridge—a kind of fold where things could be hidden.

A day without hunger. Robi breathed in the morning air—it was going to be a good day.

CHAPTER FIFTEEN

AWN ROSE brightly. The old amber windows filtered the light, and the library turned to gold.

Yorshkrunsquarkljolnerstrink, the elf boy, woke up and stretched his long arms.

The dragon went on sleeping. The slivers of amber vibrated with his quiet snores, making the light on the walls move faintly, like a breeze on a pond. The elf boy got up and shook off the hundreds of blue and gold butterflies that covered him at night, warming him with their faint heat.

He spent a few moments by the climbing plants that carpeted the ancient arches, dripping with fruit, to decide what he wanted for breakfast. The sweetness of strawberries with the harsh sharpness of oranges? No, not for breakfast. Better the resolute sweetness of a fig, along with the fresh, round sweetness of red grapes. Definitely better. Even in terms of color the effect was better. The pale pink and the dark green harmonized with each other. In the amber dish they formed a graceful contrast.

It had been a stroke of luck finding instructions on growing fruit-bearing climbing plants in an old book. The elf boy sighed. Everything was so perfect. So pleasurably perfect. Undeniably perfect. Inevitably perfect. Dully perfect. Unbearably perfect.

The dragon was a snorting mountain that occupied the whole of the enormous room with his vast bulk. His grayish and pink scales alternated to form complicated twirls and spirals. His tail was twisted like a coil of rope on a wharf. The elf boy walked past him, then approached the ancient, carved wooden door that closed off the cave. He opened it delicately. He couldn't help making a sound, but the dragon went on sleeping.

Outside, the wind was blowing. In the distance, the horizon met a dark sea, whitened with foam. The gulls were flying. The elf boy smelled the perfume of the sea as it came all the way to him. He sat down and looked at the gulls. The wind tousled his hair. Behind him, the Dark Mountains rose beyond the clouds. The scent of the sea merged with the smell of the pines. The elf boy closed his eyes and dreamed that he could touch the sea. Feel the foam on his face. The taste of the salt. He dreamed of seeing the waves breaking. He dreamed of sailing on the sea, of climbing the mountains, crossing cities, wading through rivers. He dreamed of feeling the earth beneath his feet step after step as he walked, seeing how the world was made.

The dragon's voice pierced the morning: "Thou wretched boy, how canst thou be so cruel as to hold open yon door that freezes me, sick old dragon that I am, with all my rheumatic old bones? And have you forgotten, oh most wretched one, that when the air maketh draft, the pain that afflicts my head grows to bursting? Rememberest not, oh misbegotten one, how the air doth ail me when it passes by the door and freezes me. . . . Air of door crack, air of tomb . . ."

The elf boy opened his eyes. He sighed. Once, three years previously, he had mentioned the idea of going down the steps to see the sea up close. It would have taken him half a day to get there and back. The dragon's lamentations had lasted for eleven days. With all his weeping at the horror of the prospect of being abandoned, the dragon had given himself sinusitis, which had then been further complicated by an illness of both ears, which meant attacks of dizziness that had never really cleared up and got worse on windy days. And when the dragon was seized by attacks of dizziness, it was as though his stomach was coming out through his throat and right ear, sometimes his left ear as well, but more usually the right. . . .

Yorsh sighed again.

As a child, he had sworn that he would take care of the dragon. Forever.

The elf boy politely asked the dragon if he was hungry.

He replied with a long wail of indignant suffering. Hungry? Hungry? The dragon? Had the wretched boy forgotten that the dragon suffered from halitosis; heartburn; a rumbling stomach; eructations; pains in the second, third, and sixth internal intercostal spaces; not to mention hiccups? Thus afflicted, how could he be hungry? The very thought was irresponsible and outlandish.

"You won't be wanting breakfast, then?" asked Yorsh.

This time the wail set the amber panes rattling, and the light on the wall surged like waves of the sea. How could the elf boy, with what cruelty, what malice, dare to suggest that he break his fast? Every time he spent more than two twelfths of a day without eating, he was seized by a series of contractions between his stomach and his esophagus, as though there were tiny bubbles there, not to mention the stitches in his fifth, eleventh, and twenty-sixth intercostal spaces on the left. . . .

The elf boy objected that he seemed to remember that dragons had only twenty-four ribs. The dragon started crying because nobody loved him.

The elf boy sat down on the floor and took the dragon's head in his hands. Then he remembered his oath: he would look after the dragon, *forever*. He stood up, set a slice of pink melon and a few pink grapes on a layer of pink strawberries, hoping that they would be accepted. The lamentations broke off. Pink always worked. The wind came in through the still-open door at an angle. It was a mere breeze. The reeds hanging from the ceiling vibrated, and a delicious music spread around.

Everything was so perfect.

After breakfast, the dragon went to sleep again, and his snores drowned out the music.

At last the chance to read in peace. For thirteen years, Yorsh had been effectively locked up in the library along with an incalculable number of butterflies and a dragon that was the quintessence of the most abysmal boredom, not to mention the fact that each day the creature's mind was a little more lost in the dark meanders of his increasingly spiteful frailty.

At least the elf boy could read. The whole of human and elfish knowledge: the history of the ancient kingdoms; the names of the great kings; the ruinous invasion of the ogres; herbology, astronomy, and physics—it was all contained in the library. Book after book, shelf after shelf, Yorsh had read, studied, ordered, and cataloged, room after room, stalactite after stalactite. Probably no other living creature, not among the elves, let alone among humans, had even come close to his level of knowledge. Probably not even in its distant and happy golden age, when sages had visited the library in such numbers that it had been necessary to forbid them to spit on the ground, not even then had the library been in such an orderly state. All that was left was the last shelf in the little room, the one in the far south, farthest from the great heart of the library, where the dragon snored.

Yorsh set off to the little room, raising clouds of butterflies as he passed, through climbing plants that dripped with flowers. On the single shelf there was a history book, the umpteenth biography of the great Arduin, and a book of zoology that was probably entirely fantastic, given that it showed a kind of very tall, thin cow with a very long neck, decorated with patches of yellow and brown; and a strange grayish creature, the size of a house, with an extremely long nose, with which it scratched behind its enormous ears. Then the usual books of Elfish astronomy, a book of human astrology, and a kind of extremely old and worn parchment turned by mildew into a single illegible block that couldn't even be unrolled. In his thirteen years as a librarian, Yorsh had become good at restoring ancient parchments: it would take time, steam, and the oil of sweet almonds. And he had it all in abundance—the steam from a volcano heated the library, the western side was carpeted with sweet almonds, and he had so much time that he didn't know what to do with it, and anything that could fill it was a blessing.

Yorsh wondered what he would do, now that everything readable had been read, everything studiable studied, and everything archivable archived, to get through his days without drowning in nostalgia. There were days when he had to be careful not to let his thoughts drift toward the hunter and the woman. Who could say whether they were still alive? If so, they were sure to have married! Perhaps they had children, and maybe they'd even told their children about him. Perhaps they were waiting for the children to grow up before they set off on their journey to come and find him. Perhaps they couldn't tell anyone they had met a real elf, and it would have been too dangerous to come back. Perhaps he would never know anything more about them.

He mustn't think about them. It was too painful.

The elf boy set to work. After soaking the parchment in almond oil, he tied the mildewed bundle to a stick and held it out over the crater. Now he had to wait.

He sat down and gripped the stick with both hands. It was rough, scraped, and knotted. It had belonged to the hunter. Yorsh closed his eyes and sank into his memories. He had a scrap of memory of his mother, a moment of a smile, an echo of a voice. Grandma, on the other hand, was firmly in his memory, with all her sadness and all that she had taught him. And then there was the two of them, the hunter and the woman, Sajra and Monser, their cheerfulness, their courage . . .

Yorsh smiled at the memory, but then he was filled with nostalgia, and his smile disappeared, like the last grass when the frost comes. He was overcome with longing for friendship, for tenderness, along with a faint and impalpable feeling that he found hard to define. It was, you might say, the uncertainty of things, their unpredictability. It started in the morning, and he didn't know where it would go. Everything and the opposite of everything could always happen.

His days with Monser and Sajra had been filled with fear, hope, despair, hunger, happiness, and joy.

While now, all that the days were filled with—from morning till evening, year after year, season after season, for an infinite sequence of seasons that were all the same—were petals and pink perfection.

The hope for imperfection became a more remote mirage with each passing day. Even the mud, the rain, and hunger filled him with longing. In reality his longing was for them, Sajra and Monser, the woman and the man who had picked him up, saved him, and loved him. In fact, when he thought about it more clearly, it wasn't imperfection that he missed.

He missed Monser and Sajra.

He missed being free.

"What dost thou?" asked the dragon.

"Nothing important," replied the elf.

"Then canst thou come and do it here? That I may not be left in solitude, that we may read a good book even if we have read it before, the book about the beautiful princess who weddeth the entrancing prince, he who was lost as a child and everyone mistook for another . . ."

It seemed to Yorsh that dragons' brains, after the second millennium of life, begin to develop dramatic holes. The dragon couldn't remember his own name. Of all possible shortcomings, this one struck the elf boy as being the worst. But then Yorsh discovered something even more peculiar— the dragon's passion for love stories. Not all love stories. Just really stupid ones.

"I'll finish here and be right with you," promised the elf boy.

By now the steam had softened the mildew. Yorsh very gently began to unroll the parchment. He worked slowly to avoid tearing it, oiling it with almond oil before gently unsticking the sheets from one another.

The title would soon be decipherable.

Losing patience, the dragon asked once again what he

was doing, and as Yorsh replied, he deciphered the title: *Dracos, Language of the Third Runic Dynasty*. Dragons. A book about dragons! It was the first time he had ever seen one. In the whole library, in a total of 523,826, not a single book spoke of dragons. 523,826, from astronomy to alchemy, taking in meteorology, geography, instructions about fishing, and the making of blueberry liqueur, and which included 1,105 recipe books devoted to mushrooms and 18,436 love stories, all competing for the stupidest book of the millennium, and not a single one about dragons?

Then he understood. The library of books about dragons must have contained dozens of them, or maybe even hundreds, but for some obscure reason of his own, the dragon didn't want them to be read and had destroyed them.

Once again the dragon quietly started protesting about his loneliness, the spasms in his stomach, and an itch in his fifth intercostal space on the left spreading to his hundred and fifty-seventh vertebra. . . . Then he went to sleep, his quiet snores filled the library.

Dragons (Dragosaurus Igniforus) *have one hundred and fifty-six vertebrae*, began the book. Yorsh was a bit slow at reading the characters of the Third Runic Dynasty, but he could still manage it.

CHAPTER SIXTEEN

ROBI CREPT INTO the dormitory. It was a big room that had been used in the past as a sheepfold. The morning light seeped through gaps in the boards. There were no windows, and an old sheepskin served as a door. Inside, there hung a smell that was a mixture of mildew, unwashed humans, and a hint of the honest smell of sheep, which was, in fact, the most decent part of the whole thing. On the ground there was a uniform layer of hay, which lay between the bodies of the children sleeping on the bare ground. Dust danced inside the rays of the rising sun. Robi found her place, between Iomir and the north wall, where the wood was a little more damp and a little more rotten. She covered herself with the cloak that acted at night as a blanket, brushed her finger along the tiny swelling that the second egg made beneath her jacket, and happily closed her eyes. Immediately, the image of the prince and the dragon formed, and this time she didn't dismiss it.

She was so lost in her imaginings that the sound of the wake-up bell, although foreseen and expected, gave her a start. She wasn't the only one—it was normal for the children to wake with a start from their agitated sleep. The expectation of breakfast, however meager, and a lack of confidence in the tolerance of the Hyenas for latecomers, made them all very quick, even breathless. Their cloaks were folded up and arranged on the beaten-earth floor, according to a precise order as regards to the position of the child during roll call. The hay was piled up in the corners, and the children arranged themselves, standing always in the order in which they slept. It all happened in silence, in a hurry, with the fear of not being on time. The sheepskin entrance moved aside, and the Hyenas came into the dormitory. The last latecomers dashed to their places, crashing into one another in their terror. Phlesh always smiled. She was beautiful, or perhaps it would be more correct to say that she must have been beautiful some time before, and that she was still accustomed to being so, even if she wasn't really anymore. She was small, with an oval face. She had a complicated hairdo of braids gathered at the back of her neck, filled with silver hairpins with green stones. Today she was wearing a pink jacket on which dark pink embroidery alternated with rows of glass pearls. Her skirt was a little darker in color than her jacket, and it repeated the color of the embroidery. Around her neck she wore a sumptuous circle of white lace, which made a kind of wave before crossing over itself in a voluminous knot.

Slump was much older than his wife. Perhaps in the past he'd had an intelligent face, or perhaps he had once said or done something intelligent, but that was lost in the mists of time.

"Good morning, beloved children," said Phlesh.

Slump nodded vaguely.

"Good morning to you, Mistress Phlesh and Master Slump," the children said in unison.

One of the smallest children didn't manage to finish the sentence, because she had to cough. Phlesh frowned severely, and the child immediately tried to regain her composure.

"It is the dawn of another marvelous day in which you will be able to experience the kindness, generosity, and gentleness of your benefactor. Our benefactor. The benefactor of all of us. Our leader. He who defends us. We love . . ."

"The Judge Administrator of Daligar and Surrounding District," the children replied again in a single voice. Once more, the little one couldn't finish the sentence and had to cough. The child was standing behind Robi, but she didn't dare turn around to see who it was. On Phlesh's rich and varied lists of misdeeds, turning around during the "dialogue" was classified as "impertinence" and punished with a number of blows that varied from one to six, according to circumstances. Robi had a sense that the child with the coughing fit was Iomir, but she wasn't sure.

"We are all . . ." Phlesh continued.

"Grateful," the children concluded.

"To our beloved . . ."

"Judge Administrator of Daligar, our beloved county, the only thing in the world for which it is worth living and dying. . . ."

Epecially dying. Living in this county had become a real undertaking, and the amount of luck and skill required for mere survival was growing from one day to the next.

The coughing interrupted Phlesh once again. Now Robi was certain—it was Iomir.

"Without him, you would be . . ." Phlesh went on irritably.

Robi thought once again of her father and mother: if not for the Judge Administrator of Daligar and Surrounding District, her family would still be alive—she would have been sleeping under the woolen blankets of her home, and she would have woken to a breakfast of milk, bread, apples, a little honey, and sometimes even a bit of cheese.

"Scattered and in despair," the choir replied, "the children of wretched parents."

Happy and with our bellies full, thought Robi. She herself, certainly, and Iomir, and all those who had been the children of parents who had died of hardship. Before the Judge Administrator of Daligar and Surrounding District arrived and reorganized everyone's life, it was difficult to be seriously hungry in a land that dripped with fruit trees, where kitchen gardens alternated with vineyards, and cattle and flowers filled the meadows. Not even during the Great Rains—the dark years of mud—had famine touched the county. Now it was everyday life, normality, the rule. Each summer, cartloads and cartloads of grain and fruit left the countryside and headed for the city of Daligar, where perhaps they paved the roads with it, because it wasn't humanly possible for so much food to be eaten.

"Or worse," Phlesh went on.

At this point the chorus fell silent.

"The children of selfish parent—" Iomir's voice continued on its own, but once again a fit of coughing swallowed up the final syllables.

Robi held her breath. It was her turn as a soloist: "Or selfish and protectors of elves," she added quickly, in the hope that it would be one of those mornings when everything finished very swiftly. She was to be disappointed. It was one of those mornings that dragged on and went into the tiniest details. Phlesh came over to her, and her smile grew tender.

"Exactly," she began. "Your parents were . . ."

"Selfish," muttered Robi, preferring to stick to the less serious offense, because the idea that her parents might ever have protected an elf was too horrible to think about.

"Louder, my dear, louder!"

"Sel-fish!" articulated Robi.

"Meaning?"

"That they were attached to their wealth." Robi

thought about wealth again: her mother's dried apples, her father's ducks, the orchard behind the house. Her father and mother had started working before dawn and stopped in the depths of the night, and the result had been a full larder and rows of cabbages in the kitchen garden. Then the soldiers had come.

"It's true, my dearest children," Phlesh explained while Slump gave a series of bored nods, "it's a terrible, ter-ri-ble thing not sharing your own property, being attached to your own wealth."

Phlesh broke off in annoyance—Robi's eyes were fixed on Phlesh's shoes, purple velvet run through with gold thread, with a tiny pearl shining where the seams met. It was very difficult to look down and avoid Phlesh's shoes, and the one time Robi had dared to speak to Phlesh without looking at the ground still stuck in her memory.

"The gilded shoes are not for me," Phlesh hissed icily. "They're for the functionary in Daligar that I represent. I'm only wearing them temporarily on my modest and humble person," she explained, articulating her words as though talking to the mentally deficient.

Phlesh sighed and looked at the children. Robi glanced around as well. It wasn't an impressive spectacle: they were all barefoot, dressed in mud-colored jute cloth, with dirty, unkempt hair that fell over thin and dirty faces. Once, Robi had braided Iomir's hair, but that had been considered "eccentric and frivolous behavior," an extra hour's work and no dinner for both of them.

Iomir started coughing again, and Phlesh looked at her

sadly, as though grieved by that form of irresponsible ingratitude.

"Today you have interrupted me many times, Iomir," she
said gently, approaching the girl.

Iomir tried to stop coughing and nearly choked. "No
breakfast," added Phlesh with a sad sigh of disappointment.

Then she turned around and gave orders to two older
boys, Falco and Fowlpest, to distribute an apple and a
handful of maize porridge to each. Iomir's could be divided
among the rest. Falco and Fowlpest exchanged a look of
triumph. Then, added Phlesh, they would accompany the
children to the meadows to scythe the last of the hay and
collect some wood. Iomir managed to wait for the Hyenas to
leave before bursting into tears. The children swarmed into
the open air and made orderly lines, all but Robi, who
stayed where she was, and Iomir, who crouched weeping in
a corner of the dormitory.

Robi thought about the egg she had in her stomach. For
that day, hunger was defeated.

She looked at Iomir, small and desperate, with her little hands in front of her face.

While the others went out toward the light, Robi
stayed in the shade, recovered the partridge egg from her
hidden pocket, and freed it from the soil, then went over to
the child and slipped it into her hands: "Don't stop crying
straight away," she recommended in a whisper. "And eat the
shell, too, so that it's not left lying around."

Then she joined the line and waited for her apple. She

was given a wrinkled, slightly rotten little fruit, and less maize porridge than usual, but as she ate, she heard Iomir's weeping becoming more and more cheerfully fake. It was going to be a good day.

CHAPTER SEVENTEEN

THE DRAGON demanded that the elf boy
read the story of the princess and the beans from the beginning. Surely by now the dragon knew it by heart. The
princess had been lost as a baby, during the flood, in a field
of beans, and was then brought up by the bad farmer's wife,
so that when she met the queen, unaware that the queen
was her mother, she didn't recognize her. At this point, the
elf boy broke off to give the dragon time to weep out all his
tears. Then he started up again where the princess, who
thinks she is poor, tells the bad prince he can keep all his
riches to himself. Here, there was another interruption as
the dragon covered the carpet of pink petals on the floor

with his tears. It was a joyous moment of recognition as the bean girl and the queen, her mother, hurled themselves into each other's arms. The end.

Silence.

Overwhelmed by all his weeping, the dragon fell fast asleep. His quiet snores stirred the petals and butterflies with a regular movement like the waves of the sea.

Dragons have one hundred and fifty-six vertebrae, twenty-four pairs of ribs, four lungs, two hearts. Between the uvula and the thyroid lie the igniferous glands, which contain the glucosioalcoholconvertasis, the substance that converts glucose to alcohol. When any kind of emotion raises the dragon's temperature, the alcohol ignites and a massive emission of flames accompanies exhalation. The inhalation of water infused with fresh flowers of aconitus albus, digitalis purpurea, and arnica diminishes the emission of fire, which is uncontrolled in the newborn dragon. But the infusion must be very weak, since an excess is toxic and can be deadly. Furthermore, the inhalation of simple . . .

This part here about the "simple inhalation" that put the dragon's fire out had been devoured by mildew and lost when the parchment was unrolled. It didn't seem to be important information. His dragon had never spat anything, not so much as a spark. Maybe the fire from the jaws was a rule to which there were exceptions.

If mentha piperita is inhaled, the sweetness of the breath may be improved.

Where could he plant some *mentha piperita*? One plantation or two, perhaps even three.

The soul of the dragon is also pure fire, the manual continued.

Their courage is peerless, their generosity unequalled, their knowledge is as vast as the sea, the wisdom within them embraces the sky. The only thing equal to their intellect is their boundless love of freedom and flight.

Yorshkrunsquarkljolnerstrink was so perplexed that he checked the title again: yes, it was about dragons. Terror of drafts seemed to him to be rather incompatible with unparalleled courage. The intelligence of oceanic dimensions seemed to him to be inconsistent with the tears shed over the fate of swapped princesses, not to mention its forgetting of its own name.

Most definitely, all rules have their exceptions.

There is only one word that can describe a dragon: MAGNIFICENCE.

Well, everything in the world is a matter of opinion. The author of the book was probably a fan of lamentations, a devotee of intestinal grumblings. Or else what was written in books of dragonology applied to all dragons except his.

Perhaps the library had held other manuals on dragonology, and the dragon had destroyed them for fear that his own, so to speak, lack of normality would look pale in comparison. Perhaps even as a child, that is, a puppy, yes, in short, when he had been born recently, the other dragonlets had mocked his taste for stories of swapped princesses, playing ring-around-the-rosy on volcanoes, and hide-and-seek among lightning and clouds.

The elf's heart softened. It must be terrible to be boring, unbearable, and bungling in a world of magnificent geniuses.

He unrolled the next page less successfully than the one before—at more than one point the writing was blurred and illegible.

All dragons, at the end of their lives, lay an egg.

The language of the Third Runic Dynasty was not his strong point. Yorsh reread the passage three times before he was sure. All dragons, at the end of their lives, lay an egg. But are dragons male or female? And what about his dragon? He had always taken for granted that it was male.

Like some sea fishes, dragons are born male before becoming mothers.

Interesting. But it gave neither the scientific name nor the common name of the fish in question. As a book, it was seriously lacking.

Brooding lasts thirteen years, three months, and eight or, in some cases, nine days.

Thirteen years of brooding? Plus three months and eight and a half days?

During the brood, the dragon loses its fire, its courage, and its desire to fly or to be free. Everything is drowned in the spasmodic desire for a warm place where it can stay in peace.

The dragon's knowledge disperses into a void that swallows every-thing up: first mathematics, then geometry, astronomy, astrology, prophetology, history, biology, and the art of catching butterflies. Everything is swallowed up by the void. The next skill to disappear is grammar, and the dragon speaks an obscure language, and the line of its thought resembles that of people who have taken a knock to the head. For the last thirteen years, their own name is forgotten, which is the supreme knowledge, because one's own name is one's own soul, especially for dragons, who choose their own names when they are at the peak of their power, unless that name be given them by those who bring them up.

Yorsh swallowed hard. He felt as if he had been suddenly plunged into freezing water.

The brood requires a certain quantity of heat. In the days when there were many dragons and they covered the earth, as horseflies and grasshoppers do in our own times, before commencing to brood, it would find another dragon to tell it stories. These stories were full of sentiment and emotion, because these are the only way of raising the temperature so that the egg is properly brooded. The dragon that is the friend of the brooding dragon, besides distracting and warming the brood with stories of swapped children and abducted princesses, will also have another quite serious task: that of raising the baby dragon, because the older dragon survives the brood by only a few hours, the time required to take its final flight, to feel the power of the wind in its wings and leave so that the newborn dragon, having just emerged from the egg, does not see the death of its own parent.

Death? His dragon was about to die? A dagger pierced the elf boy's heart.

This is the reason why the brooding dragon is particularly boring, tiresome, uninteresting, and unbearable, the better to try beyond all possible endurance the patience of the future tutor of his own infant, the one who will have to love it, protect it, and, above all, teach it to fly; for only when it learns to fly does the new dragon cease to be a baby.

Why hadn't the dragon told him? Why had he kept Yorsh in the dark?

Doubtless, the dragon had destroyed all the manuals of dragonology so that he wouldn't find out.

The brooding dragon is afraid of everything.

He had kept him in the dark out of fear? Fear of abandonment? Fear that the elf might abandon his precious egg?

But now that dragons have disappeared, it is always more difficult for the dragon to find a warm and quiet place with something to eat, without ever being able to move, not even for the shortest of flights, because otherwise the egg grows cold and dies. And the dragon needs stories to raise the temperature sufficiently for the brood. And if the dragon has found this, it also needs someone to adopt its little orphan, and this is why dragons are ever fewer in number, and will also be ever fewer in number in time to come. The brooding dragon knows that at all costs it must keep its condition hidden, because raising a baby dragon is terribly . . . (mildew) . . . and no one would stay for such a task. Also because . . .

Also because what? It didn't say. The rest of the writing was devoured by mildew.

The elf boy's stomach was tight with horror and emotion. And a sense of guilt. Could he have been nicer? Certainly, the dragon was stupid, tiresome, bossy, and unbearable, but that was because it was brooding!

A terribly long brood, so long and exhausting that it destroyed the spirit, diluted the mind, annihilated courage. The last act of the dragon's life. Then death would come. DEATH.

Yorsh dropped the parchment, which fell to the ground with a faint rustle. He hadn't time to do anything else— there was a terrifying crash, and the very walls of the cave trembled.

This was followed by a curious repeated rustling sound, like a parchment falling to the ground, but deeper and more amplified. Like enormous wings beating in the sky.

And finally, a deadly high-pitched *squeeeeeek* that shattered half of the amber panes that sealed the windows.

The elf boy rushed to the big hall. In the middle of it was an enormous egg, on which emerald green and gold chased after one another to create the same spirals that appeared in pink and gray on the skin of the dragon. The shell had split on one side, and from it protruded a miniature version of the old, brooding dragon. The infant's face wore a desperate expression. He was green and gold like the egg, and the tuft above his eyes was of a darker green, like the bottom of the sea when it is clear. His eyes were enormous, round, wide, and anxious. All the books on the north shelf, 846 books of analytic geometry and instructions on how to preserve blueberries and pepper, were smoking. Clearly the *squeeeeeek* had been accompanied by a spurt of fire. Yorshkrunsquarkljolnerstrink found himself thinking that it hadn't been a very clever idea to stack all the books on a single subject on a single shelf. Now the analysis of plane geometry had disappeared from the category of studiable materials, and humanity would have to reinvent it from the beginning, unless he himself could set aside a little time, fifty or sixty years, say, to write down at least its rudiments. The recipes for blueberry and pepper preserves, to be steeped in thyme, were gone forever; but with a bit of luck, no one would ever rediscover them.

The crash, accompanied by the trembling of the walls, had been the opening of the massive door. The two leaves of the door had parted, and the sea wind came in, sending petals, butterflies, and the ashes of three centuries of geometry swirling in little whirlwinds on the floor.

In the sky, the wings of the great old dragon beat above the sea. The sky was filled with his flight. The light of the sun, now high in the sky, passed through the arabesques of his wings. His golden eyes met the blue eyes of the elf boy. All the tenderness in the world lay in those eyes, and all the pride, all the possible love, all the strength and arrogance.

All the magnificence.

MAGNIFICENCE.

MAGNIFICENCE.

MAGNIFICENCE.

MAGNIFICENCE.

MAGNIFICENCE.

MAGNIFICENCE.

"Erbrow," yelled the dragon, as a streak of flame emerged from his jaws and lit the sky, giving it an orange tinge.

Yorsh understood that this was the dragon's name. He nodded, then took a deep bow.

The trail of fire stayed in the sky, dividing it in two, while the wings of the great dragon swept down toward the horizon, where the stormy waves met the sky.

The waves opened up and slowly received the great wings, which hung for a long time on the edge of the horizon, beneath clouds of gulls.

Yorsh's eyes remained fixed on the last point where the waves had flashed beneath the sun.

* * *

The elf boy's heart sank. Grief entered his soul like a blade, and there it found the other grief, the one that had always been there: the mother who had gone to the place from which you do not come back, the grandmother who had stayed in the water that rose.

The elf boy wished he could have him back, the big dragon, to be able to read once more the story of the princess and the peas, or the beans, or whatever they were. He wished with all his might that he could hear the old dragon telling him off as though Yorsh were the worst criminal in the world for having tried to climb into the oak tree outside the front door, or hear him list once again all the symptoms of external otitis, not to mention gastritis, sinusitis, urticaria, and the spasm in his thirty-second caudal vertebra, or the sixteenth, or the fortieth.

Then another terrible *squeeeeeeeeeeeeek* rang out behind him.

The little dragon was crying.

Now physics had ended up in little whirls of ash on the floor. Humanity would have to rediscover, from the very start, the laws of leverage and thermodynamics. It would take a millennia, if everything went well!

While Yorsh thought desperately about what to do and how to do it, he recalled one of the proverbs of Arduin, the Lord of Light, Founder of Daligar: "When disasters befall us, we have not time to think how sad or desperate we are, and therefore cease to be so."

The first thing to do was to pull the little dragon out of his egg. The shell was three inches thick. Yorsh tried to break it, but it was like trying to break a rock with your hands. He cautiously stretched out a hand, careful to move as slowly as possible so as not to frighten the little dragon.

His movement wasn't slow enough.

There was another little *squeek*, with the accompanying flicker of flame: fortunately, among the mushroom recipes and instructions for the making of machines, there was a manual for treating burns.

Yorsh tried again, this time with his left hand, given that his right hand now looked like one of the penny buns in *How to Cook Your Mushrooms on Embers*, fourth shelf from the south side in the third room. He moved even more slowly than before, to avoid increasing the resemblance between his face and the illustrations in *How Not to Burn Your Mushrooms on Embers*, third shelf from the south side of the third room.

This time Yorsh managed to put his hand on the little dragon's head. Whirls of tiny emerald-green scales alternated with strips of velvet-soft skin that were a darker green with a gold iridescence. Everything was smooth, soft, and warm, but through his hand, the elf felt the desperate fear of the little dragon. Inside the warm little head of the enormous baby dragon lay infinite anxiety, and the fear of something far more painful than hunger and much more frightening than darkness.

Yorsh risked being overwhelmed by that blind and unfathomable terror, and remembered himself alone in never-ending rain with no one but himself as far as the horizon.

The fear of being alone.

The fear of having no one to love you.

He knew what he had to do. With all his strength, he thought of himself and the little dragon together. He imagined himself with the little dragon's head in his lap in the middle of an endless meadow of tiny daisies. Then he imagined himself and the little dragon sleeping with their arms around each other. Then sharing sweet almonds and beans, fifty-fifty. And then, again, the little dragon with his head in Yorsh's lap in an endless field of daisies.

The little dragon calmed down, the despair faded from his features, and his eyes grew more serene.

"It's all fine, little one, it's all fine."

Little being a figure of speech—the baby dragon was huge. But no other epithet came to mind. He was a little one. He had big, dewy eyes, green and gold like a mountain lake on which the sun is shining.

"Little one, lovely little one. You're my lovely little one. You're my lovely little chick, my little chickabiddy. Chicklet, little one, lovely little dragon, tiny little dragon, lovely little chick."

The dragon brightened. For the first time in his life he smiled. Then the little dragon wagged his tail, and his giant egg shattered into tiny pieces, like an explosion of emerald-green and gold fireworks.

"Erbrow!" That would be its name. "Erbrow," the elf repeated triumphantly.

The little dragon went into absolute raptures. He hopped happily up and down. A deadly blow from his wagging tail demolished an ancient stalactite, and several boulders fell from the ceiling. This was followed by a joyful *squeeeeeek*, and fortunately, Yorsh ducked quickly enough to save his face, but his hair ended up in tiny flecks of ash that danced on the floor along with the remains of *The Art of Meridians*. Humanity wouldn't be able to tell the time for centuries to come. Even doing something pathetically easy, like predicting a comet or an eclipse would be a massive undertaking.

Yorsh sat down on the ground; the baby dragon smiled. He had a toothless smile, and his eyes lit up even more. The little dragon put his head in Yorsh's lap and immediately fell asleep, exhausted.

Peace.

Yorsh's right hand felt as if it were on fire. His forehead, too, had been scorched by the flames.

He tried to think up a plan of things to do in order of urgency: stow away all the books and parchments by cramming them into the central room, to protect them both from the baby dragon and from bad weather. Another matter of urgency: he would have to locate some arnica, aconite, and digitalis purpurea, and find a way to make the baby dragon inhale them, to make him more—how to put it—manageable. Arnica, Yorsh remembered, is also used to cure burns. He would have to plant it everywhere.

Moving slowly so as not to disturb the little dragon sleeping in his lap, Yorsh stretched out on the floor of the cave, in the middle of a carpet of daisies, stretched out his left hand, the only one that worked, and recovered his manual of dragonology, at that moment the most important book in the library.

Daisies? The floor of the cave was now covered with a field of daisies.

Some useful information about dragons hadn't been examined in the manual. The fact that the mind of a baby dragon, when it is happy, makes its dreams come true, was not mentioned.

On the other hand, perhaps it had been mentioned, but it had been devoured by mildew.

CHAPTER EIGHTEEN

THEY WORKED from early morning, picking grapes, the loveliest work in the world. It was impossible for the overseers to count all the bunches on a vine, all the grapes in a bunch. They had to sing uninterruptedly to show that their mouths were empty, but it was impossible to notice when a voice was missing. The notes of:

> *"We all love the Judge,*
> *and we trust him, too.*
> *Grateful are we all*
> *for the Judge's loooooove. . . ."*

rang out constantly around the vines. The children had learned to eat in turn, only one at a time, the one who was at that moment the farthest from Phlesh, who moved constantly between the rows while Slump snored down below, at the foot of the slope on which the vines grew, in the shade of a fig tree. When he slept, his mouth opened, the drool began to dribble down his grayish beard, and even like that he looked less stupid than he did when he was awake.

Falco and Fowlpest weren't a danger either: they were too busy trying to eat as many grapes as possible.

The sun shone down on the rows. It had been a dry summer and the grapes were perfect. In the distance the first snow gleamed on top of the Dark Mountains. It was said that beyond the Dark Mountains was the sea, which is a kind of enormous river than never ends and goes on and on until the horizon separates it from the sky. Robi thought about her father, who had always told her that one day he would take her to the sea.

Iomir was close to Robi, and even she looked almost happy; between one grape and another she yelled at the top of her voice:

". . . for the Judge's looooove. . . ."

Then all of a sudden her face froze, she brought her hands to her mouth and nearly dropped the bunch of grapes that she was picking. Robi watched as several emotions chased one another across Iomir's face: first, the greatest astonishment in the world, then the greatest unhappiness in the world, followed by the greatest fear in the world, and finally, the greatest horror in the world. Robi turned to look in the same direction as Iomir, and saw a shadow squatting among the rows. She immediately understood: one of Iomir's parents, or perhaps both, had come to take their daughter back, and the little girl was terrified by the idea that Phlesh and Slump or one of the abandoned children might see them.

You could arrive at the House of Orphans either as a true orphan—that is, the child of dead parents—or as an abandoned child—that is, the child of parents who had gone their own way, leaving their children in the care of the Hyenas.

This created two different factions, which were inevitably hostile toward one another. The abandoned children were stonily accustomed to abandonment: they had somehow survived hunger and cruelty from a very tender age. Hunger and cruelty had chosen them and had become fundamental parts of their own personalities and life in general, with a consequent and inevitable hatred for anyone with memories of tenderness and abundance. They had known Phlesh and Slump a long time, and were almost liked by Phlesh and Slump, within the narrow bounds of the benevolence of which Phlesh and Slump were capable. The abandoned children represented, by their very existence, proof that the treatments dished out by the Hyenas could be compatible with survival. They were, in a certain sense, the flower in the buttonhole of the House of Orphans.

The abandoned children were guided by a secret dream: one day someone would come to get them, a king or a queen would knock at the door of the House of Orphans to come and find their child, lost after some terrible event—swallowed up by an earthquake, swept away in a wicker basket during a flood, abducted out of pure wickedness by ogres, trolls, elves, werewolves, and the like, and then abandoned.

Day after day, not a soul knocked at the door. In fact, there wasn't even a door on which a king, a queen, or anybody at all could have knocked. There was just a sheepskin that opened to admit the Hyenas and any "temporary tutors" who came to hire the children's labor, establishing a price with Phlesh while Slump looked on, sitting under a willow tree, with one of the smaller children fanning away the heat and flies.

But for the abandoned children, there was always a chance. At the back of their minds, even the biggest of them, the majority lacking in the most elementary forms of innocence and trust, harbored the dream of a king and a queen who might one day appear outside the sheepskin in a gold carriage filled with good things to eat.

The true orphans, on the other hand, came to the House of Orphans and the care of the two Hyenas without the proper preparation. Their lack of preparation was made more obvious by their memories and their longing for times past. And on top of everything else, they had to deal with the Hyenas, whose fundamental tasks included the obligation to erase from the young minds any feeling of affection for anything but Daligar.

But in the desperate and crushed expressions of those children who had found Mother and Father replaced by the Hyenas, and bread and cheese replaced by maize porridge with worms, hidden beneath fear and hunger, stuck between desolation and humiliation, there was also a degree of hatred.

In many cases, the children had lost their parents not because of the ever-abundant poverty, epidemics, and famine, but by a more direct intervention on the part of the judge administrator, who was no slouch when it came to the sacred punishment of death by hanging, and applied it to his people for their own good. This intensified both the hatred on the children's faces and the pale delight that the Hyenas took in inflicting punishments, reducing rations, and increasing work.

The sentences dished out by the judge included both hanging and exile; those who were exiled had to leave behind their children, who were held to be the property of the county.

That was what had happened to Iomir's parents, who, had they ever come to take their daughter back, would have been guilty of abduction of a minor, a crime punishable by death.

Like a military commander planning the strategy of a battle, Robi quickly established the position of Phlesh and the most dreadful representatives of the faction of abandoned children, principally Falco and Fowlpest, and also Cala, the little girl with the missing finger, who hated Iomir with all her heart. Falco and Fowlpest were far away, on the other side of the vine; Phlesh was about halfway between Robi and Iomir and the hidden shadow, but she was facing the higher part of the hill, where one of the smaller children had fallen and possibly hurt itself, and, even worse, in doing so, had overturned its basket of grapes and was now picking them back up. The danger was Cala— she was only a few feet from the crouching shadow. Fortunately, she too had been distracted by the business with the tumbling child, but that wasn't going to last for much longer. Robi thought frantically for a moment, then set off running like a mad thing as far as possible from the crouching shadow: "A snake, help, a snake!" she began to shout as loudly as she could.

"Stop that this minute and get back to work, you stupid little girl," Phlesh yelled in reply. "It'll only be a grass snake."

Too late. Panic had spread among the vines, or perhaps it was only an excuse to stop singing quite as much and eat more grapes. There were cries of fear, and everyone ran off in all directions, crashing into one another. Robi went on running, pretending to be terrified, waving her hands and uttering horrified squeals. She actually did trip over a vine root and went crashing straight into one of the enormous panniers into which the children gradually emptied their little baskets. The big pannier wobbled a few times, then crashed to the ground, where it started to roll downhill, shedding some of its contents, but not very much. In fact, when, after one last bump against a rock, it went flying and landed on top of Slump, the big pannier was practically full.

Pandemonium broke out. Everyone was shouting. Phlesh hurried to free her companion, but the great mass of the vat lay heavily on Slump, who was trapped inside it. Falco and Fowlpest ran to lend a hand, with the two of them pulling on one side, Phlesh on the other, and Slump in the middle shouting inside the pannier, spraying grape juice in all directions. Among the rows, some of the children began laughing openly. From the corner of her eye, Robi glimpsed Iomir disappearing among the rows into the arms of a dark shadow.

She was gone.

But the problem now, was Robi. She tried desperately to come up with a way of getting out of her fix, but her mind remained blank. Slump, finally freed from the big wicker container, and dripping grape juice like a vat at harvest time, had got to his feet and was coming toward her.

"You . . . you . . ." he shouted, pointing his index finger at Robi. "You . . . you . . ." And his voice began to choke him.

Robi didn't have the slightest desire to know what was coming next. She wondered how much of a chance she had to try and escape. None at all—Falco and Fowlpest were blocking her way.

She wondered now how many blows of the cudgel she would be given, and how many times she would be removed from the line for maize porridge and an apple. For the first time, she became truly afraid: perhaps she wouldn't make it to the spring.

Robi remained motionless, devastated. Even the tiniest trace of hope seemed to have left her.

And just then, the world turned green.

Robi looked up. There was something enormous and emerald-colored in the sky, with light passing through it.

Robi was the first to figure out what was happening: the wings of a dragon had covered the sun.

CHAPTER NINETEEN

ORSH WOKE and stretched. The burns on his right arm and forehead had practically healed, but not the burns on his back. He limped as he walked. The last stalactite knocked down by the dragon's tail had struck him in the ankles. Both of them. He was stiff, and he ached all over.

The cold numbed his limbs, and his knees wouldn't respond. He felt like a crayfish that had gone to sleep in a glacier.

In Arstrid, the last village marked on the map, the hunter had bought him warm and comfortable clothes in gray and blue wool; but clothes don't grow, while elves do.

And that wasn't all: his clothes were torn and split, and in some places the fabric had simply worn away so much that it no longer existed.

He remembered the good times, when he had slept at a perfect temperature with a layer of butterflies that had kept him warm. And he had complained even then! Now he had imperfection and insecurity aplenty; in fact, his cup was overflowing. He would have given a lot to have a few days that were predictably and boringly similar to the others.

The little dragon was still dreaming. A light rain covered the larch wood where they had spent the night. Better to stay out of the library—not just to save a bit of human knowledge, but also because the little dragon was a contented soul, and always joyful. He never stopped wagging his tail, and stalactites knocked down by a sweep of the tail could be fatal.

The elf boy took a walk outside, into the clearing. Arnica grew where the mountains met the glacier. Yorshkrunsquarkljolnerstrink had done everything he could think of to try and explain to the little dragon the concept of a field of arnica, in the hope that the dragon would dream of it as he had the daisies, and Yorsh would see it grow at his feet. All that he had obtained in return was a desolate *squeeeeek* of incomprehension, accompanied by the inevitable deadly flame. His shoulder still burned when he thought about it.

Clearly, materialization worked only when big emotions were involved—piles of happiness and sheaves of affection.

And the little dragon's fangs were growing: the middle ones were a good size now, and the bumps of the posterolateral fangs had appeared. That made his gums itchy, and the little dragon eased the irritation by gnawing on things. What with the books that had ended up on the pyre and those that had ended up shredded, it looked as though the knowledge of future generations was seriously under threat. It was like sharing a house with a 1,600-pound mouse.

Yorsh had managed to limp as far as the arnica: there weren't many plants, but there had been enough to heal his back and his shoulder. To extinguish the dragon, or at least to weaken his flames, Yorsh would have needed aconite and digitalis as well, but the problem was that the book didn't tell him what dosage he needed. It recommended that *few* flowers should go into the infusion because *many* would be poisonous. Deadly poisonous. How many is *few* and how many is *many*?

Unable to resolve the issue, he had to put up with the burns. All he could do was put a check on them by making sure that he didn't cause the little dragon any kind of sudden emotion.

Yorsh finished tending to his burns. He got to his feet. Behind him the snowy peaks of the Dark Mountains stood out white against the blue sky, and the valley opened up beneath him.

He let his eyes wander. Smoke still rose from the clump of red firs where a little fox had suddenly appeared, startling Erbrow. But the fire in the patch of brambles near the pool where Erbrow had discovered a magnificent flock of butterflies had finally gone out. Yorsh limped toward the clump of larches. If Erbrow woke and noticed that he was alone, he would be frightened, and more trees would end up as flaming torches.

The little dragon was still sleeping among the larches. Yorsh sat down and stroked him. His fingers passed slowly over the soft, warm, emerald-green skin. *A newborn dragon weighs 1,600 pounds,* the book had stated.

One thousand six hundred pounds of disaster and destruction. One thousand six hundred pounds of bright little scales and affection.

The dragon woke up, stretched, and gave an enormous yawn, which reduced the tip of the hundred-year-old pine at the edge of the clearing to ashes.

Then Erbrow noticed the elf, and laughed merrily with the joy of seeing him again. Yorsh managed to dart aside just in time: by now he had the reflexes of a cat, but a rosemary bush behind him burst into flames. Yorsh went on stroking the dragon, who wagged his tail. Yorsh and the little dragon pressed tightly against one another, close to the rosemary bush, which, as it burned, warmed the air and made flickering golden lights through the fog. The little dragon looked at him happily, and the elf boy gave him a kiss on the tip of his nose. It was like having a little brother. One thousand six hundred pounds of little baby brother.

Yorsh opened the old embroidered knapsack that he wore on his shoulder belt and took out his parchment and a handful of golden beans for the little dragon. The dragon was wild about them, and settled down in peaceful delight to eat them one by one, very slowly, like all dragonlets.

The dragon ceases to be a baby when it learns to fly. Only then does its infinite wisdom begin; only then does it learn words, writing, and the correlation between its fire and the damage that it wreaks . . .

"Quhen" and not "when." After and in consequence. In consequence of the fact that it learns to fly, after its first flight, the dragon ceases to be a baby. There was also a picture illustrating the concept. The emotions of flight, along with the movements of the pectoral and dorsal muscles, are what bring the little dragon's brain to definitive maturity.

So the dragon's tutor had to teach it to fly. And until that was accomplished, it was a wise idea to keep a good supply of arnica at hand.

The problem was how? One learned to fly by imitation, but Yorsh didn't know how to fly. The closest he had come to it was an afternoon on a swing. Yorsh's first idea had been simple and brilliant. He had put his hand on the dragon's huge head, and then concentrated with all his might on a flock of flying birds. It hadn't worked. The little dragon had made a few attempts to twitter (a scorch mark on Yorsh's right arm and the destruction of eight mandarin orange plants) and had spent half the day hopping around as though convinced he weighed an eighth of an ounce, uprooting three pink grapefruit trees as he tried to jump onto them.

Shortly before Yorsh collapsed with a heart attack from all his running, Erbrow found a little frog. Initially the dragon was frightened, because the frog was the first he had ever seen, and the resultant flame had destroyed a nearby wild plum. Then the dragon started playing delightedly, hopping about all over the place in imitation.

Given his small degree of success, Yorsh tried to construct a pair of wings to improve his performance; then he climbed onto the rocks and glided down to the ground. The fact was that some time had passed since he had read the manual on making flying machines, and he couldn't reread it because it had been consumed by the dragon's second sneeze, while the texts on balloons and kites had been destroyed by the first one.

His wings clearly weren't big enough, or, in all likelihood, the sheets that he was using as outriggers were at the wrong angle to the tail plane. At his first attempt, he had crashed miserably into a meadow covered with gentians, amid a cloud of pink grapefruit leaves. The little dragon's expression went from perplexity to terror. The mountainside would bear the trace of his desperate weeping for a long time to come.

The elf boy's fingers and eyes ran over the ancient parchments, which he now knew by heart. He held arnica flowers and fresh snow in his hand, and rubbed them over all the painful spots: burns, cuts, bumps, scratches, sprains, grazes, and bruises. All of a sudden, he gave a start. There was one last page that he hadn't been able to unstick, which was finally opening up and becoming legible.

Along with the rosemary smoke, the arnica and the snow had had a powerful effect on the mildew in the parchments. This was an interesting discovery. He could have added it to the *Manual on the Conservation and Preservation of*

Ancient Parchments, if only the little dragon hadn't already chewed it all up.

There were only a few legible lines on the newly unstuck page:

There is a new line of living creatures, born of the union of elfish people and humankind. They are not like elves, who only like science books and books that explain how things are made, nor are they like humans, who do not like any kind of book because, after the collapse of the empire and the arrival of the foul barbarian populations, they became ignorant brutes, like wild boar or worse.

Yorsh read, then reread, then reread again, and then went on rereading until he was certain, beyond all possible doubt, that every word, every letter, and syllable was branded in his mind like searing iron on skin.

Erbrow finished his beans and had come to be cuddled.

Children born to elfish and human people. So marriages between elves and humans had not always been punished; the culprits hadn't always been burned at the stake. Now that he thought about it, the mere fact that the marriages had been forbidden meant that they were possible.

He had always thought he was alone. A lone elf boy. A lone youth, a lone man, a lone old man, to die alone among his books. Alone or in the company of a dragon.

And yet it wasn't so. He could marry a human girl. The very idea gripped his heart. A human girl would be human—that is, in short, yes, that is, with human characteristics. A non-elf might have hair that isn't blond and eyes that aren't blue. Rotten teeth. It would be someone who ate dead meat and squashed mosquitoes with its hands. It wasn't so much the heart as the stomach that was appalled at the prospect.

On the other hand, if he didn't destroy the library with fire and collapsing stalactites, his little dragon would be able to brood his own egg there, as well. A place of shelter, fruit, and as many revoltingly stupid novels as anyone could possibly want.

Yorsh remembered the prophecy of Daligar. It had said something about an elf who was the most powerful, the last one. The most powerful elf, the last one, would meet the last dragon. Yorsh shivered at the thought. The last dragon? The last one in the sense that there was only ever one at a time, or in the sense that this one wouldn't lay an egg, and without him his race would die out?

He also thought he remembered that it was written that he was fated to marry a girl with the name of the light of morning, the daughter of the man and woman who . . . There were another three words, but he hadn't been able to read them. The characters of the Second Runic Dynasty weren't easy to decipher, particularly when you read them while being carried by someone who is running at the time. If only he had been able to read the last three words, the ones that came after the word "who." If only the hunter who had been carrying him had slowed down a bit! He would have had time to read, and now he would have no doubts concerning his fate. They would also have been caught and hanged if they had been any slower.

If he had at least understood why the people of Daligar had been so angry with them! He was an elf, certainly, but all that his magic had done in the city of Daligar had been to bring a hen back to life. It was a very beautiful hen, with feathers of a warm brown color.

It must be he who had to marry somebody—a girl with the name of the morning light.

He had to teach the dragon to fly. He *absolutely* had to teach the dragon to fly.

There was still one idea that he hadn't tried out, one that might work.

Yorsh set off toward the snow-covered peaks. Erbrow trotted after him, nice and warm in his thick coat of emerald-green scales.

The elf shivered with the cold. Concentrating with all his strength on the feeling of warmth on his skin, he managed to avoid freezing to death. The vegetation grew ever more scattered. The snow became deeper. In the valley below, the little snow showers of the past few days had settled on the grass, while up here they settled on the previous winter's snow.

It was an ideal spot. He had seen it from the valley: a big rocky projection above a sharp spur twenty feet below. Still farther down, there was a ravine, miles of sheer drop in the middle of granite peaks as high as dozens of towers piled up on top of each other. At the bottom, the valleys opened up, with clumps of larches alternating with clearings and, still farther off, in all its magnificence, the sea.

The place was perfect. The idea was to start playing with the little dragon and get it to follow Yorsh onto the rock. At that moment, the elf would swing himself beneath the overhanging brow: there was a spot with a kind of niche that seemed tailor-made for the purpose. In its desire to follow him, Erbrow would fall into the void and, once he was in the void, he would open his huge wings and glide down to the spur of rock twenty feet below. It was a big spur. No risk of the little dragon ending up in the ravine. A simple and brilliant plan.

Yorsh started running. He waved his arms, laughed, and called to the little dragon. Erbrow squeaked with joy. Little flames of happiness melted the snow here and there, and warmed the air.

Now, thought the elf. He took a run up. Behind him he heard the ground thundering under the elephantine footsteps of the little creature. Reaching the brow of the rock, he swung himself into the niche and crouched there with his heart in his mouth. Erbrow didn't have time to brake, went over the edge of the rock, found himself in the void, plummeted in terror without opening his wings, and landed with an almighty crash on the spur of rock twenty feet below.

The little dragon stayed there, frozen, because it was the first time in his life that he had hurt himself, and he had hurt himself very badly. Even his coat and scales, which protected the dragon from everything, were scratched, dirty, and covered with blood. The little dragon didn't cry. He slowly lifted his head and looked for Yorsh. The worst thing was his eyes. They stayed, open wide, on Yorsh.

One thousand six hundred pounds of astonishment. One thousand six hundred pounds of desperation, suffering, and disappointment. Even his baby's brain understood that what happened had been deliberate. How could Yorsh have done that? *Why* had he done that?

Then the little dragon lowered his head. This time he started crying. A faint whimper. There weren't even any flames, as though his fire had gone out.

Yorshkrunsquarkljolnerstrink felt absolutely terrible. His head fell to his chest. There was nothing he could do.

He felt an enormous solitude, like a cloak of steel that kept him from breathing.

Alone, he had dragged himself through the mud and rain. A man and a woman had helped him, but they were human and he was an elf, and a wall of strangeness and incomprehension had always remained between them.

For ten years he had lived with a dragon too wrapped up in the anxieties of his brooding to pay much attention to Yorsh and his thoughts; and now, once again, he had no one. He wanted someone to comfort him, to hug him and say, "You've been good, my son, you've done everything you could, everything within your power. Now don't worry, I'll sort it out."

Never in his whole life had he heard the words "Don't worry, I'll sort it out."

He wanted someone to call him and tell him that dinner was ready.

He wanted someone to tuck him in at night.

He wanted someone to come, someone so big and clever that they would be able to help the little dragon, someone who would know what to say and what to do.

There was no one at all. Just him. And a desperate little dragon.

He had to sort it out all by himself. He remembered bringing back to life a rabbit and a hen damaged beyond survival. He had helped Sajra's lungs empty of water.

He had to go to the little dragon, take the pain from his wounds, heal them. He couldn't heal his own wounds, but other people's he could.

He had to comfort the little dragon. He had to teach the dragon to fly. He would do it. But the little dragon was just too small. He would try again in a few months, and the little one would understand everything. Certainly, that must be it: he had merely got his timing wrong. Shoulders aching, Yorsh raised his head and stirred himself to help the little dragon. He accidentally put his foot on a fallen branch, twisted his already bruised ankle, and slipped. He lost his balance and fell from the rock. He flew almost twenty feet and landed with a thump on top of the little dragon. The quiet whimpering became a convulsive scream. The terrified Erbrow gave a start, and the start sent the boy flying, a long flight in the shape of a perfect semicircle, like the arches of the First Runic Dynasty.

Yorsh landed on the brow of the spur, where the rock ended, before continuing into the void.

He managed to clutch on to a bramble bush. The rest of his body dangled above nothingness. Below him a drop of thousands of feet, and then granite.

"Help me," he yelled to the little dragon. "Help me," he repeated with all the breath in his body. "Your tail. Lower your tail down to me."

The little creature stared at him, motionless and terrified. He was frozen.

One thousand six hundred pounds of stolid incomprehension.

"Your tail," the boy cried again, "throw me your taaaaaiiiiil!"

He had hurt his hands in the fall. And on top of that, his old burns hadn't healed, and then there were the bramble thorns on top of that.

The elf tried to hold on with all his strength, but his hands were starting to give.

"I'm going to die. Don't let me die. Your tail. You can do it, you damned great thing. Save me."

One thousand six hundred pounds of absolute, stunned uselessness.

Yorsh lost his grip.

He fell into the void.

He tried to think of something, if not to save himself, then at least to suffer less when the crash finally came. Yorsh wondered how long it would take for him to die, and whether he would feel pain. He tried to think about his mother. Now they would meet. The thought didn't comfort him. The only thing he could think was that he wanted to go on living at all costs.

The world turned green. The sky, the sun, what he could see of his body, the snow up above on the peaks. Everything. A pair of huge green wings had opened up above him, and the light was passing through them.

The little dragon was flying. He was above Yorsh with his wings spread.

Erbrow's just copying me, Yorsh thought. Flying out of imitation. In a moment he's gong to go *squeeeeeeeeeeek*, and rather than smashing into pieces, I'll be burned alive.

Then his eyes met those of Erbrow's. One thousand six hundred pounds of decisiveness. One thousand six hundred pounds of determination. The little dragon was coming to save him. When the dragon had fallen, he had been badly hurt. He had worked out that falling hurts. He was coming to prevent Yorsh's impact with the ground. Flying with all his might, the dragon was coming to catch him. He had drawn level with Yorsh now. The elf closed his eyes and held his breath as he waited to feel the little dragon's claws clutch him to the bone, just to save his life. Perhaps he would be saved from falling, only to be crushed to death.

One thousand six hundred pounds of intelligence.

He felt a grip jerking him upward. Erbrow had taken him by the wrists, enclosing him between the two claws of his back feet. His grip was sure, strong, and . . . soft. Erbrow's feet were still soft, like those of any puppy. The dragon hadn't even brushed him with his claws. His brain had matured; Yorsh's plan was working!

The little dragon veered resolutely upward and aimed toward the hills beyond the Dark Mountains. They flew down over a gentle landscape, where vines alternated with apple trees. Yorsh summoned all the strength he could, contracted his abdominal muscles, and pulled up his feet in a kind of somersault. Erbrow understood the maneuver and helped him by lowering his right shoulder and, at the same time, choosing the right moment to let go of his wrists. The elf boy was on top, on the dragon's back—like two acrobats who had been training for years. Down below, among the vines, tiny figures were running away in all directions.

"Let's get away from here," Yorsh called.

Erbrow turned again and headed for the sea, beyond the Dark Mountains, which they flew over, high up, above the clouds, and then low, brushing the tips of the larches. Yorsh discovered that his library was now completely isolated. There had been two landslides, probably the spring before last, when the rains had been extremely hard and had coincided with the thaw. One landslide had closed off the steps that he had climbed with Monser and Sajra, and the other had destroyed the path that the two humans had taken when they had left. His library could now be reached only by someone with wings. Then, finally, he saw the horizon opening up before him, beyond the valley, under the clouds, interrupted only by the gulls. He felt the wind in his hair. The sound of the sea mixed with that of the wind and the seagulls.

The dragon's back seemed as though it was made just to receive a rider. There were two small inner wings, soft and warm, between the two true wings. The dragon noticed that the boy was shivering, and closed the two lesser wings around him. It was the most marvelously comfortable place imaginable.

Beneath them, the valley opened up in all its magnificence. Erbrow flew down to touch the larches, then rose again, flew down to the grass in a clearing, and then back up into the sky.

The dragon's cry could be heard in the air: much lower

and deeper than his usual *squeeeek*, and a line of fire formed in front of them. Erbrow passed through it so quickly that neither he nor the boy could feel its heat.

With each cry, the sky turned to flame and gold before immediately returning to blue and white. The little dragon flew low over the sea, brushing the waves. Yorsh felt the salty foam in his face and hair. Around him the waves followed, the gulls flew, the horizon was unbroken.

Erbrow closed the lesser inner wings tighter around Yorsh, then plunged in. Once again Yorsh dreamed of being a fish, and the salt water around him became pure pleasure. They met a school of dolphins that looked at them curiously. A mother dolphin was close by, with her baby dolphin, and for a moment Yorsh's heart filled with longing for the childhood he had never had. But then Erbrow turned back toward the sky, right through the middle of a cloud of gulls, and the boy's longing dissolved in the drops of foam that were left behind and beneath them.

The dragon called again: his low, strong call, like a hunting horn. No flame burst forth.

Yorsh began to laugh—he had found the missing element. To put out the dragon's fire, much simpler than aconite, digitalis, and arnica, what one needed was simple sea water.

And he didn't stop laughing, because flying up toward the sky, down toward the horizon and back up toward the sky, with the wind in his hair, the gulls close by, and a baby dolphin watching him in the water, was the very essence of happiness. And beside him, or, to be more precise, beneath him, he had a true, big, strong brother.

It was the circle of the horizon that he and Erbrow had broken by flying together, the circle of sadness, the circle of loneliness.

He leaned over and hugged the dragon. He plunged his face into Erbrow's emerald skin and stayed there. The dragon called out with joy. This time its golden flame pierced the sky like a long sword of light.

The sun sank low on the horizon, then disappeared. The sky filled with stars. A tiny island with an enormous wild cherry tree on it was the only land in sight. Apart from that, the horizon was a perfect, unbroken circle, a meeting of sky and sea.

CHAPTER TWENTY

ROBI LAY stretched out in the sun, time passing over her like water over a rock. Since the dragon had
filled the sky with the green of its wings, the children
had not done a day's work. No one was on Iomir's trail.
They were eating a little better, too. The incredible had
happened. In fact, despite the fact that only a few days
had passed, the memory of what really occurred had now
been contorted and twisted into countless different ver-
sions.

In the end, the most popular theory was that a dragon
had appeared in the sky, carried off poor Iomir, and that the
rest of the orphans had been saved by the valiant fighting of

Slump, who had finally, heroically and blood-drenched, sent it packing. The funny thing was that after the third repetition of that story, they really believed it. The truth had disappeared into the earth like the juice of crushed grapes. And Robi hadn't been punished. In fact, in the different repetitions of the story, she had become the one who had sounded the alarm—if not exactly a hero, she was at least a protagonist.

A few feet away from her, leaning on the fence, Phlesh told the story to the envoy from Daligar: ". . . and then this child, Robi, gave the alarm. She's the daughter of the most terrible people, really the worst," she sighed. "Fortunately, justice has taken care of them, and thanks to the morals she has learned here, Robi did exactly the right thing. Admittedly, the love of justice wasn't the only thing involved. There was also fear of the dragon, certainly" —a chuckle—"but thanks to our influence, she has done the right thing. And you should have seen him—Slump, I mean"—moments of emotion with eyes gazing into the void, and a vague smile—"he leaped to his feet, took an enormous pannier full of grapes and, brandishing it as a makeshift shield . . ."

No punishment for Robi, then. No bloodhounds unleashed after Iomir, who was officially dead. And four decorations for Slump: courage in the face of the enemy; generosity in his treatment of minors (who had been saved from the beast despite their unworthiness); heedlessness of danger; and capacity to honor Daligar, because in the moment of chasing the monster, throwing a pannier of grapes at it . . .

". . . Slump yelled, 'For Daligar and her Judge Administrator' and hurled himself at the dragon. Just like that, my husband flung himself forward with his pannier, shouting like a hero"—a little sob of emotion, a few tears— "The monster was so terrified that it fled: it spread its enormous wings, with what remained of little Iomir in its jaws and . . ."

Robi was glad that Iomir was free and with her family, but she also felt her loss very acutely. More than ever she yearned to speak to someone, to remember what had really happened, to understand it.

A real dragon had appeared in the sky. Green. Just like in her dream. Dragons weren't extinct, and her dream wasn't a fantasy. The dragon had stood out against the light, but despite the sun in her eyes, Robi had managed to see a human figure hanging from its feet, dangling dangerously into the void. He could perhaps have looked like prey, something that had been plucked from the ground. But as Robi watched him, the dangling figure had somersaulted and settled on the dragon's back. He had stayed there for a few moments. Black against the blazing sun, he had spread his arms, as though to embrace the world. That had been the last clear image, and then the dragon had turned toward the Dark Mountains, quickly disappearing into them.

So the dragon did exist, and was carrying someone on its back.

The prince? Who, if not the prince? Robi's mind was split in two. One part believed that the dream was true, the dragon had come to save her with its mere presence. The other part of her believed that there was no logical sense to it—she wasn't a princess or anything of the kind. A dragon still existed; that was it.

A dragon still existed, with a person on top of it, and by pure chance it had arrived at the moment when she had been desperate and in danger, and also by pure chance it was very much like the dragon she had dreamed about every night since her family had been destroyed. A coincidence?

But there was also a third thought spinning around in her head. It was a worm-thought, a caterpillar-thought, hairy and poisonous, like the worms she found in June, in cherries that looked lovely but weren't. Perhaps the things Phlesh and Slump said were true. Perhaps they weren't just lies. Perhaps she wasn't just anybody. Perhaps it was true that her family was . . . bad. A family that—Robi found it repugnant even to pronounce the words in her head—a family that had helped elves. It was horrible, it couldn't be true. Her mother and father were good. It wasn't possible that they could have done something so filthy as to protect an elf, and for money. That had been the accusation: protecting an elf in exchange for gold coins that were then used to buy the house, the farm, the cow, the horse, the sheep, the chickens, and the orchard. Anyone who protected an elf might have connections with a dragon. And the one protected wasn't just any elf, but *The Elf*, the one who had come to terrorize Daligar the year before her birth. It had been the judge administrator who had saved the city from the fury of the terrible individual, a bloodthirsty beast who would have delighted in slaughtering all the soldiers, the women, the children, the dogs, and even the chickens, if the judge administrator hadn't stopped the monster, with his courage and his valor.

The details of that business had never been properly explained. And Robi did have some doubts about what precisely had happened. If the elf had been so powerful as to rout the soldiers just with the sound of his terrible name, how had the judge administrator been able to confront him? Perhaps the same way Slump had bravely confronted the dragon? Robi laughed. She felt cheerful once again. And what if it was not true that dragons are bad, that elves are wicked? If it had all been as false as the heroic battle on the hill of vines?

"A heroic battle, h-e-r-o-i-c," Phlesh's voice went on. "The blood dripped from his back like . . ."

Perhaps dragons really were good, and a dragon had been coming to get her. Robi closed her eyes; hunger and sadness vanished, and beneath her eyelids the image formed again: the dragon was so close that its wings filled everything. Robi could make out the swirls of golden skin alternating with the emerald-green scales.

Even with her eyes closed, she was aware of someone's presence. Robi opened her eyes and found herself face-to-face with Cala. Falco and Fowlpest were standing a few feet away from her, arms crossed, while Cala was on her knees, watching her with a mixture of disgust and fear, as though watching a nest of red ants.

Robi realized she was in trouble again. She got to her feet and looked at the three of them.

"Where has Iomir gone?" hissed Cala. She was small, with blond hair that fell into her face, emphasizing her grim appearance. Without the two heavies behind her, she would never have dared to confront Robi, but with them, she felt strong.

"The dragon ate her, don't you remember?" Robi replied serenely.

"That's not so," Cala replied in a whisper. "You know something. The dragon appeared at precisely the right moment." She looked her up and down. "At your house you were friends of the elves," she added poisonously, "so why not dragons as well?"

"All right, then, let's ask Phlesh, and find out if what she's saying is true, or if it's all made up," Robi suggested angelically. She turned around as though she really was going to address Phlesh. Falco and Fowlpest looked at her, then pursed their lips, shrugged their shoulders, and after one last furious sidelong glance, they left. Only Cala remained.

Phlesh wouldn't let go. ". . . the dragon groaned with terror. Between its claws it still had one of the poor little girl's hands. . . ."

"That isn't true," Cala whispered, still full of hate and fury. Her eyes were filled with tears, filled with all the rancor in the world. Someone had risked their lives to take back Iomir, their child. No one had ever come for Cala.

Robi looked at her for a long time. Then she said something ridiculous: "Sooner or later someone will come and get you as well." It was if it had come out of her mouth all by itself. She listened in horror as she said it. It was meaning-less, and it was cruel, too, because having nothing is infi-nitely better than having an illusion and seeing it shattered. She looked into Cala's face, half hidden by her filthy blond fringe, her eyes furious and desperate. Once again, words reached her lips as though of their own accord.

"Sooner or later someone will take you away from here," she confirmed.

Cala turned pale beneath her layer of dirt. Her eyes grew wide. She brought her hands to her mouth as though to stifle a cry. Or a groan. Her left hand was missing its thumb, the most important finger of all. Suddenly, in Robi's head, behind her eyelids, the image formed of Cala's little hand with all five fingers attached. She bit her tongue till it bled to keep from saying that her hand might return to nor-mal, because that would really have been too ridiculous and cruel.

"Are you a real witch?" Cala asked in a whisper. "Are you from a family of witches? Is that why you are friends with elves? But . . . listen . . . you really know things, don't you . . . ? Don't you?"

Robi didn't reply.

"Slump was dripping blood and mud, you should have seen it, blood and mud . . ." Phlesh was saying. Then her story broke off with a strangled cry. Above their heads, enormous, splendid, and menacing, flew the dragon with emerald wings. On its back a tiny white figure could just be seen. Howls of terror spread, and people ran in all direc-tions. Forgetting his warlike and heroic precedents, Slump suddenly roused himself from his snores to dash to the nearest barn as fast as his legs would carry him. The envoy from Daligar, who had brought Slump his decorations, was too intent on escaping in the opposite direction to notice Slump flee. Phlesh, too, ended up in the barn, but before she got there, she stumbled over one of the smaller children, and her dust-blue tunic with its points of silver thread was now a mess of mud and straw.

Falco and Fowlpest ran into the distance. Robi stayed where she was, watching the dragon. A vague smile formed on her lips. The dragon, after circling once more, wheeled around toward the Dark Mountains, flew over its peaks, and disappeared behind them. Clearly, its lair could not be far away. Cala was standing close to Robi and went on watching her, frozen. She hadn't run away, either. Finally, she dared to ask, "Now that Iomir isn't here, can I sleep near you?"

Robi didn't need to think about it. "Of course," she replied.

CHAPTER TWENTY-ONE

HE PROBLEM was *how*.

The little dragon was sleeping wrapped up in two coils of his tail, like a little bird in a nest. Outside, the wind was wailing. In fact, it was wailing inside the grotto, too, because baby Erbrow's squeaks had shattered all the amber windows, one after another, and Yorsh had no idea on how to repair them. But there was less wailing inside than out, and the steam from the volcano helped keep the place warm. The temperature was far from perfect, but overall, it was compatible with the survival of a half-naked elf.

Yorsh watched the dragon sleep and tried to size up the situation. *How* could he get ahold of some clothes? He couldn't walk around half naked. Winter was just around the corner. The snow, which had only appeared on the highest peaks for the time being, would soon submerge the world. Besides, humans didn't like elves. In all probability they would like half-naked ones even less; and above all, they would recognize him even more quickly. A hood to hide his hair and his ears would also keep him from catching a cold and protect his head in the not-unlikely situation of people throwing stones at him.

How was he to teach the little dragon to read and write? He tried to recall how his grandmother had taught him, but his memory didn't go back far enough to remember a time when he hadn't been able to do it. Had there really been such a time? Or do you come into the world already able to read? Probably not. You come into the world not knowing how to do anything. Then you learn to speak and, only after you have learned to speak, do you learn to read. Yes, that was definitely the sequence. First speaking, then reading. Monser and Sajra didn't actually know how to read, but they could speak. Theirs was a rather rough eloquence, leaving aside the irrationality of the thoughts that inspired them, but it was undoubtedly intelligible.

How to confront the world of humans without ending up stoned to death and/or flayed and/or hanged and/or burned alive or even killed first in one of the fashions outlined above and then burned as a corpse? The answer was an easy one: he had to find Sajra and Monser. They would take him in, help him, protect and advise him. Now the problem shifted to the next stage: how to find Monser and Sajra?

He could ask. For years and years he had spoken to no one that wasn't a dragon. He had to prepare his speech.

"Excuse me, Excellency . . ." or was it fool? Which of the two was the polite formula? He was still confused about it.

No, back to the beginning; his speech would have to be prepared in an impeccable fashion. If he made a mistake, he would end up having stones thrown at him, which was never a desirable prospect.

"Excuse me, noble sir (noble lady), do you know the dwelling place of two characters called Sajra and Monser, who are humans?"

Better to leave out the bit about humans. Otherwise the person he was addressing might begin to have doubts about his membership in the human race, and he would end up having stones thrown at him anyway.

"Excuse me, noble sir (lady), do you happen to know the dwelling place of a woman called Sajra and a man by the name of Monser?"

That might do. With a great deal of luck and a few years at his disposal, perhaps even a few decades, sooner or later he would find them.

But what was he to do with the little dragon? Abandoning Erbrow would be intolerable. Take the dragon along?

How do you go about hiding a green dragon that must now weigh about two thousand pounds, and that will have doubled in size by the end of the month? Impossible. He would have to abandon it. But not like this, not as the dragon was today, lost in the silent desert of ignorance. He had to teach it to speak and read. Once the dragon was sufficiently instructed, he would be able to spend his time teaching himself. Even without the books that had been burned to a frazzle and the ones that had been chewed to pulp, there were still enough books to help him pass the time, without suffering from abandonment or solitude. So Yorsh could leave the dragon in the library for long enough to go in search of Monser and Sajra; find himself a wife; avoid stonings, hangings, and burnings at the stake; and come back.

A decade or two at the most.

His human wife would certainly be happy to spend her life at the top of an inaccessible mountain, along with a dragon, because you don't come across a dragon every day, and a dragon can be useful when it comes to lighting a fire and cooking a few beans, since human beings always have difficulties in that respect. And what situation could be more perfect than spending your entire life in a library filled with the whole of human knowledge, or at least what was left of it? He would bring up his children to read and write, and to know astronomy, geometry, zoology, and dance, feeding them on golden beans and pink grapefruit, so that by never eating dead rabbits they might grow up less uncouth than their mother, and perhaps even smell a bit better than humans usually do.

The plan was perfect. The problem was *how*.

Yorsh tried to get down from his stalagmite. It wasn't easy, because Erbrow had eaten his shoes, which had been woven from wild mandarin twigs. It had been a few days after coming out of the egg, two weeks before, when the dragon's lateroposterior fangs were emerging. They must have been giving Erbrow a great deal of trouble. And as if that weren't enough, the floor of the grotto had replaced its carpet of yellow and gold butterflies with a thick layer of bird excrement.

Yorsh wasn't the only one who had noticed how much warmer the inside of the grotto was than the frost outside, and anyone could seek refuge in it through the shattered windows. The tops of practically all the stalagmites were occupied by some kind of nest: there were wrens and a few starlings, but by far, the greatest number were magpies. As Yorsh couldn't help noticing, these were the most cackling, noisy, and quarrelsome of the birds, and the ones that produced the greatest volume of excrement.

Tiptoeing and hopping from one clean spot to the next, the young elf reached the vines of golden beans. In a corner, a small magpie was chasing one of the last terrified butterflies, which were valiantly battling against extinction. The little bird was cackling contentedly, when an enormous owl swooped down and snatched it.

The little magpie didn't even have time to call out; feathers and blood were scattered everywhere, over the golden beans, all over the floor, and over the chest of the young elf.

The uproar had woken the dragon, who opened his eyes and lifted his head from his tail. Yorsh joined Erbrow, darting between piles of excrement, feathers, and the remnants of bones stripped bare by the owls.

After their magnificent flight over the sea the previous day, they had come back to the library. Only the central room, isolated from everything, closed and stuffed with books, was still clean and decent, but apart from the books, not even a little canary could have got in there, let alone the two of them.

Yorsh calmly got himself ready. The dragon was watching him, sleepy but alert.

None of the books he had read referred to little babies, but many of the philosophical texts dealt with their education. About two thirds recommended raps on the knuckles as improving the learning process, while the remaining third relied on the theory of play to focus the pupil's attention. Dragons don't have knuckles, and cudgeling a creature of more than two thousand pounds might prove incompatible with his survival, so Yorsh decided to follow the gentler methods. Education was to simulate play.

He put some beans on the ground: one bean on one side, two on the other, then all three together, and so on, up to six. He might be able to teach language and mathematics at the same time.

"BEAN," he said, indicating the isolated bean. He smiled and clapped his hands. "BEAN. B-E-A-N."

Another smile, a little skip, and a clap of the hands with each letter.

The dragon had raised his head and looked at Yorsh, perplexed. Perplexed but interested—it was working!

"BEAN," Yorsh repeated. "B-E-A-N: one bean, two beans. Bean, beans. One, two. One bean. Two beans. More beans." A little skip, two little skips, more skips. Hand claps and laughter.

The dragon's eyes stayed firmly on him. More and more perplexed, but more and more interested. This was clearly the right method.

"Bean, beans. One, two. One bean, two beans. Bee Ee Ay En. Bean!" Yorsh smiled.

"Have you been transformed into an idiot this night, O elfling, or have you always been so, and I merely failed to notice?" the dragon inquired politely. "And pray excuse me, is there nothing to eat but gold beans and pink mandarins? Should I see them again, I fear I may void the contents of my stomach, and this floor is already so disquietingly soiled that it could be said to resemble a latrine."

CHAPTER TWENTY-TWO

THE INCOMPLETE book on dragonology had left out quite a number of things. The elf boy's ideas about dragons were limited, sparse, incomplete, and lacking as leaves in winter or apples in times of famine. With great patience, the dragon re-explained everything from the beginning.

"Through the egg?" Yorsh asked.

"Through the thickness of the egg," the dragon confirmed. The young elf's intellect seemed as narrow as the cupboards in which brooms are stored. The dragon was stunned—he seemed to remember some book or other that categorically asserted how astute and intelligent elves were.

"If it were not the case, then why, in your view, would a dragon sit on the egg for years on end?"

"To keep it warm. As birds do," suggested Yorsh.

The comparison made the dragon shiver like there was cold snow on its back. The scales of its tail straightened. Like birds? How dare he? Erbrow's ancestors would have made the elf pay for such an insult with blood, indeed with fire. A bit of fire and a bit of rosemary. Fire, salt, and a bit of rosemary. He seemed like a tasty youngster. No, absolutely not. Whatever nonsense he might say and think, you can't roast someone who has pulled you from the egg, taught you to fly, and helped your parent while it was brooding you. The dragon sighed, then started to explain again, in a calm and even voice—really scraping the barrel of what remained of his patience. Erbrow explained that birds are just birds, which is to say that they have the brains of a chicken. A bird sits on an egg because, being a bird and hence incurably idiotic, it has no other way of keeping it warm. If it was a dragon, on the other hand, it would calculate the temperature required for the time required and obtain it by means of combustion, refraction, exploitation of seismic steam, or some other means.

Dragons chose to sit on their eggs rather than going around exploring the universe and improving the world with their presence because, during the process of brooding, thought was transferred directly from the parent dragon to the child dragon. In fact, the dragon's reproductive system was truly marvelous—halfway between that of the phoenix and that of elves, humans, dogs, cats, canaries, dolphins, penguins, and sharks . . . yes, certainly, of course, and butterflies—it might be an improvement if Yorsh could keep from constantly interrupting. The dragon hated being interrupted. A loathsome thing. LOATHSOME! Had Erbrow already mentioned the fact that dragons are magnificent, nature's masterpiece, the very essence of creation? He didn't want to forget it, continuously being cut off midflow by frequent and pointless interruptions. Who had taught the dragon to speak? His father, obviously, who else? "Father the Magnificent," if Erbrow were to call him by his correct title, had taught him from memory. The memory of the parent dragon is concentrated to that of the baby, and communicates to him all his own knowledge and memories so that the newborn, barely emerged from the egg and instructed about flight, is already, well, there's really only one word: "perfect."

"To return to the beginning," the dragon went on, "the dragon's reproductive system is halfway between that of the phoenix and that of elves. Have you ever met a phoenix? No? Clearly not; the last ones lived between the Third Runic Dynasty and the Middle Era, and you elves, miserable creatures that you are, do not absorb the knowledge of your forebears. Through fire, the phoenix regenerated its own being, always as the same individual. Fire was, you see, their philosopher's stone, their route to eternal youth. Until someone wrung their necks to put them in a stew, phoenixes were immortal. Luckily the stew was good, the rosemary abundant, and we wiped them out."

"You wiped them out? You wiped out the phoenixes?

They were immortal? And you . . . you . . . you . . . wiped them out. . . ."

But what was happening to the young elf? Had he forgotten how to speak? Yorsh was utterly speechless. It was as though he had just fallen into cold water. He took a step backward, one of his bare feet slipped on a bone half stripped by an owl, and he fell bottom-first into the layer of excrement of various birds that covered the ground.

Perhaps intelligence came to elves when they were a little older.

"Are you feeling quite well?" Erbrow asked him.

"You wiped them out. . . ." he stammered again. "How could you?"

"Well, it wasn't difficult." The dragon remembered with emotion: it wasn't Erbrow's own memory—he had absorbed it from the parental memory—but the dragon's mouth still watered. "A few bay leaves and a bit of sea salt. Cook just for a few moments, like fish."

"But they must have been magnificent birds!"

"Precisely. Strawberries are magnificent as well, and we eat *them*. Phoenixes were the most wretchedly obtuse, smug, dull, and utterly brainless creatures ever created. When someone is born completely witless, his extinction can hardly come as a surprise. The only things that a phoenix has in its head are its tail feathers and the wrinkles under its eyes. You could only have an idea if you'd met one.

"Talking to a phoenix is an act of desolation, like finding yourself in the middle of a field of dry grass and flowers that have never blossomed. The very memory of such desolation fills my brain. And it was an act of mercy, for their existence was one of pure suffering. Predisposed to burn alive so as not to age. No new phoenixes were born, you see. What was reborn was the same chicken, over and over again, with its head full of nonsense!"

The dragon sighed.

"For dogs, cats, canaries, chickens, elves, boar, dogs, and, now that I come to think of it, butterflies, the system is different. There are a father and a mother, and they unite and have a child or two or five—in the case of rabbits, even eleven or fifteen—and these children are neither their father nor their mother. They are a new creature: father's nose, grandma's eyes, mom's big toe, other grandma's back teeth. The child is new, unique, and unrepeatable; and to teach them, you have to start from zero. From the elements of written and oral communication to peeing in a potty and pooing far away from home, it's all a matter of upbringing and education. Do you follow? While we're on the subject of excrement, my son, are you aware of what you're sitting in?" Surely the elf must have bumped his head. As a child. Against something very hard, this youngster. And to think that someone had written that elves are the most brilliant creatures on the planet.

Yorsh nodded. He was fully aware of what he was sitting in.

He struggled to his feet and set off out of the cave. There was a little puddle of water not far off, where he could wash himself. The dragon followed him.

On the one hand, Yorsh was relieved, infinitely

relieved. On the other hand, he wanted the baby dragon back, squealing and disastrous, and looking at him with adoring eyes. Now the dragon didn't squeal and he didn't burn things, but there wasn't much in the way of adoration, either.

Fog engulfed the world. The horizon was lost in the haze. The water in the puddle was icy but clean. Yorsh stripped off his dirty, filthy, stinking rags and then resolutely plunged in.

"The dragon is not his own father, but a very similar copy of him. He absorbs science, knowledge, and the memory of roasted phoenix through the shell of his egg. Mother Nature never ceases to be amazed at his genius," the dragon concluded in an inspired and emotional tone. "Since the dragon is a perfect creature, there would be no sense in altering anything, while your system always leads to different children, with a hope of . . . sooner or later . . . a possibility of"—the dragon looked benignly at the elf as he sought his words—"improvement," he finally suggested with a benevolent smile.

Clearly, Yorsh should have enjoyed the adoration while it had lasted. Now that he came to think about it, it was the fate of his life to notice good things only after he had lost them.

The water really was cold. He dreamed of being a fish. The cold became a pleasure. The water slid caressingly about him.

Now the dragon was in his stride. "The egg is laid and the brood begins at the end of the dragon's life, precisely so that the dragon can put all his knowledge, all his experience, all his memories, into the new creature," he added in an inspired voice. "While brooding, the dragon uses only a small part of his brain, the occipital part, which is also the most . . . how should I put it . . ."

"Stupid?" suggested Yorsh. He was really starting to have enough.

"You realize that I could burn you like a thrush, roast you like meat on a spit, make you blaze in the glory of the flame?" the dragon asked irritably.

"You'd never do that."

"How can you be so certain? Surely you can't read my thoughts, not from this distance, at any rate!"

"You wag your tail when you look in my direction," the elf boy shot back.

The dragon looked a little hurt. He sat down on his tail so as to keep it from moving.

"I find your love for such crude terms contemptible," the dragon announced haughtily. "The occipital lobe is the more . . . primitive, while the superior, frontal, parietal, medial, and limbic lobes are the seats of courage, of knowledge, of intelligence, of magnificence, and of . . . how should I put it?"

"Unbearable self-importance?" Yorsh suggested.

"Pride," corrected the dragon. "Pride. Superiority, and awareness of one's own superiority." This time the dragon was really annoyed. "I was saying that the parent dragon uses only its inferior brain to think, eat, sleep, and live, because the superior one is constantly in contact with the new dragon's brain to communicate all its knowledge. So that when the dragon is born, it has all its father's memo-ries, and the moment the first flight connects the various parts of the brain, the dragon is ready to be . . . ."

"To be . . . ?"

"Perfect. Absolutely perfect! Excuse me, but when I speak of our perfection, ah, how it moves me!" A tear of emotion fell down the dragon's cheek. Having reached the edge of his lip, the tear detached itself, gave a little jump into the void, and fell with a *plop* on the water, where it made a series of concentric circles.

Now that he was clean, Yorsh came out of the water. The icy wind swept over his soaked skin. He shivered. He sneezed. The dragon's eyes, lost in the celebration of his own magnificence, looked down and came to rest upon him.

"You're shivering like an autumn leaf in an icy wind," he observed. "That means you're cold," he concluded, smug and triumphant in his own wisdom.

"I knew I wouldn't be able to hide it from you," Yorsh agreed. He hated the dragon's superior tone.

"I can only imagine and perceive by intuition, you know. We dragons don't know what cold is," the beast went on, still smug and pompous. "Scales are excellent ther-mal isolators, not to mention the two inner interscapular, leather-clad wings. . . ."

"I'm breathless with admiration," replied the elf, who was growing colder and colder, frozen, in fact. He had to get out of the open air and try to warm himself somehow in that cold cave covered with bird excrement. Perhaps he could create some warmth by burning the excrement, but it wasn't the most pleasing prospect. If only he could stop his teeth from chattering!

The dragon looked at him for a long time, then stretched his wings, and the two enormous inner pockets opened up, warm and very soft, like a double marsupial pouch.

"Climb up," he suggested. "Let's go flying."

"Flying?" For a few moments Yorsh was confused. He was so irritated that he had even forgotten how lovely flying was. Lovely? Magnificent!

"Flying," confirmed the dragon. He stretched his wings a little more. "You're warm here," he reminded him.

"Flying!" Yorsh agreed, jumping into the middle of the soft, warm leather. "Toward the mountains this time."

The dragon had transformed abruptly from an unbearable little brother into an unbearable big brother, but all in all, flying made up for the fact that he was no longer a baby!

As Yorsh climbed onto the dragon's splendid back, his mind raced with questions for the dragon. "Now, I wanted to ask you, dogs, cats, canaries, chickens, and elves reproduce like butterflies, you said. Does that mean I came from an egg as well? Really? Did my mother or my grandma brood it, in your view? Grandma, of course, since I lost my mother immediately. . . . Will my wife brood our egg, I mean our child, or will I be able to do that, too? Do elves brood like dragons and chickens, or do they leave the egg somewhere to brood itself, as butterflies do? And spiders! I once saw a spider laying . . ."

The dragon gasped. "Sorry, my son, but have none of

the people you've met, none of the books you've read, explained the facts of life to you?"

Yorsh realized that one of the things he hated most in the world was being called "my son." "Of course!" he replied, annoyed. "Grandma explained the Decree for the Protection of Elves, and the Special Laws for Elves, not to mention the twelve books of law and the forty-six books of history. . . ."

The dragon exploded with long and unbearable laughter. Every now and again he managed to stop laughing, then he would look Yorsh in the face and start again. Unbearable.

"Make yourself comfortable, my son" he said finally. "I'll explain a few things to you on the way."

Definitely, Yorsh thought, a kind of big brother.

CHAPTER TWENTY-THREE

THE DAY WAS pale. The fog made the world vague and magical, like the shadows of the big pines that alternated with the pallor of the peaks.

Erbrow soared resolutely upward. He asked the elf boy what the plan was. It was an interesting question, because it meant Yorsh was forced to come up with one.

They would go in search of Monser and Sajra, the two humans who had picked him up, saved him, protected, and comforted him. And find him some clothes as well. . . . No, it would be better to do it the other way around: first the clothes, then the humans. Once he found the woman and the hunter, he would, with their help, find himself a wife, a

{ 208 }

human one, obviously, who would be happy to go with him, to spend all her life in a wind-battered cave on a mountain, eating golden beans with a dragon.

In order to get ahold of some clothes, he had thought of going to the village of Arstrid, just beyond the mountains. The people in the village were kind and didn't hate elves. It wasn't impossible that the hunter and the woman had settled there. It was a good place to live. The problem was how to get the clothes. He would have to give something in return, but he had nothing, and it was hard to strike a deal when you were stark naked.

As they flew toward Arstrid, Yorsh thought about what might be traded. Perhaps the treatise of multiple astronomy by Gervaise the Astronomer, the fourth king of the Third Runic Dynasty. No, he'd forgotten that an illiterate humanity would find Gervaise the Astronomer's treatise on multiple astronomy an item of dubious worth. . . . They could always look at the pictures, there were some engravings in that treatise, perhaps not the finest quality. . . . No, he had forgotten that when you're shivering with cold and all you have to eat is maize porridge and chestnuts, your aesthetic sense is sterilized.

Finally the fog parted and they realized they were flying over Arstrid. Yorshkrunsquarkljolnerstrink was worried that he might be seen, naked as a newborn baby, flying on the back of a dragon, but he quickly realized that his worries were pointless—little was left of Arstrid, and its only inhabitants now were some crows.

There were more houses than he remembered, but they

had been destroyed by fire; their roofs had caved in, and what remained of their broken doors creaked uselessly on their hinges. Where once there had been vineyards, there were now only a few strands of vine that had returned to their wild state and were growing on what remained of the charred trellises. The apple trees had been chopped down. A boat lay on the little beach, upside down and with a hole in its bottom, along with the rotten carcass of a cow and the partly stripped bones of some smaller animal, perhaps a sheep or a dog. In the middle of what had been the square of the tiny village was the pot of concord, dented, blackened, and unusable.

The dragon landed.

Yorsh felt as though a friend had died. In all his long stay in the cave, he had fantasized about his return to the world of humans, given that the world of elves now existed only in history books. And his fantasies always began here, in Arstrid. He would arrive, he would buy some clothes in exchange for an old book and a few golden beans, he would ask the whereabouts of Monser and Sajra, the inhabitants of Arstrid would tell him, because they couldn't be too far away. It was the prettiest village they had come across, and the farthest from the menacing soldiers of Daligar—his friends were sure to be there. He would find Monser and Sajra, who would say, "Oh, how handsome you are, how you've grown, how happy we are to see you." He would say, "But of course, I'm happy to see you, too, I've come to thank you for saving my life when I was a child." Then he would open his knapsack and show them his golden beans, and they would say that they were marvelous, and then they would hug each other—

The dragon's voice made him start. Yorsh had been lost in his fantasies once again.

In the whole of his life, Erbrow had never seen anything but a cave, a few mountains, a forest, and the sea, but that had been enough to know that the place they were in now was desolate, to say the least. It was a horrendous place. Clots of fat white worms and a pestilential stench spilled from the cow's carcass. Crows circled around, cawing.

The young elf was furious. Loneliness seemed to gnaw at him, like the death of some beloved person. The dragon searched through his various memories, those of his father and his father before him, to work out what you have to do to comfort someone, but he couldn't find anything of the kind. He tried to imagine what would have comforted the elf.

"The people who lived here are not dead," the dragon said firmly. He pointed at the carcasses. "The bones are the bones of cattle, sheep, and dogs. No human bones, either from an adult or a child. They have gone. Or been chased. Or else they've been taken somewhere else. . . . I remember this—it is a habit among humans to move from one place to another, and if one of them says, 'No, thanks, I like it here,' they hang him from a tree with a rope around his neck, and that is bad for his breathing."

It worked. The young elf immediately sprang from his state of motionless desperation. "It's true!" he said. He ran around what remained of the burned-out shacks. "There's no one here, either dead or alive. They must be somewhere else! Perhaps they've escaped, or perhaps they've been . . . what's the phrase they use? Hmmmm, yes, *deported*. It's true, you know, it is a human custom to deport people; they did it with the elves, too. They put them in some horrible places—Elf Camps, they were called, where we died, one after the other."

"Of what?" the dragon asked.

"Hunger, I think, and eaten alive by lice."

"But aren't elves magical?"

"Well, they have some powers. But so what?" The young elf was growing irritated by the dragon's questioning.

"Couldn't you have done something?" The dragon pushed on. "Burned the aggressors, made them burst into flames? Given them the plague? An itch?"

"It isn't as simple as that. Not all elves are magical. My father wasn't magical at all. Most of us only know how to light tiny fires and bring midges back to life."

"Bringing midges back to life? What kind of power is that?"

"That depends on your point of view. It's pretty important for the midge. But elves can't cause any kind of illness, nor would they want to. Only some of us, some rare cases, have powers that might be useful in a war. But humans are afraid that's true of every elf, so they directed their hostility at all of us. Elves couldn't avoid deportation, and by the time they realized that death by starvation awaited them in the Elf Camps, it was already too late—there were hardly any of them left, and they were sad and wretched. Magic drowns in sadness, you know. When a mother's son dies, she loses the power to do magical things forever."

"You could have used your old weapons—swords, arrows, halberds. Elves were great warriors, terrific archers!"

Yorsh didn't know how to respond. They had been warriors, certainly, but that was before—before they learned to read the pain and joy in people's minds. If a midge feels such happiness at coming back to life, think of a man's horror when you kill him. That must have been what had paralyzed the elves; and there were so few of them, and they were divided. There had already been persecutions in past centuries. Deadly persecutions. They believed they were just moving from one place to another. They were allowed to take their books with them. It can't have seemed all that serious. By the time they had realized what was happening, it had already happened. They were so far in that there was no point in fighting; it would only have increased their suffering. . . . There was another thing, and the more he thought about it, the more he realized how fundamental it was: everyone wanted them dead.

"So you died out of politeness toward humans? So as not to disappoint them? Very kind, really." The dragon's tone was turning sarcastic again, but this time Yorsh didn't take offense.

By talking about it, Yorsh was beginning to understand. "Magic drowns in hatred. No, wait—thought drowns in hatred. The desire to see, to fight . . . when everyone is barking orders at you, it's easy to take the easiest route, let yourself slide . . . no, not the easiest route, the only one open to you. The hunter and the woman risked their lives to save mine. That means that they . . . well, yes, they loved me. Perhaps they loved me in spite of the fact that I was an elf, not because I was an elf, but it doesn't matter. Where they were concerned, it was worth risking their lives so that I would live. There you are . . . yes, when everyone is barking at you, it's enough for someone to fight on your behalf, and you get your strength back. The ability to fight . . . if you don't, you're dead, and your people die with you. . . ."

The elf boy shook his head, frustrated. The breeze grew into a wind. A half-door clattered furiously. The young elf shivered.

The dragon spoke gently, "Perhaps you could just look around and see if there's anything that might fit you here."

"Wouldn't that be stealing?"

"No." The dragon's tone was compassionate now. "Certainly not. It would just be taking things that are no use to anyone anymore."

The young elf walked all the way around the village again. Everything was destroyed or burned. In what must have been the biggest shack, he found the remains of a toy boat and a rag doll, which he took with him. They plunged a new dagger of sadness into his heart. Outside, something white emerged from the haze. It was a big, old, emaciated dog. Until that moment it had been crouching among the reeds, perhaps frightened by the dragon, but when Yorsh touched the toys, it had managed to get to its feet, and now it was dragging itself toward him, its tail wagging weakly.

"Fido!" yelled Yorsh. "Fido, Fido, Fido. It was their dog! Monser and Sajra's dog, I mean. Fido. Fido. Fido!"

The dog had recognized him, too. Yorsh knelt on the ground and wrapped his arms around the old neck covered with stiff, gray, dirty fur. The dog licked his face all over. When Yorsh's hands touched the dog's forehead, confused memories reached his consciousness: cries, bitter smells, flames, fear. The dog remembered a kick from a horse that had seriously lamed him as the village burned. Then there were other memories, other smells: hunger, solitude, nostalgia, days spent competing with the worms over old carcasses, in the hope that someone might come back. Now someone had. His guard duty was over. His task was complete. Yorsh had come, he had found the house; in a way he had put things right. Now the old smells would come back, the smells of the old days: dried apples, roasted partridges; good smells of people who love each other. For a moment, Yorsh saw, in the dog's memory, the figures of the woman and the hunter, and for a moment, a small, vague shadow: someone who had played with the doll and the little boat.

Yorsh hugged the dog tighter. The elf became aware of infinite exhaustion and a single desire now that his watch was over: rest. He felt the dog's breathing grow slower and slower, until it finally stopped completely. He felt a twitch in the dog's heart, then another, more feeble, then, after an interval, another one, and finally the last. And then nothing.

Yorsh stayed for a long time with his arms around the

dog, feeling the warmth fading, the muscles beginning to stiffen. There could be no doubts anymore: Monser and Sajra had lived here, in the village, in the house where the toys were. Something terrible must have happened to them. Now more than ever Yorsh had to go in search of them.

He broke away from the dog, ran his hands over Fido's eyes one last time, and then buried him in a hole, quickly dug by Erbrow with a swish of his tail. The search for clothes resumed.

Yorsh was about to give up, when he had an unexpected stroke of luck. In the furthermost shack, he found an old trunk hidden beneath a piece of staircase, which the stone steps had protected from the fire. It was a small trunk made of fine walnut. The cast-iron lock, carved with flowers, was shut, but the dragon resolved the problem with a blow from his claws. Inside was a long, white dress, made of real linen and covered with little embroidered flowers. It must have taken years of work. Around the sleeves and on the lower rim of the skirt were pieces of fabric with patterns made of little holes that the dragon said was lace. On the lower part of the body was an embroidered letter T.

Yorsh got tangled in all the layered veils, before finally managing to slip it on. That was one problem solved.

The dragon seemed to remember that among humans, males never, for any reason, wore white dresses full of lace, embroidery, and veils, and that women wore them only once in their lives, on their wedding day. But since it didn't seem important, the dragon decided to forget about it. Dragons are born naked and remain naked until the end. The complex human customs concerning wardrobes were somehow stored in his various memories, but like a useless frill, an eccentric and debatable tradition, there was nothing worth getting into an argument about.

CHAPTER TWENTY-FOUR

I T WASN'T that Robi really knew how to read. And it wasn't that reading was actually forbidden.

Phlesh and Slump could read. It was with great self-importance, genuine pomposity, in fact, after puffing out their chests like turkeys, that they read the rare dispatches that came from Daligar. For anyone who had nothing to do with the Administration, reading was, so to speak, not recommended. In fact, it might have been more correct to say that it was actively discouraged. In Arstrid, the village of Robi's birth, a few, very few, people had known how to read, and there had even been a kind of school. The delightful little town sat right in the middle of things to eat: on one side there were the trout in the river, on the other, the apples in the orchard. In between lay kitchen gardens with chickens pecking about in them, and at the back there were hills with cows, which meant milk, which, in turn, meant butter.

Twice a year, the head of the village noisily summoned the children together and tried, without any method to speak of and in an inconclusive and chaotic fashion, to teach them the alphabet, which was all he knew. The lessons took place amidst the laughter of the pupils, the comical grimaces of the head of the village, and were brought to an end by the cries of mothers coming to pick up their children to send them to take the cattle to the pasture or to collect apples. Or smoke trout. Or put the grapes on the trellises to dry and turn into raisins to be put in honey bread for the winter festival.

The village head's knowledge of letters came from a mysterious and legendary figure with an unpronounceable name who had visited Arstrid years before Robi's birth, and who had supplied the mythical smoking pot.

From those absurd lessons, Robi had remembered little more than the four letters of her name: ROBI.

R for Rose. Rose petals could be soaked in honey and turned into sweets.

O for Oranges, delicious with roast duck. They had eaten the last one the day before the soldiers of Daligar appeared like ravenous wolves, claiming from them what they had and even what they didn't have, over some obscure story of overdue taxes. That had been during the last summer. The following winter the village was destroyed and her parents arrested. In fact, first her parents were arrested and then the village was destroyed, but that was afterward, once she was already in the House of Orphans; Phlesh had told her. In the summer the soldiers had come, wanting a lot of things: grain that they didn't have, an exorbitant amount of smoked trout, more than they could put together in a whole year, for the county and its administrative judge. The head of the village wasn't there. He had died the previous winter, shortly after his daughter's wedding, so it had been Robi's father who had stood up to the soldiers, saying that the county of Daligar had never given them anything, and that they owed nothing, adding that in any case you could ask people for a part of what they possessed but not everything, and certainly not more than they had ever had. It had been then that one of them, one of the soldiers, a tall, pompous one with an idiotic face and a thick, snowy beard, had looked her father and her mother straight in the eyes and recognized them—they were the ones who had brought the elf. The protectors of the terrible elf who had devastated Daligar years before. Robi didn't believe it—her parents couldn't have protected something so disgusting as an elf. It must be a mistake.

B for Beautiful things to eat. And beautiful things to drink, like milk or cold grape must.

I for Indigestion. When Tassya, the daughter of the head of the village, had put on her lovely dress, made of veils over veils, and with the T of her name embroidered on the front and the crimped lace collar, they had eaten so much that Robi had given herself indigestion. She'd had to turn down a third portion of walnut tart. When she thought about it, even today, her eyes filled with tears of regret.

Without the knowledge of those letters it would have been a morning like any other, a morning made slightly different by the arrival of the cart from Daligar with its usual load of new beloved guests for the House of Orphans. The new beloved guests were two pale, blond-haired little boys, clearly brothers, both with ears that stuck way out and freckles on their faces. The two boys were crouched among various provisions, including a big copper pot, dirty and dented, but intact, which had clearly been brought to replace the one in which they made their endless quantities of soup. Crammed around the pot were many closed wicker baskets, each with something written on it.

Robi's heart leaped. On the smallest basket were letters that she recognized, one of them repeated.

There was no doubt about it. BUTTER.

Butter was absolutely the most precious possession of all: white as milk, soft as a caress. It was what her mother put on the maize porridge on feast days.

Butter was the taste of abundance. Dishes were made of butter when things were going well, like the biscuits eaten at the winter solstice celebration, to greet the lengthening light.

Robi couldn't even imagine what the punishment might be for the theft of butter. When you chase after anyone who dares to eat one miserable little blackberry, what would you do to someone audacious enough to lay their hands on the supreme pleasure: butter?

One of the two boys, the younger one, began to cry. Robi was ordered to bring him down from the cart, and because she was abominably stupid and clumsy, as Phlesh had told her for ages, she knocked against the copper pot, which toppled from the cart with a terrible crash. By the time everything had been put back, the butter had disappeared. Phlesh searched everything and everyone, especially Robi, but the basket of butter had vanished into thin air. In the end, the only explanation was that there must have been some mistake: perhaps it hadn't been sent from Daligar. Robi was searched again, and beaten again, and at that point the case was closed, because there was nothing else to do but close it.

The two new boys were called Merty and Monty. By the time evening fell and they found themselves in the dirty, stinking sheep pen, the two of them had no tears left to cry. Falco and Fowlpest had distributed apples and maize porridge, and the children were huddled in their cloaks, trying to drag dinner out for as long as possible. Robi looked at them all for a long time: the two new arrivals, Falco and Fowlpest, Cala, all the others. Then she looked at her bruises, the ones she had earned that afternoon. Then she looked at the others again, and then once more at her bruises. Merty and Monty were starting to cry again; Cala tried unsuccessfully to comfort them, and Falco and Fowlpest told them to shut up, which didn't work; in fact, it only made things worse. Finally, Robi had had enough.

She got to her feet and left the room before Falco and Fowlpest could stop her, and when she came back she was holding her little pat of butter.

"Damn it all," she announced, "I was going to keep it for myself, and I'd have deserved it! Look at these bruises. . . . The trick is to distract attention: when the pot fell, everyone looked the other way for a moment, and I hid the butter under the cart. If you distract attention for a moment, you can do anything at all. You just have to be quick and then steal whatever it is. I could steal a king's crown. . . . I went and recovered the butter when no one was looking. . . . But . . . stop crying now . . . a finger of butter for each of you . . . on your porridge . . . like at home. . . . If I try to eat it all by myself it'll take too long and sooner or later I'll get caught. . . ."

There was an ovation.

There was a celebration.

It wasn't like being at home, but, at least for an evening, there was no sadness and no hunger. Even Falco and Fowlpest were too stunned, too admiring, and too happy to threaten and pester, to menace and confiscate as they would normally have done.

The crying stopped. Even the two newcomers, pressed against one another, calmed down.

Robi explained again and again how to steal things. She even gave a few demonstrations. Then they asked her how she had worked out where the butter had been, and she explained that as well: the B from Beautiful things to eat, the R from her name, and there, in the middle, the

T that she remembered from Tassya's wedding dress. That was perhaps even better than when she explained the essentials of the art of theft. The fact was that everyone, some more, some less, had always considered being able to read as a kind of . . . how to put it? . . . a kind of magic! An inscrutable, inexplicable, and inaccessible ability that divided the world between those who could do it—beings who were in some way superior—and those who, like them, couldn't do it and would never be able to. Now Robi, squatting on the beaten earth on which they slept, went on tracing the four letters, and the magic became possible. The two new arrivals stopped crying for a moment, while they too, with their fingers, drew the two hills that were the first letter of their name. Robi also remembered the A from the beginning of "Arstrid," bringing the number of letters up to six.

Everyone spent a long time drawing the letters before finally going to bed, and Robi had a sense that those seven letters might be important in some way, even more important than the butter—as though, at that moment, they had all become richer.

Then they put out the candle and went to sleep. As soon as Robi closed her eyes, everything behind her eyelids turned green, with complicated gold arabesques.

CHAPTER TWENTY-FIVE

TO AVOID dirtying the lower edge, Yorsh had pulled up the hem of his gown and fixed it at his waist with a kind of knot. It was the most uncomfortable piece of clothing he had ever worn. Even the horrible yellow canvas "elf" rags that he had worn at the beginning of his life, which somehow managed to be very heavy and cold at the same time, were more comfortable than this floating cloud of white linen. But he had done everything he could to avoid dirtying or tearing it, and had slept on the sill of one of the windows where the amber had remained intact, which he had dusted carefully, using a makeshift feather duster made from some tail feathers that had fallen from the many magpies that had taken up permanent residence under the ancient arches.

He woke up in the morning with terrible anxiety, after a night of horrid dreams in which he had seen the village burning and heard cries for help rising vainly through the darkness. The elf joined the dragon outside and told him of his firm intention to go in search of the woman and the hunter as soon as possible. Then, calmly and with their help, he might be able to find himself a wife. He was a little young, admittedly, but it was the custom among elves to start looking for their future wives very early, even if they then waited years before getting married. And elves only had a single love for their entire lives. They saw love as something too important not to dedicate one's whole life to. Often in the history of elves there was a toy that parents had shared as children, and the children they had brought into the world would then play with it. In his case, it was the blue spinning top. His father had given it to Yorsh's mother, and then it had become his toy.

Yorsh was full of doubts about the next step. He asked the dragon if his dress was right for looking for a wife, and the dragon calmingly reassured him that anyone who would love him dressed like that could only be a jewel of tolerance and open-mindedness.

After which the dragon lowered his eyes and once more set about stripping flesh from the bones of some kind of roasted bird.

"What are you doing?" the elf asked.

"Breakfast," the dragon replied cheerfully. He showed him the long spit made from the whole trunk of a young pine tree, on which lay the remains of the carcasses of a dozen magpies, owls, and capercaillies. "I've given you a hand with your wedding. I've done half the work on clearing up your house. Your spouse, when you have one, will be much more comfortable here. I've cleared the birds away. The only thing you need to do is clean the floor. I've halved your workload."

Yorsh stared at him in horror and dismay. He had eaten the magpies! And the owls! Those splendid little owls, clumsy and fierce-looking, those sweet magpies. They had made a terrible racket, admittedly, not to mention the incredible amount of excrement that they produced. In fact, if one were being perfectly honest, they were unbearable, but that didn't authorize anyone to wolf them down like a series of peas in a pod.

"How could you do that?" Yorsh asked, with as loud a voice as he could muster.

"With rosemary," the dragon replied serenely. "There's a basket of it just behind the door."

The dragon yawned and then started to clean his teeth using the remains of a capercaillie's thighbone as a tooth-pick.

"Now then," the dragon said. "When are we setting off?"

"We?" asked Yorsh in a puzzled voice.

"We," the dragon confirmed.

Yorsh hadn't expected that. Going into the world of

humans with a dragon? How? "You're not very presentable." Yorsh stammered. "You're very beautiful, I'd even go so far as to call you magnificent, but I must go among humans unobserved. They'll be scared enough already by the idea that I'm an elf, without adding the terror of a dragon to their suspicions." He didn't want to offend the dragon, so he gave him a beaming smile. "Now you know how to fly, you can go and . . . how did you put it once? Go off to explore the universe and improve the world."

"Exploring the universe on your own isn't much fun," Erbrow objected. "We'll just be careful. We'll fly at night, and by day I'll stay hidden among the crevasses, or in clearings in the big forests. Don't worry, we'll make sure no one finds me. If they do, we'll fly away beyond the clouds. Both the road and the steps leading from the library have collapsed, remember? We watched them go. And then, you see, I'm a dragon. The fact that I'm nearby, trust me, really will limit the number of people who might potentially cut your throat, hang you, or otherwise do you harm."

It was decided they would journey together to Daligar. Yorsh thought of the strange prophecy he'd discovered there, and knew it would be a good place to start. The prophecy was his fate carved in stone to point his way. He had neither mother nor father, and only the distant memory of his grandmother telling him to go and never turn back. But somewhere in centuries gone by, there had been someone who had known about him, who had dreamed of Yorsh while seeking to trace the future in the orbits of far-off constellations. Someone who had carved in marble the prophecy that he would be the last one—and also that he would not. He would have a wife. That was what he seemed to remember. He struggled now to make sense of the prophecy. The first few lines he was sure about:

> WHEN THE WATER COVERS THE EARTH,
>   THE SUN WILL VANISH,
> THE DARKNESS AND THE COLD WILL COME.
> WHEN THE LAST DRAGON AND THE LAST ELF
>   BREAK THE CIRCLE,
> THE PAST AND THE FUTURE WILL MEET,
> THE SUN OF A NEW SUMMER WILL SHINE IN
>   THE SKY.

But what followed, he was less certain of. Perhaps it was written that he would have to marry a wife with the name of the morning light who could see in the dark, a wife who was . . .

> . . . THE DAUGHTER OF THE MAN AND THE
> WOMAN WHO . . .

Who . . . ?

And what was it that strange book of dragonology had said about the children of humans and elves, who become the authors of strange stories about princesses switched at birth? Perhaps elves and humans can join in matrimony. Clearly they had done so in the past, and their children had produced the novels so beloved of brooding dragons. Perhaps being the last elf didn't mean he had to be lonely forever. Perhaps he had a road and it was a path of flowers, not a dark alley.

His road, Yorsh knew, was written in the stone of Daligar.

There was a brief consultation on the direction to take. Either Erbrow's father or his ancestors had been to Daligar, because the dragon was able to mention names, nicknames, patronyms, and birth years of all the stone carvers who had built the walls, and yet, he simply didn't know where Daligar was. Yorsh had a map, but it was rather basic and sketchy—all he could work out was that Daligar lay to the south.

They decided to fly back upriver, and sooner or later they would reach the city.

The water shone beneath the moon and provided an adequate trail to follow, even at night. When they thought they saw the rectangular light of a shack, they flew down over the tops of the larches. There were different kinds of darkness: the black dark of the sky, the even blacker one of the forests beneath them, and the yet blacker darkness of the ground where the watery ribbon of the river span out its silvery iridescences.

If Erbrow flew high he didn't really have to follow all the loops of the river—they cut across them, which made the journey shorter. They reached Daligar before dawn. The city walls, bristling with pointed tree trunks, like the prickles of an enormous hedgehog, rose up grimly, casting their shadow over the water of the river, which sparkled with gold in the morning light. The city was even more densely filled with towers, castellations, and arrow holes than Yorsh remembered.

Erbrow glided gently down onto a little clearing covered with grass and clover, hidden among tall chestnut trees. The prophecy was on the southern side, opposite the side with the big gate and the drawbridge. The plan was simple: the dragon would stay crouched in the shadow, barely distinguishable in the low, uncertain light of early morning, while Yorsh would slip into the city, hidden among the crowd and avoiding the guards before the drawbridge, at the drawbridge, and beyond the drawbridge. When he reached the southern wall of the former palace of justice, he would find the ancient prophecy.

Yorsh approached the drawbridge with a carefree air. One of the veils of his complicated white dress covered his head like a hood, hiding his pointed ears and his unusually light-colored hair. His heart was thumping. The very presence of such a large number of human beings made him unsettled. On top of that, there was the fear of being attacked, the hope of finding a trace of his destiny, and the memory of Monser and Sajra. He was a few feet away from the gate when he was somehow spotted. Everyone stopped doing what they were doing: people interrupted their conversations, those who were crossing the bridge came to a halt, the two street vendors selling apples and cabbages immediately stopped calling out the price of their merchandise and turned to look at him. But the word "elf" did not resound.

Everyone just started roaring with laughter. A group of ragged little boys, led by a boy with impossibly sticking-out ears, suddenly appeared and started jeering at him. They were all talking at the same time and Yorsh couldn't understand a thing, but he didn't hear the word "elf." So why were they troubled by him?

A few stones were thrown, but they all missed—by concentrating on the trajectory of each stone, Yorsh managed to dodge it. After an initial moment of fear, he figured out how to do it, and almost began to find it amusing. Finally, a soldier at the gate had enough, and with a few hoarse shouts he halted the stone-throwing and even managed to obtain a little silence. He was a tall, thin man with a big grayish beard. He turned toward Yorsh and beckoned him to follow. The elf entered the city behind the man, saving him from further attacks.

Daligar struck him as vast, and Yorsh was as stunned as he had been as a child. It was full of enormous buildings, with ancient columns and big intersecting arches that divided the sky into strange geometrical shapes. Many of the arches were broken, and the vaulting had crumbled. There was a terrible stench. Enormous jasmine bushes hanging from the crumbling walls mixed the scent of their flowers with the stagnant smell. Yorsh wondered how they could still be flowering at the end of autumn.

He recognized the cobblestones of the city, the facades of the pastel-colored houses with their pointy roofs, their shutters all painted with dark red-and-green diagonal stripes, forming a pattern of rhomboids when closed. Now, though, everything was peeling, and there were no longer any geraniums at the windows as there had been when he was a child. They passed close by a fountain, topped by a wooden sculpture of a rampant bear, now headless, while the water was nothing but a foul-smelling trickle. Opposite them was a very high wall of square stones that alternated with blocks on which little ferns and tiny pink flowers grew. It was the palace of the judge administrator, which extended into the tribunal where the prisons were. Perhaps Yorsh had come to the right place for news of his human family.

The palace towered over the city. Its base was some kind of asymmetrical polygon, the exact shape impossible to identify. One part was higher than the other, giving the whole thing an unbalanced and provisional appearance, halfway between something unfinished and something that had already begun to fall to pieces.

Unlike the Daligar that he remembered, there were now no chickens in the street, except for one. It appeared suddenly, emerging from a dilapidated door. The very old chicken moved itself along with difficulty on its claws, heading for Yorsh, who immediately recognized it. He had brought the chicken back from death thirteen years ago. The strange fact of being brought back to life may have saved the chicken from the pot and the spit, but the link forged between chicken and elf had kept it alive. It had felt Yorsh's presence: its mind had fused with the elf's when it had come back from death, and that was the tie that bound them. The chicken made its way to Yorsh. The elf boy leaned over and picked it up. They looked at each other for one last time, and finally, the chicken allowed itself to die. The boy felt it filling up with peace, its heart coming to a stop. He looked up and noticed the crowd of people around him. He wasn't the only one who knew the story of the chicken, and he wasn't the only one to have recognized it. The word "elf" rang out loud and clear. The stone-throwing began again, and much more seriously this time. It was impossible to avoid all the trajectories.

Yorsh wondered where to run. All escape routes were blocked—all that remained was a wall. He had only to imagine that he was a grasshopper, and already he was on the top, enveloped in his dress like a cloud and pursued by shouts and stones. On the other side of the wall there was a garden with enormous trees, gushing fountains, and a pond with swans mirrored in it. Enormous wisterias grew against the walls, and their knotty trunks made it easier for Yorsh to climb down. The abundance of flowers gave him the sense of being in a kind of paradise, but it was a strange, almost excessive paradise. Once again Yorsh wondered how such an incredible amount of blossom was possible on the brink of winter. He knew nothing about wisterias, but even their scent struck him as overdone. Not far away, a girl, also dressed in white, was playing on a swing, singing an ancient song about girls, boys, and new love. Still hidden in the shade of the wisterias, Yorsh approached. The girl was tall, slim, and very beautiful, with white skin and big green eyes. She was wearing a pale-colored dress patterned with gold, her blond hair in a series of braids that intertwined like the backstitches of her high stiff collar, with a gold ring where they met. Apart from anything else, the girl struck him as being a bit too grown-up to be spending her time fiddling about on a swing and singing little songs to herself. Finally, the ambiguous deception of the scene was shattered: close to the girl on the swing was a little dark-haired girl who, when the fair-haired girl had finished her song, plucked up the courage to ask a question. A kind of pandemonium broke out and Yorsh managed to pick up a few scraps of the conversation that followed. The subject was the possibility of taking turns on the swing. Or rather, it was a monologue and the subject was the impossibility of taking turns on the swing, which was apparently an inalienable and permanent right of the fair-haired girl.

". . . Because I, you see, am the daughter of the judge administrator, but how can you . . . you unspeakable little daughter of an . . . insignificant and ordinary . . ."

The little girl wept desperately.

"You're fat, ugly, and stupid. And you're ordinary. Ordinary. My father, you know, my father is the one who . . ."

What an unbearable, preening bully. Yorsh was tempted to run to the younger girl's defense, but he was already in quite enough trouble, and it wasn't the time to increase it still further.

Was that the daughter of the judge administrator? Another reason not to be caught in that garden. Shouts of "elf" still rang out on the other side of the wall. Yorsh calculated that if the north wall, the one he had just climbed, overlooked the main street, then the one on the other side, facing the south, must look out on the river. Too late: the entrance had been opened and dozens of soldiers were rushing in, while the fair-haired girl, screaming with terror, ran to the wooden construction covered with climbing roses that stood at the end of the garden. The roses were blooming as well. Yorsh wondered if the younger girl would be able to have a turn on the swing now.

The problem was how to get across the garden. Yorsh climbed back onto the wall and tried to move, but one of his feet got caught in a wisteria branch, and he dropped back to his starting point on the main road. The soldiers had scattered; they were now in the garden, but there were many more ragged boys than before. Dense showers of stones rained down. More and more stones hit Yorsh. His forehead began to bleed, his pale dress was drenched in blood. He tried to run. He ran as elves run: by dreaming that he was a plunging eagle. He should easily have been able to shake off his aggressors, but he tripped over his frothy dress and fell heavily. He managed to get back up and drag himself toward the high part of the city, where the shanties climbed on top of each other like a gigantic termite mound, covered with caper bushes and some rickety vines with a few bunches of stunted grapes hanging from them. The houses were made of earth and tree bark, the streets were covered with mud, interrupted by puddles and intersecting streams that formed an uninterrupted network of dirty water, which reflected the white of the clouds and the sky.

In the muddy streets, abandoned children rolled about

with stray dogs, fighting over bits of cabbage and apple cores. None of them broke off to jeer or chase after him. Yorsh ran down narrow alleys that were barely wide enough for a single person, which climbed up an intricate sequence of uneven stairs. None of the wretched inhabitants he encountered—a very bent little old woman, a crippled young man supported on a rough-hewn crutch, and a woman leading a little boy by the hand—attempted to stop him; in fact, they pressed themselves against the walls so as not to obstruct him, before tripping up the soldiers. He guessed that this was the inviolable solidarity of the people from those parts—they clearly approved of anyone who had problems with the judge's notion of justice. Yorsh managed to lose his pursuers and get far enough away to reach a flat area overlooking the loop of the river. From there he could see Erbrow. And the dragon could see him.

The world turned green. The shouts turned from triumph to terror. Erbrow the Younger had come to save him. There was a roar, and a tongue of flame shot through the air. The flat area was big enough for Erbrow to land without difficulty; Yorsh climbed onto his back and they flew over the terrified city to the south gate. He recognized the portico and the steps; he found the arch with the prophecy. The dragon flew down and circled slowly in midair to give him time to read. The prophecy was gone: it had been chiseled away. Lest there be any doubt, the marks of the chisel remained like incoherent scars on the stone.

One of the archers recovered from his terror: he slipped the arrow on to his bow and fired. Erbrow gave a start, and blood began to pour from his chest. Yorsh understood why there were no other dragons left: the bottom part, the one which the dragon presented to the world as he flew, was utterly defenseless, being covered with little scales no harder than those of a snake or a dragonfly. The dragon immediately flew higher into the upper air.

They flew toward the Dark Mountains, over the hills of vineyards and orchards that they had flown over the first time, and this time, without the light in his eyes, Yorsh managed to make out lots of little figures running among the green. Close to a fence, two tiny people had stayed to watch them as closely as they could. Then the dragon and the elf boy turned and plunged behind the peaks of the Dark Mountains. There appeared the peak on which their library stood and, behind it, the sea.

CHAPTER TWENTY-SIX

ERBROW'S INJURY was neither serious nor deep; it had taken Yorsh only a few moments to heal it. By the time the dragon had risen above the city of Daligar, the arrow had already been removed and the blood had ceased to flow. Before they reached the library, a scar had formed, and shortly afterward it had disappeared. During the rest of the day, Erbrow, who was in fine fettle, spent his time on the snowy mountaintops, happy as a little finch, sliding in the snow and hunting the yellow partridges that he proceeded to cook on a crackling fire of pine and rose-mary.

Yorsh lay on the floor of the cave. All his strength had

left him; he felt ill, and couldn't stop shivering. The energy required to remove the arrow and treat Erbrow's wound seemed to have left him exhausted. And his chest remained acutely painful, as though he himself had been the one pierced by the arrow. To make matters worse, there was also the terrible disappointment of not having discovered where Monser and Sajra might be, allowing that they were still alive.

Yorsh didn't feel any better until evening, when he dragged himself out to the puddle of cold water and drank from it. His dress was spattered with mud, the blood that had flowed from his forehead, a few splashes of Erbrow's blood, and, above all, the excrement of various birds, chiefly magpies and owls, which lay on the floor of the cave. Only a few tiny fragments of lace near his neck had retained their whiteness.

The following day, Yorsh was a great deal better, and the exploration resumed. They decided to go back to Arstrid.

They set off at sunset to be less visible. The evening wasn't exactly clear, but it wasn't cloudy, either. They flew over the forests of larches, which stood as motionless as statues in the fading light, and then over the forests of chestnuts, whose yellowing leaves fell like a slow, light rain, and shone in the faint gleam of the few stars.

The dragon's wings beat lazily as he gently lowered his altitude and began to fly in wide circles over the plane of Arstrid. A small moon shone over the loop of the river. The ashen remains of the village stood out in all their desolation against the light reflected between the sky and the water. A cloud hid the moon, and the world turned dark.

The dragon landed. They consulted one another on what was to be done. They had no idea.

The cloud lifted. The moon shone again. Yorsh lowered his eyes. Half hidden in the grass, something gleamed at his feet. He bent to pick it up: it was a little white stone that caught the light of the moon. He looked up. He rummaged in the grass with his hands. A foot or so away from the first, there was a second stone, then a third, then yet another. They couldn't be seen from above, but when you walked on all fours, the little white stones glowed in the moonlight.

Yorsh showed the dragon.

"They've left a trail for us," he said triumphantly.

"For us? But they haven't even got an idea of our existence in the world!"

"Well, maybe they didn't leave it for us, but they have left a trail!" Yorsh said obstinately.

"But who could be so silly as to leave a trail of stones without anyone to leave them for? What would be the point?"

"To find their way home. It must have been a child. When I abandoned the place where my grandmother was, I left a trail of stones so that I could find my way back to her. The rain submerged them, and they disappeared within half a day. It's something a child does when it's forced to leave a place it doesn't want to leave. It leaves a trail of stones so that it can find the way back, and that gives it a sense of security. Or it might dream of finding the trail again. When everything is frightening, you need a dream even more urgently than you need something to eat. But this points the way for us, right now. We have to follow it on foot. The stones are too small to be seen from above."

"Are you sure? I hate walking. Dragons don't walk. They can do it, certainly, but the very structure of their knees and metatarsals . . ."

The moon shone. Ahead of them a path broadened into a mule track. The little stones lay in the grass, by the side of the road, so as not to be confused with the stones in the middle. But there they were: all the same, all round, all very white. The child who had scattered the stones must have spent years collecting them, gathering them from the shores along the river, must have collected and kept them as a treasure, which it had then dropped at intervals along the way in exchange for the dream of returning.

At first the mule track went in the opposite direction of the Dark Mountains, toward the city of Daligar, and then it swung off toward the east. The stones began to thin out, as though the person distributing them had decided to save them. Fewer and fewer of them, farther and farther apart. Not for a moment did the dragon stop complaining about the pain in his back feet, not to mention his back, and to explain how clearly superior flight was over walking.

The moon set and dawn arrived. The stones only appeared at very occasional forks in the road, when the mule track divided, to show the right direction. The rising sun shone on one last stone, pointing toward a narrow, muddy path half invaded by bramble bushes. After a while, the path turned boggy and could no longer be distinguished.

There were no more stones. A marshy terrain spread in front of them. They were engulfed by clouds of midges. The sun rose decisively, and with the light of the new day, the flies awoke. The elf and the dragon struggled on.

Finally, a kind of valley opened up before them, and at the end of it they saw a hovel made of twigs and mud and, to judge by the smell, cow and goat excrement as well. There were no windows. The door was a hole covered by a sheepskin.

"There are no more stones," said Yorsh, "and we've arrived somewhere."

"Well," replied the dragon, "that is good news. My back feet are like two sausages that have been rubbed through a grater, my knees are creaking—not to mention my back. My stomach is rumbling like the wind among the tree-tops. We can camp, rest, sleep, and get our breath back. Or even better, I camp, rest, sleep, and get my breath back, and you have a look around and see what's going on."

Yorsh was extremely tired, but no amount of fatigue could have stopped him. The dragon crouched in the upper part of the little valley, under two big oak trees, managing to make himself look as though he were part of the land-scape. The long walk through the night had left him covered with dust, and he was further streaked with mud as he lay down. The complicated whirls formed on his back by his scales, in various shades of green, made it even harder to distinguish the dragon from the surrounding marshland.

The young elf set off toward the hovel. Every now and again he turned around to check that the dragon was still a vague patch in the greenery. As he drew closer, he became aware that, beside the hovel, there was a charming cottage of delightful white-and-pink stones, with a granite architrave carved with a long line of tiny goslings, each with a little bow around its neck and a bunch of flowers in its beak. There was also a wooden door painted with a long line of multicolored hearts, and a chimney from which a pillar of smoke emerged, and a reed fence, within which a little flock of geese and chickens pecked the ground. On the other side of the fence, there was a clearing surrounded by a cruel and wretched palisade, bristling with old rusty lances, pointed pieces of wood, thorns, and bramble bushes, with two sentry boxes for archers placed at intervals. In the clearing, a strange scene presented itself to the young elf's eyes: a group of dirty children, all wearing the same torn and ragged clothing, digging long trenches in the muddy earth.

CHAPTER TWENTY-SEVEN

EAR HAD TAKEN hold of the world. Everyone seemed to have gone mad. A dragon carrying an elf on its back had reappeared in Daligar, where it had exterminated all the poultry in the county. Thousands and thousands of dead chickens were piled up under clouds of flies in a rotten stench of putrefaction. Or at least that was the rumor going around.

Robi had never been to Daligar, because her father and mother had always avoided going there, but Glamo, one of the bigger children, tall and thin, with black hair falling over his face, came from the city, and he said that there weren't really any chickens left in Daligar; the judge administrator didn't want them because they made the streets untidy. A few of them walked about in the high part of the city, the least desirable area in the county, where even the soldiers were seldom seen. Even there, however, there were only a few chickens, as many as you could count on the fingers of one hand, more or less, not enough to make a mountain. A pile of them wouldn't have filled a sack. The problem was that Glamo was the biggest fibber the children had ever met. He was the son of vagrant parents who had gone from market to market selling trinkets before they had been finished off by the cold and coughs of a worse winter than usual. Like all vagrants, Glamo had the pomposity of someone who has seen everything, because he had seen lots of things, and also the conviction that the others were so stupid as to believe everything he said.

It was he who maintained that there was only a single chicken alive in the lower part of Daligar, and no one dared to wring its neck because it was a special chicken, a magic one that had already died and been brought back to life.

Glamo had been beaten various times by people who were exasperated by all the nonsense he came out with, particularly Falco and Fowlpest. But he insisted on talking about the chicken of Daligar that had been to the realm of the dead and had come back from it, when he wasn't making up all kinds of other fairy tales, such as saying that there were plants in Daligar that flowered all year round, or the time he met a troll that was working as a woodcutter along with two human giants in the Dark Mountains, and they had helped his father to repair his cart. His father had given them half a ham in payment, and before eating it, they had buried it and dug it up again. Glamo had been beaten for that story as well.

Even if you considered Glamo to be unreliable, the story of the mountains of dead chickens didn't make a great deal of sense. If the dragon really had exterminated stacks of them, couldn't they have eaten the chickens rather than leaving them to rot? Or given them to the children? In the House of Orphans, the chickens would have been eaten even if they were riddled with maggots. That story of piles of dead and rotting chickens stinking up the air seemed to be on a par with the abduction of Iomir.

Still, according to rumors, the dragon had been confronted by the judge administrator's guard of honor, who, after a tough battle, had chased it away, dripping blood and practically at death's door. But clearly dragons recover from mortal wounds more easily than children from blisters on their hands, given that the creature had managed to soar over the House of Orphans, fast and powerful, almost as high as the clouds.

Stories went flying about, growing ever more outlandish as they did so. The only certain thing was that there was more work to do, and less maize porridge, and when they weren't picking apples to send to Daligar, they were digging trenches in the mud. Since poor Iomir's abduction by the beast, everyone had to work strictly in pairs, each member responsible for the other, and answerable to Phlesh and Slump. Fortunately, Robi was with Cala. Of all the terrible jobs that Robi had ever done, the trenches were the worst. The mud was soft. Robi slipped, and slipped, and slipped again. There were worms in the mud and a kind of hairy caterpillar that looked as though it had gone to sleep, but when it woke up, it gave you nasty bites that hurt for hours.

Slump had come up with the idea of the trenches. He knew as much about military strategy as he did about astronomy, which is to say absolutely nothing. But having developed the habit, over a number of decades, of never giving anything a moment's thought, it occurred to him that you could confront a winged creature while knee-deep in mud and unprotected by anything at all.

When the dragon had appeared for the second time, the celebration of victory had yielded to the most intense and total terror. Slump, who had already faced the dragon, and who had been routed with a pannier of grapes, and who thus had a certain amount of experience in this area, was appointed camp commandant with responsibility for the defense of the "adjacent district," which meant everything outside the walls of Daligar. The result had been a series of hysterical panics, alternating with the umpteenth retelling of his rout of the dragon. First they had dug trenches around the moors, then they had abandoned them to dig them under the vines, then they had started to erect a rampart that was never completed but abandoned shortly after the beginning, to return to the initial idea: trenches around the moors.

Robi stopped for a moment. She couldn't go on. Her arms hurt and she had blisters on her hands. She was hungry, too. There was nothing to steal when digging trenches. She was tired: she really couldn't go on.

It was said that the dragon had been injured. Perhaps it wouldn't come back. Perhaps everything was lost. Perhaps the dragon they had seen and seen again had been nothing but a crazy dream. Perhaps no one was coming, no one would save her, not her and not any of the others. Everything would stay as it was.

Suddenly, an image of paradise came speeding through the mud; hope was rekindled and spirits lifted: the fattest rat that Robi had ever encountered. And not just her: Cala had seen it, too. The two little girls swapped glances. Meat. And lots of it. A whole rat, a big fat sewer rat.

When Robi had been sent to the House of Orphans, they had taken away her clothes, her shoes, and the big rough woolen shawl her mother had wrapped around her, but Robi had managed to save her slingshot. Her father had made it for her. It was a strip of leather with a wider part that held a stone. Robi had managed to hide it, inspection after inspection, in the pocket sewn with threads of straw inside her filthy jacket.

Phlesh and Slump were at the other end of the long trench, and neither Robi nor Cala had yet been granted permission to answer the "call of nature" that was granted to all "infant workers" once a day. The two little girls went dashing after the rat, which took refuge behind the whitethorn and blackberry bushes that bordered the clearing before the forest. Robi was able to take out the slingshot, pick up a stone, and fire without anyone seeing her. *Bam.* A clear and precise shot. The rat collapsed. The two children hurried back to their place in the trench.

The day passed slowly until lunchtime, when every digging child would stand in line to receive the six chestnuts and half an apple provided by the generosity of the county of Daligar.

The rat was a communal meal. Grapes, blackberries, nuts, eggs, and apples were things that you could wolf down all by yourself, without having to say a word to anyone. But a rat, if it was to be edible, had to be skinned and roasted, two tasks that could only be accomplished by the whole community of "beloved guests" at the House of Orphans. Moving as though at random along the trenches, Robi managed to end up standing beside Falco and Fowlpest, and tell them of her catch. Her heart broke as she did it. It meant that those two would have half of the rat all to themselves. The other half would be shared among everyone, because the skinning and cooking would be done in the dormitory, using the little brazier that heated it up, and that would mean a tiny piece for everyone. But a tiny piece is still better than nothing, not to mention the fact that it would be a kind of party.

When the time came for the food to be distributed, Fowlpest went to do it by himself, while Falco, with Robi and Cala, slipped off to the blackberry bushes to recover the prey. They carried the sack that had held the chestnuts, and which was empty by now, in such a way as to make the rat disappear inside it, and to smuggle it into the dormitory in the evening. A rat was not a "theft," and there were no punishments set aside for it, but equally, it would be confiscated as a "distraction from work," and would attract all kinds of accusations of ingratitude and barbarism.

"How could you?" Phlesh would squawk. "With all the good things you get to eat at the House of Orphans, all in great abundance and so beautifully cooked!"

"They're barbarians!" Slump would snort as he roused himself from his usual cataleptic state. "The children of barbarians, with barbarian practices . . . It's a good thing that we're here now, and that being intelligent, we can teach them. . . ."

The rat was no longer in the clearing. Or rather to be more precise, it was still there, but it wasn't where they had left it. Instead of being on the ground, stone dead, it had been picked up by a character who looked like a cloud with hairy legs, because he was wearing an incredibly filthy wedding dress pulled up and knotted at the waist. This character was very young—a boy—a little older than the children themselves. Robi wondered whether, if the dress had been less dirty, the ensemble might have been any less ridiculous. The problem wasn't so much the dirt, it was the unbearable and unmistakeable stench of bird excrement emanating from it. Even the children, who slept in an old half-dilapidated sheepfold without any opportunities to wash except when they had to work in the rain, found it unbearable. The stranger was holding the rat on his knees, and as he stroked it, he spoke as if it were a relative or a dear friend. The rat looked at him beatifically as its tail swung gently back and forth. Clearly, Robi had only stunned her prey, and equally clearly, the smell of bird excrement was doing the rat a great deal of good. The stranger and the rat sat looking at one another for a long and tender moment, and then the rat slipped to the ground and crept lazily away, past the whitethorn bush. Not even in the two years she had spent in the company of Slump had Robi witnessed a scene so full of idiocy, of a guy dressed up as a filthy bride, stinking of bird excrement, cuddling a rat as though it were his own child.

Cala took a step backward, and Robi reassured her by giving her arm a quick squeeze.

The stranger noticed the gesture and smiled.

The first to recover was Falco: "Stupid, snotty, cretin girl-child, you don't even know when you've killed a rat and when you haven't," he sneered.

"But it *was* dead," Robi protested, her humiliation matched only by her astonishment.

"It isn't now," the stranger said.

Cala started crying. For hours she had been thinking of that roasted rat, dreaming of sinking her teeth into her little piece of meat, and everyone would have said that she and Robi were really clever—two real huntresses. And everyone would have been happy, and the roasted meat of the rat would have gone *scrunch* under her teeth. . . .

"Robi did kill it," Cala insisted. "We would have eaten it," she added disconsolately.

"Don't eat anything that has ever thought," the stranger reproached her gently.

This assertion was so wildly eccentric that Cala immediately began to wail.

The stranger got to his feet, still smiling. He was the handsomest boy Robi had ever seen. If only he had been less stupid and didn't give off such a pestilential stench!

"Do rats think?" Falco asked in a puzzled voice.

Robi replied with a vague shrug. If Slump could think . . .

"What does that mean?" Falco asked again.

Robi gave an even vaguer shrug.

"Do you think he's an elf?" Falco asked, lowering his voice. The veil had fallen from the stranger's head, revealing very pale hair and pointed ears.

"No," Robi replied firmly.

"How can you be so sure?"

"Elves are swine, but they're also supposed to be intelligent," Robi whispered back.

The stranger looked at them and smiled even more broadly, then he bowed and said, "Yorshkrunsquarkljolner-strink."

"Bless you," Robi replied politely, as her mother had told her to do when someone sneezed.

"Bless you, too," said the stranger. "You can call me Yorsh, if you like. I'm looking for someone from the village of Arstrid."

Cala and Falco both pointed at Robi, with their arms straight and their index fingers outstretched.

The stranger's eyes remained fixed on Cala's little hand, which was missing a thumb. He looked at it for a long time before coming out with the idiotic statement: "Your thumb's missing!"

Cala lowered her arm and then her eyes, mortified. The tremble returned to her lower lip, and she was shaken by a few silent sobs. Robi looked at the stranger with hatred in her eyes. She dreamed of being big enough and strong enough to give him a good thump.

The stranger approached Cala and took her left hand between his two hands, and held it for a long time, gazing into nothingness. Cala was frightened, yet she didn't move or try to pull back. She stood there, her eyes lost in the blue of the stranger's eyes, which were in turn lost in the void. The stranger started to turn pale, then white, and a vague tremor began to shake him. Robi wondered if it mightn't be a contagious disease, and approached to pull Cala away. There was no need—the stranger's hands opened, and Cala's filthy, mutilated hand was free again. The stranger fell on his knees in the mud, unable to stay upright, and then came out with a second idiotic sentence: "Your hand will be all right, do you know that? Adults don't heal, but children do."

Cala stared at him in fascination, and Robi's fury mounted.

The stranger turned toward Robi once again.

"I knew there was a child from Arstrid here," he said. "Someone left a trail of stones, and that's something only a child can do!"

A child? Falco glanced at Robi, the unmistakable look that people give to idiots, and Robi felt that she hated the stranger with all her soul.

"My compliments, my dear lady, pray tell me what happened to your laughing village, and for what reason you are here now, and what you are doing."

At the words "my dear lady," Robi had hastily turned around, imagining that Phlesh must be behind her. When she was sure that the stranger was speaking only to her, her rage and frustration with this unbearable clown—he said his name was Yorsh—who had not only robbed her of her dinner, but made her a laughingstock, far exceeded her already limited patience. She bent forward to pick up a stick and waved it at the stranger. "I'm smaller than you, but I can hit harder," she told him threateningly. "And don't you dare touch her again," she added, nodding toward Cala without taking her eyes off him.

The stranger looked extremely ill. He trembled and gasped for breath. "Forgive me, my dear lady. If I have offended against your customs, it was far from deliberate! Mmm, Excellen—no. Imbeci—no, not that either. . . ."

Robi's expression became more menacing; her hands gripped the branch more tightly. The stranger suddenly remembered something and opened an embroidered blue velvet bag on a strap around his neck. He took out a little wooden boat and a little rag doll, its hair made of sheepskin dyed with walnut juice to make it rich and black, like Robi's.

"These are yours, aren't they?" said the stranger, holding them out. "I found them in Arstrid. I've brought them back to you."

Robi wished the stranger would disappear, sink into

the bog, vanish into the mud, or that a dragon would come and take him away. At the same time, she looked at her little boat and her doll with a fierce desire to touch them once again. Her mind filled with the memory of her father carving the hull of the ship from a block of beech, and her mother cutting from her very own cape the material for the doll's little dress. It was all that was left of her parents.

She stretched out her hand and silently took them.

"What happened in Arstrid?" the stranger asked gently.

Robi went on looking at him sulkily, then slowly, brought the stick down.

"It was destroyed," she murmured.

"Why?"

Robi said nothing. She didn't want to remember. She didn't feel like talking.

"Why?" repeated the stranger.

"Sel-fish-ness," Robi said in a tired voice, detaching the syllables from one another.

"What does that mean?"

Robi said nothing.

"They didn't pay enough taxes," explained Falco, breaking into the conversation. "They didn't want to pay," he added, sounding pompous and leaning on the word "want" in an imitation of Phlesh.

"They couldn't!" Robi protested desperately. "They couldn't."

The stranger nodded thoughtfully. "Are the inhabitants of the village alive?"

Robi nodded.

"And where are they?" the stranger went on.

"They escaped to the other side of the Dark Mountains, beyond the waterfall. Now they're living on the seashore." It wasn't a secret. The soldiers knew. They had never gone in search of the defectors, simply because they were too frightened of the waterfall.

"Do you know a man called Monser and a woman called Sajra?" the stranger asked.

Silence.

"Do you know a man called Monser and a woman called Sajra?" the stranger repeated.

Robi's eyes filled with tears. She gripped the little boat and the doll. "They were my father and mother," she said softly.

"Were?" insisted the stranger.

"They were hanged," said Falco.

The stranger turned pale. "Why?" he asked in a strangled tone when he managed to get his voice back. "Why?"

"Selfishness," Robi said between sobs, "and . . ." Robi couldn't go on.

"And . . . ?" the stranger said encouragingly.

"And they say they had protected an elf, but I know it isn't true, it can't be . . ." Robi couldn't finish.

"Nooooooooooooo!" screamed Yorsh. "No, no, no, no. They gave life, they are dead, they left you as an orphan for saving me!"

The stranger covered his face with his hands. He knelt on the earth, huddled in on himself, shaking like a leaf on a branch in the winter wind.

Falco smiled triumphantly. "He *is* an elf!"

Robi stopped crying. She raised her head and then looked down at the weeping creature at her feet. Was he really an elf? *The* elf? The one for whom . . . Had her parents really died and left her an orphan for this? For this thing here? Because of him she didn't have a father or a mother? No dried apples and partridges on a spit, or a warm bed and milk with honey in the morning, for this wretched creature who couldn't do anything but mock a group of hungry children and make fun of somebody's mutilated hand? It wasn't true, it couldn't be. And now Robi recognized the dress he was wearing—it was the wedding dress of the village head's daughter! Her mother had even helped to embroider the T on the front. Rage overcame her grief, and a very modest kick from her bare foot made contact with Yorsh, who was already too upset to notice.

"Go away," yelled Robi. "None of what you have said is true. Go away!" She spat on him, but Yorsh remained motionless—he had fainted.

Robi hadn't time to think of anything else to say or do: Phlesh's shouts behind her let her know that break time was over.

"He's an elf," cried Falco, pointing to the prostrate figure at their feet.

The words rang out until they reached the soldiers. A few arrows flew. Robi, Cala, and Falco threw themselves to the ground and covered their heads with their hands. Yorsh remained motionless; he was barely breathing. The hill that could be glimpsed behind the House of Orphans suddenly moved. It was a dragon crouching in the grass. He was very close, and he was enormous. Everybody ran in all directions, apart from the three on the ground, who couldn't see properly because of all the things in the way, and who remained stretched out on the ground with their hands over their heads, unable to work out what was going on. They understood when a hot and stinking wind blew over them. Looking up, they found themselves staring into the dragon's jaws, and it was suddenly clear that the wind was the breath coming from a mouth with fangs as long as an arm.

Fortunately, the dragon hadn't even noticed them—he was trying to find a way of taking Yorsh between his jaws with a secure grip but without hurting the elf boy.

"Robi!" Cala called out.

"Sshhh. Shush, now."

"Robi, I've wet myself."

"It doesn't matter; in fact, it's quite a good idea," whispered Robi reassuringly. "It'll make you less good to eat. Now be quiet."

But the dragon wasn't even slightly interested in them. He was still busy working out how to transport Yorsh. After a few attempts with his fangs, he opted to use his claws. He would hold the boy's ankles with the claws of his left foot, and his wrists with those of his right foot. Then the dragon spread his enormous emerald-green wings and rose slowly upward.

When he was high in the sky, very high, a few arrows flew up improbably after him.

Robi stayed on the ground, not knowing what to do,

until Phlesh's hands took her by the shoulder and pulled her to her feet.

"You . . ." Phlesh began, her voice choking with rage, "you . . . you miserable . . . elf-lover. . . . Yes, that's it, elf-lover . . . like your father and your mother, glory be to Daligar for putting them to death . . . miserable scoundrels . . . but I've had my eye on you, you know. . . . I knew . . . you're the one who drew them to us. . . . It's your fault, isn't it?"

Robi didn't even try to reply. She knew it would only increase Phlesh's rage and the fury of her blows. She tried to protect herself as best she could. She felt so terrible that Phlesh's slaps were really the least of her problems. Her mother and father had condemned themselves to death and her to unhappiness, all for a miserable cretin. The dream that had pursued her since her life and her family had been destroyed, a dragon with a prince dressed in white, had come true, and an elfish villain wearing a wedding dress covered with bird poo and various kinds of dung had descended on her to make her wretched life even more complicated than it was already.

By the time Phlesh had calmed down, Robi was covered with bruises. Slump had arrived as well, and was deciding what needed to be done. He himself would go to Daligar and request the reinforcements necessary to bring the little witch to the city.

"Yes, witch," he added, turning to Robi. "A real witch—that's what we call elf-lovers. . . ."

The journey would take half a day. He couldn't risk his

precious life by escorting her himself. The dragon and the elf would attack again. They had clearly attacked the place to free her.

Fine, Robi thought bitterly. She was about to leave for Daligar, for a prison cell, which would probably be followed by a gallows, just as she had reached the minimum age, which made her eligible for hanging, although she wasn't yet considered an adult in other respects. The second part of her dream was about to come true as well. Thanks to the dragon and the prince, she would be leaving the House of Orphans forever.

She allowed herself to be carried to one of the sentry boxes, where she was put in chains. The two archers would keep watch over her as they waited for the other troops to arrive. Robi hunched up with her head between her elbows, the boat and the doll clutched in her hands, letting time slip over her, while her thoughts went on milling around inside her head like a flock of crazed crows.

Time passed. Every now and again Robi's eyes closed with exhaustion, but no images formed except, sometimes, a little left hand with its five fingers spread. Slump came back. He had an entire garrison with him. They had come to get her. They removed her chains and made her put on a lighter kind, suitable for travel. Then they sat her on a donkey. Robi had never ridden before, but she was too desperate to bother about the fact. It was a sad and foggy day, softening the colors of autumn.

The other orphans were crowded around in silence in

the clearing in front of the old sheepfold. A hand was raised in a gesture of farewell and remained open in the air with all five fingers spread. Phlesh barked something, but the little hand remained stubbornly in the air, and finally Robi realized that it wasn't a wave. Cala was holding up her little left hand with the five perfect fingers attached to it. Including the thumb—the one that the hatchet had cut off two years before.

Robi looked at Cala's hands, both of which were raised now. She felt short of breath, and for a moment her vision grew hazy. Finally, she figured it out: a creature kind and powerful beyond imagination had crossed her path, and all she had done was kick and spit at it. She went on staring at Cala until the little girl was out of sight. The donkey walked on, escorted by a garrison of soldiers that would have been large enough to fight an army of trolls.

CHAPTER TWENTT-EIGHT

ORSH WAS in despair. He had been an idiot, an absolute idiot. He felt sick at the thought of how stupid he had been. His idiocy was profound, cosmic, titanic, gigantic, epic, infinite, mountainous. Incurable. Irreparable.

"All right, you've been a bit daft, but it's not true to say that it's hopeless. Only death is hopeless, and yesterday no one actually died. . . ."

The dragon's words were lost in the wind, which blew furiously in from the stormy sea.

Yorsh was still too ill to do anything but lie on the ground, hunched in on himself, quivering like a leaf in a gale, while a pain as unbearable as a red-hot knife ran through the thumbs of both his hands. He was burning up with fever: the cold wind was a relief to his fiery skin. He lay on the wet grass with his hands plunged in a little puddle of icy water that formed among the rocks outside the cave when the rain fell.

Obviously, the little girl had to be their child, the daughter of Monser and Sajra. She had her mother's features and the dark skin of her father; he should have been able to work it out all by himself. She had the generosity and courage of her father and mother. She had never stopped protecting and reassuring the smaller girl. A shame that, like her mother and father, she grew angry in a matter of seconds, and for reasons that were incomprehensible! Yorsh should have noticed all by himself that the little girl was desperate, malnourished, miserable, broken with exhaustion, and the first thing he should have done was to protect her and bring her to safety, rather than leaving her where she was, after putting her in mortal danger.

The fact was that the pain of the other girl, the smaller one with the mutilated hand, had struck him like a rock, and he hadn't immediately worked the right order in which things should have been done: first bring the children to a better place, then heal their wounds, cure their afflictions, and console their miseries. . . .

The dragon nodded with conviction as he attacked the third capercaillie that he had slipped onto a willow-branch spit, which was browning nicely over a delightful little fire of rosemary and pine, so that the smell of the burning twigs merged with the odor of roasting meat.

"How can you eat that stuff?" the elf asked plaintively.

"I bite with my front teeth and chew with my back teeth," the dragon replied politely. "Let's go on with the story: why did you faint?"

"Rebuilding the little girl's hand was terrible. I should have known, I should have remembered how exhausting it had been to heal your wound, and multiplied it infinitely. I should have foreseen that it would put me out of action. I should have figured out that this wasn't the moment. But the worst is over: knowing that the man and woman died and that it was my fault . . . my fault . . ." Yorsh's eyes were lost in the void. "All this is so . . . so . . ." He couldn't find words.

"Stupid, ridiculous, and laughable," suggested Erbrow as he tore into his fourth capercaillie. He even started snickering.

"How dare you? . . . How can you? . . ." He groped around for words that might deliver a wound to match his own. "Stupid, blind beast, son of an even stupider beast, more insensitive and brainless and, what's more, fond of idiotic fairy stories. How can you laugh? That marvelous girl is desperate and an orphan because . . . because I . . . because they . . . because they saved me!"

The dragon remained quite composed. He plunged his teeth into his fifth capercaillie.

"I'm laughing at you, not her. If that marvelous girl is desperate and an orphan, it isn't your fault; it's the fault of the criminals who put a noose around her parents' necks, and, not content with that, locked her up in a place that makes a snake pit look like a picnic site. We are responsible for our actions, and ours alone. Marsio and Silla, or whatever their names were, chose to save you, and that was their right. Their choice. Among other things, without you, they mightn't ever have come together, and their marvelous child wouldn't exist. But that's not the point: you remember the story of the dwarfs from the Second Runic Dynasty? First, people persecuted them because they wore beards, then because they'd stopped wearing them. They just wanted their mines. They were setting off to explore the eastern coasts and they wanted the money for their ships."

The dragon broke off to swallow his sixth capercaillie, then went on: "The people in charge of Daligar want stupid and miserable subjects, and those two didn't have the vocation for either stupidity or for misery. If it hadn't been because of you, it would have been because of something else, and they would have been destroyed anyway. So remember that you owe your life to them; enjoy it and use it. Stop flapping like a capercaillie that's lost its tail, get off your bum, and go and save the little girl—what was her name?"

"Robi. The other girl called her Robi."

"Robi? Humans clearly have a gift for names that don't mean a thing. They are unaware of the concept that a name is important. What's the plan? How are we going to go back and get her?"

Yorsh was starting to feel better.

"We'll go at night. A moonless night. A night like this one." Yorsh noticed that his strength was growing by the moment. Nothing was lost. The dragon was right. "Let's go back tonight," he said firmly.

"I'll just finish my snack," the dragon sighed. He was on his seventh capercaillie—on the spit there were twenty-one. "You just can't eat in peace in this place."

Yorsh devoured a few golden beans and picked up his things again: the bow and the elfish arrows, because, as Erbrow insisted, "You never know." The mythical embroidered velvet bag containing his mother's poetry book, and the spinning top he'd had when he was a child—the toy that his parents had played with when they were children, before him.

"That seems like basic luggage to me. If the archers attack us, you'll always be able to read poems and make them play with the spinning top," Erbrow observed sarcastically.

Yorsh didn't reply. He filled any remaining space in the little bag with golden beans, so that at least one of the children's problems—hunger—would be quickly resolved.

Yorsh's dress still smelled of bird excrement—although the previous night's wind and rain had made them slightly less pestilential—and Yorsh now had an ever-stronger sense that there was something wrong with his way of dressing. Since he had no alternative, he limited himself to a few variations. He took off the top layer of the dress, the one with the embroideries and little patterns made of holes that were called lace. He took off the puffy sleeves that got in his way, and shortened the cape to just above the ankles, so that he didn't have to keep it tied at the waist. The result was a kind of habit of a vague gray color and an almost passable smell, not unlike the clothes of the alchemists or the ancient sages.

The dragon was growing fatter with each passing day. By now, he was almost the size of Erbrow the Elder, and his outstretched wings were wider than the clearing that held the rocks and the little pool. He took the elf boy between his wings and rose steadily and securely into the wind and storm. In the total darkness of the night, in which the rain formed great walls of water, they lost their bearings, then had terrible arguments about which was the right direction, then they got lost again, and finally they argued about who was to blame for getting lost. Finally, toward dawn, the light arrived, and the pale shadow of the hills emerged from the dark, and the half-dilapidated sheepfold with its ferocious-looking palisade appeared on the horizon. Yorsh was dry and warm, but Erbrow's wings were so soaked with rain that he could barely fly. After landing in the little forest alongside the clearing where Yorsh had resurrected the rat, they wondered what to do next. Yorsh had read about military tactics and strategies, and it was with ill-concealed pride that he began to illustrate his two plans, the main one and the one he held in reserve. The first idea was the far more discreet of the two, which is to say, Yorsh would silently penetrate the old sheepfold, while Erbrow would stay at the rear, ready to intercept any outflanking maneuvers and cover the escape route. . . .

At that point, the geese started honking. In a grayish universe of mud and rain, inside Phlesh and Slump's poultry pen, outside their charming little wood-and-stone house with vines climbing over it, the snow-white wings of four geese were reflected in an overflowing puddle. The moment Yorsh approached, they began to make the loudest noises he had ever heard. The young elf remembered that the ancient kings used geese to guard their palaces against intruders, thieves, and invaders, and now he understood the wisdom of it. Phlesh and Slump came flying out into the courtyard in their underwear. The soldiers flung themselves out of their sentry boxes, wearing their armor and with their bows at the ready. For a moment, they all stood and stared, before the dragon moved. He opened his mouth and emitted a terrifying roar, sending out a long tongue of flame that shot through the rain, making the mist evaporate into a thin strip of fog. Everyone fled: Phlesh at the front, then the soldiers, hampered by their armor, and last of all Slump, his enormous bottom swathed in a pair of pea-green underpants.

The only ones left were the children still hidden away in their filthy dormitory.

"Now what's the plan?" the dragon asked.

Yorsh opened the door to the children's quarters. A dozen terrified children were huddled and weeping in a corner, looking at Yorsh and, more to the point, Erbrow's shadow on the other side of the door.

"I've wet myself," one of the littlest children whispered.

"Good idea," Cala said comfortingly. "It means you won't be so good to eat."

"My name's Yorsh," the elf introduced himself. He'd had enough of being told to bless himself, and decided to limit himself to the short version.

The children were still huddled and terrified. Their weeping continued, becoming shriller now.

"Do something to reassure them," the elf said to the dragon.

Erbrow rummaged around in his various memories for an idea. Then his mouth widened into a kind of smile that revealed his inferomedial and posterolateral fangs, and the worried wails of the children rose to another level.

"Surely you can do better than that!" groaned Yorsh.

The smile widened: the posteroinferior fangs appeared as well. Besides being longer, they were also more curved. Some of the children hurled themselves to the ground, begging not to be eaten.

"What absolute nonsense! Dragons never eat people!" Yorsh said, exasperated. Now he realized that Robi was missing. He had to reassure the children quickly to find out what had happened to her.

The uproar continued and got even worse. Cries alternated with pleas for pity. Now they were imploring Erbrow not to eat them, and begging the terrible elf not to kill them with his rage.

Yorsh didn't know what to do. All the things that came to mind—shouting, waving his arms around, lighting the little torch that hung near the entrance—only frightened the children all the more.

Finally, a mighty roar drowned the hubbub, and the

light of a new flame lit up the darkness. A smell of meat, half roasted and half burned, filled the air. There was sudden and total silence.

"Who wants a bit of roast goose?" asked the dragon. "A lovely fat goose. Hey, you two, the biggest ones," he said, turning to Falco and Fowlpest, "one of you go and find a bit of rosemary, and the other a branch of willow or pine so that we can put the rest of the geese on the spit and—"

He didn't have time to finish: the boys darted out toward the fence from which there rose the unmistakable smell of something warm into which they could plunge their teeth, and then feel their stomachs filling up.

"The only thing that can drown out fear and hunger," the dragon hastily explained. "It applies to dogs, cats, humans, goldfish, dragons, and trolls. I don't know enough about elves to deliver a judgement about them in this respect."

Cala stayed behind. She went over to Yorsh, took a long breath, swallowed, and then stayed there. Yorsh knelt down to bring his head level with the girl's.

"Where have they taken Robi?" he asked gently.

Cala calmed down, swallowed again, then managed to speak: "To Daligar, they've taken her to Daligar. I heard Phlesh and Slump talking about it. They took her to a place called 'the old palace dungeon.'"

"I know where that is," said Yorsh. "I was there, too, as a child."

Cala swallowed again.

"They said . . . they said . . . I think they're going to hurt her. . . . Phlesh beat her . . . very badly."

"Don't worry. I'm going to get her now. Don't worry, it'll all be fine."

Yorsh repeated it several times—not just to calm Cala down, but for his own sake, too.

Cala nodded. Her eyes filled with tears, but she choked them back and didn't cry.

Yorsh turned to go. He was in the doorway when Cala mumbled something.

"Pardon?" he said, turning around.

Cala shyly raised her left hand, with the fingers spread, and took another big breath.

"Thanks for my hand," she said. This time he heard her.

In the few moments that Yorsh had spent with Cala, Erbrow the Younger had already organized the children. He had put the smallest ones safely in the little house dec-orated with hearts and goslings, which Phlesh and Slump had left with the door half open, while the bigger ones helped him organize a mammoth spit, in spite of the rain. In Phlesh and Slump's house, the children had found some real bread made with real grain, and a yellow thing with a very special smell that they called beer. Goose and chicken feath-ers flew everywhere, and Yorsh watched with horror as they wrung the poor creatures' necks.

"Anyone want some golden beans?" he asked.

No one even replied.

"Do you really eat people sometimes?" one of the young-est children asked.

"Only very rarely," replied the dragon pompously. "The

flavor isn't terribly good, and the shoes are a further compli-
cation. . . ."

"Could you eat Slump?" the little one asked hopefully.

"Is he the one with the big pea-green bottom?" asked
the dragon.

"Dragons don't eat humans anymore. Dragons never eat
humans. NEVER!" yelled Yorsh.

If nothing else, he managed to get everybody to be quiet
for a moment.

"I'm going to Daligar to get Robi back," he said to the
dragon.

"Is Daligar that nice place where the soldiers fire
arrows? Do you mind if I stay here and defend the children?
Things could get dangerous here. I don't know . . . I don't
want the geese attacking them. . . ."

Yorsh thought about it.

"Yes, it's a good idea. You stay here and protect the
children. The soldiers might come back, or those two horrible humans who were, shall we say, entrusted with the task
of looking after them." He turned back to the children.
"When I come back, anyone who wants to can follow us to
the sea beyond the Dark Mountains."

Although he hadn't really thought about it yet, he
knew what he had to do: get Robi back and then bring
everyone to safety on the seashore.

"There are shells on the seashore, which might think
and write poetry, but you can still eat them," he said, quot-
ing Monser, the hunter, and not speaking so much as thinking out loud.

Cala started laughing. "That was what Robi used to say, too. Her father said it to her."

"Really? How long would it take to get from here to Daligar? A day's walking?"

"On foot, I would say, yes," replied Cala. "But there are horses, too. The last time Slump went to Daligar he came back on a horse. It's tethered at the back of the house."

"Then I'll take the horse, and I'd better get a move on before it ends up eaten with rosemary along with everything else," said Yorsh with one last glance at the dragon and the flock of ravenous children. "Now you go along and . . . well . . . eat your piece of meat."

"Even if it has thought?" Cala asked.

Yorsh looked at the little girl's pale cheeks, the big circles under her eyes, and her skeletal legs, and knew that the geese and chickens would be turned into strength, blood, and flesh.

"Yes," he said, "even if it has thought."

Cala smiled at him and ran off.

Yorsh went to get the horse. It was a magnificent bay with big hazel eyes. Yorsh put a hand on its forehead and felt its soft fur, while a series of sensations ran through the horse's mind: longing for its mother when it was a colt, horror at the thought of saddles and reins, a grudge about the long journey from Daligar with the huge bottom and riding crop of his previous rider, and a great desire to kick him.

"Fine," he whispered, "no saddle and no reins. We elves don't need them."

The horse looked into his eyes and understood. Yorsh

leaped onto his back, and the horse sped off immediately. It was like being as one with its strength and speed; the most beautiful sensation he had ever felt, apart from flying on Erbrow.

In the rain-soaked light of dawn, finding his bearings was easy. Before midday, the menacing walls of Daligar were in view.

CHAPTER TWENTY-NINE

HE PRISON WAS much colder than the House of Orphans. It was made of stone and there weren't any other children breathing together and keeping the place warm. On the other hand, it was drier, the straw for sleeping was better, and you were given more to eat. And there was no work to do, either. If it hadn't been for the word "hanging" that sounded periodically, it could have been a kind of holiday for Robi.

She had been shut up in there since the previous evening. Shortly after her arrival, an icy wind and beating rain had begun, and showed no signs of abating. Robi wondered if that terrible weather would delay the prince, or if he would come anyway; for now she knew that the prince and the dragon were not just a fantasy. She wondered what power the prince would use to save her. Perhaps he would knock down the walls by playing a trumpet, or fly there on his dragon and break open the roof by dropping rocks on it. Or . . .

The two prison guards came in: Clover, small and thin, and Beach, big and fat, red-faced, always in search of a pint of beer. They were two middle-aged men, probably fathers and family men, who hadn't treated her too badly. In fact, they were actually kind, and certainly much nicer than Phlesh and Slump. They had even let her keep her doll and her little boat, and had found her a blanket for the night-time.

Now they were scared and excited—the judge administrator was coming down to the dungeon to speak with her. It was an absolutely extraordinary event—it had never happened in living memory. The guards darted about like two streaks of lightning in a desperate bid to make the place look slightly respectable after years of filth and abandonment. A ridiculously long time was devoted to the discussion of whether to let Robi keep her blanket and toys, or take them away. In the former case, it would be clear that they took care of their prisoners; in the latter that they didn't treat them too indulgently. In the end, they decided to let her keep everything, with an order to hide the toys under the blanket, in the darkest corner of the cell. They lit the torches, which hadn't been illuminated for years, and some of which were damp or mildewed. That operation also took an excessive amount of time and filled the dungeons with an annoying and bitter smoke that was a curious shade of yellow.

The piles of straw in the corners, with fat rats running over them, didn't look much better in the light. The two guards tried at least to take the straw away, so that perhaps the rats would scatter as well, and the whole thing would start to look more like the dungeon of a palace with regal pretensions, and less like a pigsty. Then they realized that the really urgent thing to do was to drag out the empty earthenware bottles that were piling up beside the guards' office, indisputable proof that the main activity during guard service was the consumption of beer. Finally, Beach, with his arms full of straw, and Clover, laden down with empty pots, hurried toward the exit, and it was at that precise moment that the judge chose to come in, so they crashed into each other. Beach and the judge ended up on the floor. Clover just about managed to stay on his feet, but failed to keep hold of the pint pots, which rained down on the two men beneath him, and since Beach was smart enough to dodge, it was the judge who took the brunt. The last bottle to fall on him still had some beer in it, so the judge's jacket stopped being lily white with a delicate hint of ivory, and turned the unmistakable yellowish color of beer. The judge's mood turned from "really furious" to "give me someone to strangle, and do it, please, before dinnertime."

Robi burst out laughing. She knew she shouldn't have. After all, three people had collided and two of them had fallen and hurt themselves, but when the tension is high and you haven't slept for a long time, you do stupid things like emitting squeals of high-pitched laughter when someone falls over. When she had managed to collect herself, the judge was standing in front of her, with his hands gripping the bars. He was now truly in a rage.

"It was you, wasn't it? You provoked this! I know it was you," he hissed.

The judge was tall and thin, with a silver mustache and beard, and hair that would have curled into soft ringlets if the rancid beer hadn't plastered it into a foul-smelling heap. "You put a spell on them and they fell, isn't that right? I know it! You came here with the sole purpose of making me look a fool, isn't that so? Discrediting me and my job!"

Robi wondered whether she should reply and clear herself. Apart from anything, she hadn't gone to the judge of her own accord—she'd been dragged there—and if she had ever had any power she would have used it to open the cell and eliminate the problem as quickly as possible. But the judge started talking again, without leaving her the time to respond. "You do know who I am, don't you?"

Robi was doubtful for a moment. Half of her mind, the part where pride and courage prevailed, wanted to reply: "The murderer of my parents, the one who signed their death warrants, the wretched, cretinous criminal who spreads injustice and misery as a candle spreads light." The other half of her mind, the one that wanted at all costs to continue the life that her parents had left her, thought about supplying his official title: "You are the judge . . ." followed perhaps by some additional qualifiers: "the great . . . noble . . . judge."

Again she didn't have to make a choice—conversation with the judge was not a dialogue, but a monologue enlivened by interrogations. Her answers weren't required.

"I'm the one who came to bring justice to these parts, to eradicate greed, covetousness, and pride. It is too elevated and too noble a task to be hampered by pity. I know! Like a surgeon valiantly amputating a limb when it is infested with gangrene, I will restore health to the body of this wretched and beloved county. Do you know why I lowered myself, even though I represent the county of Daligar, to come down here and talk to you?"

This time Robi didn't have to make an effort to keep her mouth shut, because, frankly, she had no idea.

"Because I want you to understand. It might seem cruel, I know, to kill a child. That's why you won't be hanged in the public square—like your wretched and insignificant parents—but here, sheltered from eyes that might fail to understand. I want you to understand, because otherwise I know that in that wretched and insignificant head of yours, you might accuse my magnificence of injustice, mightn't you? That would be intolerable. You will be aware that the last thing your father dared to say out loud was that all that interested him in the world, more than Daligar and me, you understand, *more than me*, were his wretched and insignificant wife and his even more wretched and insignificant daughter?"

Robi was growing more and more puzzled. She had

often thought about the judge administrator, and she had seen him as a sort of lord of evil, with a kind of pride about his own ferocity; more or less like an ogre, but more intelligent and civilized. She was clearly wrong about the intelligent and civilized part.

"We have arrested your elf!" the judge informed her with fierce pride. "He handed himself in of his own accord to our guards a short time ago. He knows that we're invincible, and he didn't even try to fight. I know it—this is the moment of our glory! Is it not?"

So this was the path chosen by the prince to rescue her. Turning himself in—a simple, brilliant plan. Robi heaved a great sigh of relief. Luckily, the only thing that matched the judge's ferocity was his stupidity. Obviously, he considered it perfectly normal that a gentleman with extraordinary powers who, among other things, rode nothing less than a dragon, wished only to make the aforementioned judge administrator happy by turning himself in of his own accord, permitting himself to be hanged without further hitches.

Never had Robi felt safer than she did at that moment—the prince was coming to get her. He would certainly know what to do, and how to do it.

CHAPTER THIRTY

ORSH HADN'T the faintest idea what to do or how to do it. Turning himself in to the soldiers at the great gate was the only idea that had come to him, and he wasn't entirely convinced that it was a brilliant one.

He had done a swap, turning himself in without a fight in exchange for the girl. Not just because he owed it to Monser and Sajra, but because he had seen her, and she was now the only thing that meant anything to him. He didn't know how to fight. So what else could he do?

Often in the complicated fairy stories that he had read to Erbrow the Elder during the brood, something was exchanged for something else: I give you half a pound of courgettes and a quarter of a pint of beans and, when she is born, your daughter will be mine. Or: if you bring me three tail feathers of the golden vulture, you will have half of my kingdom or, alternatively, seven eighths of the magic carpet and five elevenths of the pot of abundance. And everyone kept to their agreement. So he was unaware that pacts are sometimes not respected, and that you have to make your contract from a position of strength before giving up that position. He should have freed Robi first, and then turned himself in. The fact was, he now realized, that it had seemed *rude* to him to suggest that they might not be men of honor, and to take precautions accordingly. And turning up all by himself at the garrison by the gate, where they were all armed to the teeth and with arrows aimed, hadn't been particularly clever. He should have threatened reprisals by the dragon. Too late now. He had been arrested. And now the plan was: hanging for everyone. Yorsh in the square and Robi in the depths of the dungeon.

Yorsh was wrapped in so many chains that he had trouble breathing. He was surrounded by so many soldiers that he couldn't count them. His only consolation was that they were taking him to the dungeons of the palace of Daligar and he knew that Robi was there. He'd think of something. He had to—if there was an ancient prophecy about his future, it meant that he still had a possible future ahead of him. And he wouldn't escape without taking Robi with him.

He was taken down stairs that became more and more narrow and steep, passing along corridors that became lower and darker, deeper and deeper into the earth, farther from the daylight, until finally, the walls widened and, in the torchlight, he saw a figure dressed opulently in white, smelling strangely of rancid beer, whom he recognized as the judge administrator.

Behind him, the darkness beyond the bars concealed the barely perceptible little figure of Robi.

The judge wasted no time.

"I've been waiting for you, elf," he said. "You've come in search of your future wife, haven't you? I know it."

Yorsh was speechless. How did he know? Certainly, Robi was little more than a child and he was still a boy, but elves choose their wives very young, and forever. Each time he thought of Robi—her face, her tenderness, and the courage with which she had tried to protect and comfort the younger girl, the one with the missing thumb—he knew she was the one!

"I know it," the judge continued. "I, too, know how to read the ancient tongues. I, too, read the prophecy before having it destroyed, along with all the other writings that sullied the walls of this place. Reading does the people no good—not that anyone here can do it! I have taken precautions to avoid that misfortune. The prophecy was written by Arduin, the great wizard, the Lord of Light, the founder! Daligar was once an Elfish city, you knew that, did you not? After the ogres destroyed it, Arduin reconquered and reestablished it. He was completely mad, Arduin; he loved elves. And he was not without a certain degree of military acumen. Certainly, freeing the city from the ogres when they were at the peak of their power, attacking with an army that was not even half the size of his adversary's and defeating them nonetheless, was an undertaking that required a certain level of skill, a certain level of wisdom, too, I grant you, but nothing comparable to mine. I am the true founder of Daligar—its true liberator. I am liberating Daligar from passion, from selfishness. I am leading it back to virtue and humility. With my justice and my severity I am purging it. And I am making it more beautiful! I, too, am a magician, much greater than Arduin, who could only predict the future and destroy the spell of the Shadow, with which the ogres had enslaved the world. I have done more than that. Haven't you noticed? Haven't you seen my extraordinary marvel? My triumph?"

Silence. A long silence. Yorsh wondered if he was expected to say anything. He probably was, but honestly, he had no idea of what the judge administrator's extraordinary marvel might be. The only thing that came to mind was that Daligar had struck him as an extraordinarily miserable place, and it was somehow marvelous that it could be so after such a splendid past. The embarrassed silence continued and finally the judge went on.

"The flowers!" he exploded in exasperation. "The wisteria that are always in flower, the perfume of the jasmines! By rotting down enormous quantities of fruit and grain that we are sent from the countryside, we obtain a special fertilizer, which gives us permanent flowers, and perfumes of great intensity. Isn't it extraordinary? It's really extraordinary, is it not?"

Yorsh stared at the judge in fascination. He was mad, completely and spectacularly insane. There could not be the slightest doubt about his madness. What he failed to understand was the reason why the many armed onlookers remained at attention in the face of his madness rather than taking him by the hand and leading him politely but firmly to a place where his delirium might be cured, or at least rendered harmless.

"I also had to destroy Arduin's old royal palace—arches all over the place, those dull old arches and columns alternating with those dull flower beds, surrounded by those ludicrous cedar trees. I, the judge, knocked almost all of it down, leaving only the porticoes, because a new era had dawned. An era unlike anything ever seen before, an era of which my palace was the very symbol."

"Arduin," the judge went on, "before he died wrote his prophecy: 'The last elf will marry a girl, his descendant, the heir of Arduin himself. The girl will be endowed, like her forefather, with the power of clairvoyance and will have, in her name, the light of the morning. She will be the daughter of the man and the woman who' . . . and here a word was missing, weathered away by time . . . 'who "something-ed" the elf,' I guessed the word was probably 'hated.' When they told me you had entered my garden and had seen my delightful daughter, Dawn, I understood that you would come back and take her, and that I would then be able and obliged to destroy you."

Dawn? The judge's daughter? The awful girl he'd seen on the swing? The judge's daughter was called Dawn, the light of sunrise! That jewel of malevolence, arrogance, and bossiness had the light of morning in her name?

"My daughter, Dawn. In her name the light of morning. I brought her up to absolute perfection. She is the perfect girl. She plays the lute, reads ancient poems, and sings as she sits on her swing, like the princesses of kingdoms past. At least as they are represented in images on parchment. So, since she reached the age of reason, she has been allowed to do nothing, Dawn has, I mean, except play the lute and swing and sing among the flowers, because for a girl that is perfection. . . ."

Lute playing and singing on a swing from morning till night, day after day. Yorsh began to feel a spark of sympathy for poor Dawn, forced as she was to live like the perfect imitation of that absurd story about some princess who might never even have existed! That was why she was such an unbearably silly goose: perfection must be an unbearable burden.

"Dawn is my daughter and thus, the heir to Arduin, because since I am, like him, the head of the city, I am his successor." The judge's voice had risen, and now he was uttering his words more precisely, as though to lend them greater weight. "And Dawn has the ability to predict the future, did you know that? Once she predicted that she would have the gold necklace that belonged to the wife of the head of the guards, and guess what? He turned out to be a traitor. He was hanged, his goods were confiscated, and the gold necklace is Dawn's. . . . And when she predicted that sooner or later the dryness of last summer would come to an end and that it would rain in autumn—she was right again!"

For a few moments a vague smile disfigured the judge's features. Yorsh's brain was in torment. Dawn! The awful, nasty, stupid girl on the swing? The girl who could make a little child cry for hours on end? He felt sorry for her. In her own way she too had had a difficult—in fact, unbearable—fate, but there was really no question of founding a new tribe with her. Never. He'd rather have the gallows. Never. Not for anything in the world. His destiny stopped there, along with his patience with Arduin and his prophecies. Perhaps poor Arduin, the Lord of Light, had been feeling the effects of age: the light must have blinded him from time to time, and the shadows had blurred in his head. Waging war against the ogres couldn't have been a picnic—during some siege or other Arduin must have bumped his head against something very hard, and got it into his mind that the last elf could, under any circumstances, marry Dawn.

Now the problem was how to get Robi back and quickly cause a disturbance, leaving the judge and his delightful daughter with their brilliant predictions.

The judge was holding his bow with the three arrows and his little blue velvet bag.

"Let's see what you brought, elf, to destroy us. Your bow and your arrows are in my hands. What else have we here?"

The Judge squeezed the velvet bag. The golden beans fell to the floor.

Their scent was too subtle for humans, but not for an elf. As the beans scattered, Yorsh smelled their perfume, faint but unmistakable, sweet and penetrating, like freshly baked bread.

Yorsh remembered the rats.

The big, fat rats of the prisons of Daligar had helped him once before, when he was a child.

They, too, were able to smell the scent of the beans, and their minds would fill with it. Rats' minds are easy to control. There were thousands of them. Yorsh felt them. He felt their eternal, insatiable hunger; their fury; the grudges they bore over all the kicks, the stones, the darts thrown for fun, the poisoned bait. Thousands of them in all the cells— hungry, angry, mean.

Yorsh breathed and felt the air filling his lungs, felt his strength increasing—he knew what to do. He would use the rats. He intensified the perfume of the golden beans, and with it, he sought the minds of the rats and guided them.

"A child's toy." The judged dropped the spinning top to the floor and smashed it with a kick. "And . . . a book! Interesting, is it not?"

The rats were starting to emerge from the darkness behind the bars, from the darkness behind the corridors off to the side. Some of them ran along the walls, using the frieze ornaments between the torches. There were not yet many, a few dozen. Yorsh took the fear from their minds. Others arrived, and behind them, yet more, and then more. They made straight for the beans, heedless of the soldiers and utterly fearless: a wave of flesh, hair, and tiny teeth that submerged the men's feet like an incoming tide. The soldiers tried to dodge, to escape, crashing into one another as they did so.

The judge was holding the poetry book that had belonged to Yorsh's mother, and was concentrating on it too hard to notice anything: "What are they, spells? Poetry? What nonsense! 'Fol . . . low the . . . the . . . blue . . . i . . . vy . . . branch.' '. . . Follow the blue ivy branch.' I know your language, elf, are you aware of that? You should always know the language of your enemies.

'Follow the blue ivy branch.'

"Ivy's green, I know that. Elves always lie, is it not so? Even in their poetry.

> 'Follow the blue ivy branch:
> It will lead you to where the gold gleams.
> Find where the water gurgles.
> The future depends
> On our strength . . . and . . .'"

The rats had begun to bite, not only the golden beans, but everything they could find. That is, the feet and legs of the soldiers and the judge, who dropped the book with a shriek. Only Yorsh and Robi were unharmed, their feet free of the uniform layer of rats that covered everything like a swarming, treacherous, shifting carpet with teeth.

Some of the men started to run away, pressing themselves against the walls so as not to lose their balance. Yorsh concentrated on the locks. *Clank*. The lock holding Yorsh's wrists opened, and his chains fell at his feet. *Clank*. His ankles were free, too. The tide of rats swept over everything. The judge tripped over the remains of the spinning top and fell to the ground. The few remaining soldiers hurried to try and protect him and lift him up, leaving Robi's bars completely unguarded. *Clank.* That lock was open as well. Yorsh took her by the hand and pulled her out. Then they left slowly, walking backward so as not to lose sight of the soldiers and the judge, while the sea of rats parted obediently as they passed. Yorsh pulled a torch from the wall and glanced one last time at the group: the judge was on his feet again, but he was too busy defending himself to worry about them. The stairs swarmed with soldiers, and above them were more stairs with more soldiers, and yet more soldiers, and yet more.

In the minds of the rats, however, there was an image of a vast, labyrinthine, subterranean world that stretched beneath the city and beneath the river. Yorsh saw what the rats saw, and he and Robi turned and started to run in the opposite direction of the stairs. Bars blocked their way, but fortunately they were closed with a lock that opened easily, and the corridor continued on the other side. Yorsh slammed all the locks shut behind him to hold up their potential pursuers. He ardently hoped for a glimmer, a blade of sunlight to show them some way of escaping to ground level, but nothing of the kind appeared. The corridor ran downhill, always downhill, through tunnels that grew darker and darker. The rats became fewer on the ground. More gates, more locks, more corridors, farther and farther down, deeper and darker. Whoever had built the old royal palace, probably Arduin, had decided to exploit the ancient elfish underground passages by transforming one part into a prison separated from the rest by ancient and impassable gates. His old royal palace had then collapsed, and on top of it had risen the curious Palace of Justice with its incomprehensible shape, but the prisons had been preserved intact.

Yorsh and Robi stopped, breathless. Yorsh was frightened; he wasn't sure he would be able to get them out of there. Sooner or later, the rats would be distracted, or else someone would remember that it took only a torch to scatter them, and they would find themselves discussing their chances of survival with the army of Daligar, and the discussion would not be a friendly one. Or they would simply be lost in the middle of half-dilapidated tunnels, waiting for hunger to do the gallows' job.

"I don't know where to go," he admitted, as soon as he was able to speak.

Robi smiled at him and gestured with her hand toward the ceiling of the tunnel, where the flickering torchlight illuminated a long fresco showing a shoot of blue ivy. His mother's poetry book was another map! They had only to follow the path!

The fact was that the ivy was everywhere: where the tunnels forked; where they went off in three, four different directions; in the tunnels that led nowhere, growing more and more cramped so that they had to crawl back; in the ones that came to a dead end with walls richly painted with images of fountains and gardens.

Looking carefully, Yorsh noticed that at some points,

the shoots assumed the shapes of Elfish letters: when the word formed was GO, the path was not interrupted. They were in an ancient maze. There were lots of crossroads with different tunnels bearing the same kind of fresco, and they had to reconstruct the trail with the letters hidden in the pattern of the ivy shoots. Sometimes there was the word NO, sometimes a mocking verse: IF THESE PAINTED WORDS YOU SEE, LONGER STILL YOUR PATH WILL BE, or: IF ATTENTION CLOSE YOU PAY, YOU WILL NEVER LOSE YOUR WAY.

To anyone unfamiliar with the Elfish language, the maze was inextricable, but someone armed with patience, time, and a length of string that could be unrolled to find their way back, would be able to explore and defeat it. They needed to get a move on. It would take them some time, but sooner or later the judge's soldiers would arrive.

The game became more complicated. The word GO began to lead to blind alleys or stairs leading nowhere. One of the walls showed the game of Elfish chess: white nymphs and two black dragons fighting around a queen wearing a crown twined with blue ivy. The key was the book—poems alternated with riddles:

> Four we are,
> In our hearts
> A warrior's bravery;
> Sword in hand,
> Proud-eyed,
> We protect the queen.

{ 293 }

The nymphs! Yorsh looked very carefully. At the spot where the nymphs' hands grasped their swords, there were four slender, almost unnoticeable cracks concealed by the painted shadows of the hilts. Slipping in his hand, Yorsh found some levers, which his fingers managed to touch but not to move. It didn't matter. The important thing was that he knew where the movement was supposed to occur, so that he could guide it as he had done with the locks. *Clank.* The wall was a panel, and it slid away. But the levers, worn by time and moisture, broke as they opened, and the panel couldn't be slipped back into place behind them. They were opening up a path for their pursuers, guiding them into the ancient underground passageways.

Another wall led abruptly to a dizzying spiral staircase that brought them so far down into the earth that Yorsh started to think they were somewhere beneath the river. The sea was painted on the wall.

"When we get out of here, we'll go and live by the sea," Yorsh said to Robi, perhaps more for his own reassurance than hers.

. . . Little fruits sun-reddened, splashed by salty spray . . . the book read. Looking closely at the painting, Yorsh located a little island with the wild cherry tree growing on it, the one he had flown over on Erbrow's back. Had it existed centuries ago, with a cherry tree growing on it, the great-grandfather of the present one, or had the painter simply imagined it, dreamed it up? In the tree, the cherries gleamed with a shiny red that darkened toward the shadows: there, once again, he found the cracks that concealed the mecha-

nisms. *Clank*. Once again the panel opened up, and once again they couldn't slide it back behind them. The only important thing at this point was to move on.

They were going farther and farther down, under the bowels of the city, into what had been the underground passages of the royal palace of the Elf capital.

Enormous cobwebs veiled their path. Little stone falls that made it narrower alternated with floods of water that widened it: more and more often they found themselves crawling in the mud, as the air thinned and filled with dust and old smells of earth, water, and rotten leaves. Yorsh was terrified. It was quite possible that he was heading for death and, infinitely worse, that he was taking Robi with him. Until that moment, he hadn't really been afraid of anything because, in a sense, the prophecy protected him. The fact that someone, in this case Arduin, Lord of Light, had mentioned his fate, suggested that at least he had one. But now he knew he had escaped the prophecy! Spend his life with that horrible girl Dawn? He'd sooner be eaten by a troll. Or die in the underground passages of Daligar. If the prophecy was only partly true, even his right to survival became a matter of opinion: Arduin was in favor, the judge administrator absolutely opposed, and the latter was much closer than the former, and had far more people at his disposal. If only he could save Robi!

The tunnel stopped abruptly. They were advancing on all fours through the mud when they came face-to-face with a set of bars. On the other side, the darkness widened and the air was cold and clean. The tunnel ended in a cave. The bars consisted of complicated swirls that imitated ivy: the leaves were of silver, the shoots of gold, and they twined into coiled arches. They were clearly a piece of Elfish workmanship and were not made to be opened: there were neither locks nor hinges. They were bars, plain and simple, not a gate.

"I've got a question for you," said Robi. In the flickering torchlight, her dark eyes shone like stars and a smile lit up her face. Yorsh gave a faint smile of encouragement, hoping that it wasn't a request for information about their survival, because that wasn't something he wished to talk about at any length.

"Now?" he asked.

Robi nodded. Shyness filled her face, erasing her smile, but stubbornly she nodded.

"All right, then, what do you want to know?"

"What the judge said . . . 'descendant,' he said. Does that mean doing the same job, or having the same blood? Meaning the daughter of the son of the grandson of the daughter . . . something like that. Do you see?"

Yorsh was puzzled. Puzzled and moved. The girl's thirst for knowledge was so intense that even now, with the prospect of choosing between a new meeting with the judge and the gallows, or a more peaceful death from starvation, she had lost herself in questions of semantics.

"It could mean either," he explained.

Robi nodded.

"Did he have lots of children, that lord, the one with the light?"

"You mean Arduin?"

"Yes."

Yorsh tried to remember.

"Mmmm . . . yes, I remember now. He had a son who succeeded him and then died childless, Gesein the Wise, and at least six daughters, two of whom went to live away from Daligar when they got married."

"And those daughters had sons or daughters who had more sons or daughters, who had more sons or daughters, so that now there's no way of knowing who's a descendant of Arduin! He might have descendants who don't even know they are!" she concluded triumphantly.

Yorsh thought about that for a moment. As conversations went, it was actually a bit ridiculous, but at least it deferred the moment when they would have to admit that all hope was lost.

"Yes. I think that's right," he agreed.

"And clair . . . clairvosomething . . ."

"Clairvoyance?"

"That's it, clairvoyance. It means when you close your eyes and images of things that are going to happen form all by themselves?"

"Yes," Yorsh replied firmly. He had had enough of the conversation. "There's no way of getting around these bars."

"But of course there is," Robi replied calmly. "There must be. There can't not be. It's just that you haven't thought hard enough about it yet. Haven't you even got anything to eat? Even stupid stuff, if you like!"

"Stupid stuff?" The conversation was becoming more and more absurd.

"Of course!"

Yorsh had stitched two secret inner pockets into his tunic—thanks to the instructions from twenty-six books on sewing and embroidery in his library—and now he looked inside them. There was still a handful of golden beans. He gave them to Robi, and their hands brushed in passing. Yorsh felt a strange sensation in his stomach—something halfway between hunger and a hiccup, and it was the first time he had felt it.

Robi filled her mouth with beans. Yorsh knew how good they were. He smiled at the ecstatic expression on her face, the happiness with which she ate. He felt her joy within him. It was like a hurricane. Of course he would get her out of there. He was outside the prophecy, but he was also still an elf. The last one, and the most powerful. He was in an ancient Elfish royal palace. The path was there, they had only to find it. And to find it they just had to be certain that they could. He was tempted to tell Robi how much he loved her, that she was the only thing in the world that existed for him; but fortunately, he stopped. Robi was not an elf but a human being, and human beings choose their companions not when they are children, but when they are adults. He would have to wait and hope that Robi would eventually accept him. That might be more likely if he put it off for a few years. And besides, he was an elf. The majority of humans hated elves. Even Monser and Sajra hated him at first! He would have to wait for Robi to know him better if he wanted to have a chance.

Then Robi asked him about Dawn. Did he know her?

Had he seen how beautiful she was? Yorsh was about to tell her how hateful he thought she was, when another thought came to him. Robi was so incredibly unafraid because she was sure of the prophecy, and that their survival was therefore guaranteed. If he told her the truth, fear would grip her in its claws like a sparrow hawk. He confined himself to a vague nod of agreement.

CHAPTER THIRTY-ONE

HE MOMENT the elf had come in surrounded by guards, Robi's heart had started beating faster. He was even more handsome than she remembered.

He had come for her: he had assumed the task of freeing her.

Since her mother and father were no longer alive, Robi had experienced the acute suffering of no longer being someone's child. Her life, her death, her hunger, her grazed knees no longer interested anyone. Now, all of a sudden, she was at the center of the world. A real boy with immense powers, and handsome as the sun, was risking his life for her. He was there with his hands tied behind his back, afraid of nothing because he was sure he would be able to save her.

Then the judge administrator had spoken of the prophecy, and Robi's heart had flooded with light. It was her! She was the one who had the visions that told her what was about to happen. Her father and her mother had given her a name that contained the magical moment in the morning when the light begins to spread across the world and the hope of a good day to come is still intact. Her mother told her that every morning when she woke her—even if it was raining or snowing outside and there was no light. Robi was a nickname. She was Rosalba, the pink light that is reborn, each morning, promising a good day ahead. Fortunately, caution had silenced her, and then the judge had begun to talk about his own daughter, Dawn. The ray of light that had filled her heart now turned into a flood of icy mud, and all that remained was a strange sensation in the upper part of her belly, like something halfway between hunger and a hiccup, like when Phlesh noticed that she had stolen something.

Robi knew Dawn. She had seen her when, escorted by half the county's army, she had entered Daligar. Their paths had crossed just past the great gate, Robi on her donkey and Dawn on her crimson-and-ivory litter. Robi had been speechless. The other girl was the prettiest she had ever seen. She had the face of an angel, framed by her blond hair and the collar of her gold brocade dress. Her hair was wound in a series of braids that echoed the pattern embroidered on her bodice. Robi had sat gazing at her with her mouth agape, and the girl had given her the unmistakeable glance of someone looking at a cockroach. Robi had felt just like a cockroach. Well, yes, actually, she was a bit of a cockroach. Two years had passed since the last time she had had her hair done. She hadn't washed since the second-to-last shower of rain the previous summer. The last one had happened at night, and she had missed it. The autumn rains soaked your feet and froze them, but you stayed dirty. And Dawn was at least a foot taller than Robi.

When her parents had still been alive, her mother told her that she had her father's eyes, and her father told her that she had her mother's smile, and the faces of both lit up when they looked at her. But now her parents weren't there for their faces to light up, they weren't there to say such things.

Until a few moments previously, all she had wanted was to be able to go on living. Now it wasn't enough for Yorsh to save her, she wanted him to be hers. But the other girl was infinitely more beautiful than Robi.

But no, it was she—Robi, Rosalba, the pink light of morning—who was the wife heralded in the prophecy. She knew it. What the judge had called "the predictions of Dawn" were stupid nonsense. She was the one who saw things: yes, that was what "clairvoyance" meant—seeing things before they happened. The daughter of the man and the woman who *hated* him? What kind of prophecy would that be? Half the people in the world hated elves. Everybody hated elves. Everybody but Monser and Sajra. The word was "saved," not "hated."

The daughter of the man and the woman who saved him, the daughter of Monser and Sajra, the one who bore the name of the morning light.

Clearly, she was the granddaughter of a granddaughter of the Lord of Light! That lord must have been somewhere among the grandparents of her grandparents or her great-grandparents or the great-grandparents of her great-grandparents' grandparents, and anyway, who knows anything about their grandparents and their great-grandparents? They could be anybody, why not the Lord of Light (as they said he was called)? Robi asked Yorsh for confirmation: "descend" could mean having the same blood, and clairov . . . clairvo . . . well, that thing, meant that the future formed inside your head and you knew it before it happened. Now that the young elf had talked to her about the sea, she had finally understood the meaning of the blue that filled her head every time she closed her eyes.

As they dashed along ever-narrower and ever-darker tunnels, where magnificent Elfish patterns pursued one another across the walls, Robi felt her joy and calm growing from tunnel to tunnel, from ivy leaf to ivy leaf. That man, Arst . . . Ard . . . the guy with the light wouldn't have dreamed of them so that they would die hanging from a gallows or in the bowels of the earth like a pair of rats. She was about to tell Yorsh about her name, about her visions, when her joy grew numb inside, turning into a kind of cold stone in the upper part of her belly. Would he be hers because she wanted him to be, or because it was written on the wall? That is, did the Lord of Light, Ard . . .

anyway, that one, did he see the things you were *going* to do or the things you were *supposed* to do? And what if he, Yorsh, spent his life with her, thinking about that other one? Dawn! Once again that face passed through her memory. Almost as beautiful as an elf! That other girl wasn't all knees and elbows and sticking-out teeth. Once Phlesh had looked Robi up and down and told her in a sweet and disappointed voice that, dark as she was, she really did look like a cockroach. A cockroach with the teeth of a rat. She had said with a sigh that we can't all be born beautiful. And besides, she, Dawn, probably knew how to write, and she would eat her beans like a lady, she wouldn't just gobble them down as Robi had done. When Yorsh had given them to her, their hands had touched: his long, pale, perfect hand had touched her little, dirty one with its chewed and blackened nails. Robi looked at her skeletal, muddy, grazed knees, and felt like a cockroach once again. She asked Yorsh about Dawn, and the nod he gave in reply drowned her in dejection.

Once again she closed her mouth. She wouldn't tell him that she was his future wife. Never. She would rather not become his wife than know he had chosen her "to fulfill the prophecy."

Finally, after examining it carefully and for a long time, Yorsh had grasped how the set of bars worked. The central part was connected to the rest by four tiny, slender gold stalks twined around a copper wire. As he explained it to Robi: they would have to increase the temperature so that the gold stalks "melted," melted away like the last snow in the spring sun. He managed to make the heat with his head—not in the sense of banging his head against the bars, but in the sense that he thought of heat and some of the little metal rods that held up the bars heated up until they melted away, just like snow in the sun.

Once enough of the bars were gone, the world was wider. On the other side, there was an enormous grotto with big columns of rock, some of which rose up from the ground while others fell from the ceiling. There was a loud sound of water. Everything was encrusted with gold, which sparkled in the torchlight as though it had been sprinkled with stars. As Yorsh explained to her, these columns were called stalagsomethings, the ones that rose from below, and the ones that came from above were called something almost the same. The cave was underneath the river Dogon. The water had dug everything out, and because the Dogon is a river that contains gold, speck by speck, the cave had been covered in it. Robi didn't really understand how the water could have dug anything, because to dig you need a spade and two hands to hold it, and water hasn't got any of those three things. But she didn't ask for explanations: Yorsh's voice and his smile when he explained things were magnificent. And besides, probably "the other girl" would have understood, and Robi couldn't let herself look stupid.

The unmistakable noise of the soldiers' clanking armor rang out behind them.

Beach had gotten stuck in the bars, and Clover was pushing him with all his might.

Still crammed in the middle of the swirls of gold-and-silver ivy, Beach smiled.

"We followed you step after step," he told them triumphantly. "We followed your voices."

"Otherwise we'd have got lost in the maze," Clover finished.

"The madman wanted to have us hanged!" Beach went on, red with effort. "For pouring half a pint of beer over his head!"

"You don't mind if we join up with you?" asked Clover. "Just to get out of here? After that we'll go off and mind our own business."

"Apart from anything else, if they come after you, we'll have slowed them down!" Beach concluded, happily showing them the big bunch of keys. "We've got the keys! They'll have to find themselves a blacksmith, and that isn't going to be easy. The last one left was hanged two days ago."

"We've brought you your things as well," said Clover, holding out the little boat, the doll, the bow, the arrows, and the book. "You will bring us to safety, as well, won't you?"

Yorsh and Robi were speechless. They stared silently at the two newcomers, just as they might have looked at a talking fish or a donkey with wings. Clover, still pushing Beach with all his might, but without managing to shift him an inch, asked with a hint of impatience whether, by any chance, rather than staring at them like two pretty statuettes, they couldn't perhaps take the trouble to give them a hand.

"What made you come after us?" asked Yorsh, as soon as he had his voice back.

The two men started talking over one another: "I told you—he would have hung us. . . . Half a pint of beer on his noggin . . . You don't know him . . . Well, no, when I think about it, you do know him . . . We don't want to die. . . ."

"And besides," they finally concluded in unison, "you're magical. Even Arduin knew that you were destined to live. If we're with you, we'll live, too, and get out of here alive!" they added triumphantly.

For some mysterious reason, Yorsh made a strange face. It was the face of someone who isn't happy—but more or less the face of someone who has just discovered that the only thing he had found to eat has just been brought back to life, or that he's been told that there are trenches to be dug. The face, that is, of someone who isn't just dissatisfied, but has a fever as well. Yorsh walked over to the bars and started to look for another point where they might be demolished. The original Elfish workmanship hadn't anticipated soldiers trying to break their way through. In the end, the matter was resolved by Yorsh tugging with all his might while Clover pushed with all his might and Beach cursed with all his might, and with everybody's might all together, the soldier came free and fell to the ground with a disconcertingly loud clank, although he suffered no serious damage.

"Fine," said Beach, after struggling back to his feet. "But now could we please get going? The moment we're outside we will go off to mind our own business, and our business is that we've got to pick up our families."

"I've got four children and he's got five," explained Clover. "We have to go home to get them or the moment they notice we've escaped, the madman will take it out on our wives and children."

Yorsh's expression grew even darker: it looked like the expression of someone who's developed a fever and septic boils and a desire to throw up.

CHAPTER THIRTY-TWO

HE CAVE was vast. Hidden among the verses was a description of it:

> . . . *in the dark and stony wood*
> *doves sleep enchanted, calm and good.*

There it was, on the right, the stalactite where the water and gold had formed the outline of four turtle-doves. They had to reach it and, from there, find the next step:

> . . . *the dream will fall from above* . . .

The dream? What dream could that be? In Elfish, "dream" and "veil" are the same thing: the veil of dreams, the slender and transparent stalagmite down at the left, and then back to the right, where they would find:

> *. . . the mirror of the girl so proud,*
> *the mirror of old age, bent and bowed.*

The little pool formed by the water that dripped from above, in which were reflected the stalactites in the shapes of a young woman and an old man with a walking stick. Yorsh had often wondered about the meaning of the poems his mother had left him, which, if truth be known, had always struck him as rather insipid, but which had now acquired a precise meaning about showing the way. For a moment, he had been filled with horror that had turned his stomach into a frozen lump, at the idea of the number of lives for which he had assumed responsibility, and the incalculable pain that his failure would cause. He wasn't just risking the life of Robi, who was already the light of his own life, but also of these two unfortunates and their wives and children.

As he made his way across the vast cavern, dug beneath the whole of the city of Daligar by the waters of the River Dogon over the past millennium, Yorsh got his spirits back. The ancient verses describing the way through the stalagmites provided a safe trail to follow. He was certainly going somewhere. He was in the places that had belonged to the elves. He was the last of his tribe, and perhaps the most powerful. If not him, then who?

The watery mirror reflected the torches, his own and Clover's, a hundredfold, so he didn't immediately notice that the light was getting brighter. Finally, a ray of sunlight appeared among the gilded stalactites, lighting up the dust as though it were a swarm of stars.

Inside the light stood a golden throne on which the blue ivy drew swirls that alternated with Elfish letters.

On the throne sat an ancient king. His skeleton was covered with golden vestments and, on his head, a glittering crown of gold with blue ivy leaves. In his hands he still held his sword, its gold hilt likewise enameled with blue shoots of ivy. The blade was sunk into the stone floor. The chain around his neck and the rings he wore on every finger were also of gold and blue ivy. Yorsh walked over, and the light of day fell upon him, too, giving his hair the gleam of a halo for a moment. He tore at the cobwebs, which fell away in showers of dust, and read:

HERE LIES

HE WHO WORE THE CROWN

AND HELD THE SWORD

Four gold columns flanked the stalactites. Above them, too, the blue ivy writhed around to form a relief so deep that it could be used as a single, very long spiral staircase. Yorsh looked up. Dazzled by the light, he glimpsed an opening edged with ferns. The topmost part of the column closest to the opening was covered with moss and a few small ferns glistening in the sun.

"It's stopped raining," said Clover.

"We can go. These columns are proper stairs," added Beach.

Robi had approached the throne as well. Its glow lit up her eyes, which shone like stars.

With Robi nearby, Yorsh felt his strength growing and his fear almost fading away. Or perhaps it was the ancient king who emanated that strange feeling of power. Yorsh looked at the empty eye sockets covered with cobwebs and felt a strange sensation akin to that of belonging. He put his hand on the hilt of the sword, which stonily refused to budge. The sword was stuck so firmly in the rock that it seemed a part of it. Yorsh was puzzled for a moment, then he began to laugh. But of course: it was meant for an elf. It was a trick to ensure that only the right person could remove the sword, a simple question of thermodynamics: by reducing the temperature you also reduce the volume. Once it was cold, the blade would become imperceptibly smaller, but small enough to slip out of the rock as easily as it had entered centuries before. Fortunately, the need to put out the countless fires started by the newborn Erbrow had trained him in the extraction of heat. He put his hand on the hilt, closed his eyes, froze the blade, and then pulled it out. The old sword gleamed in his hands. The ivy-swirled hilt fit his palm as though made specially for him. Perhaps the trick of extracting heat was exceptional even for an elf. Perhaps the sword had been made not for an elf, but for the most powerful of elves. The last one.

All traces of fear disappeared. But a wave of exhaustion

passed through him, and he sat down at the feet of the throne, waiting for his forehead to stop burning. It was less painful than putting out Erbrow's fires, but all the same, he needed a little time to recover. When he got to his feet, he looked at the king. The crown, the neck chain, and the rings had disappeared. Yorsh stared in puzzlement at the two soldiers, who stole a sidelong glance at him.

"I have four children and he has five. . . ." they began sheepishly.

"They're not much use to that corpse; he doesn't have to put bread on anyone's table. . . ."

"He doesn't know what it means to come home without anything to eat and to have everybody crying. . . ."

"If we don't take this stuff, someone else will. . . ."

"Even the judge—the judge might swipe the lot. . . ."

Yorsh flashed them a look of fury, but there was nothing he could do. Slowed down by the gates, dispersed by the labyrinth, the judge's soldiers had finally arrived. They hadn't been able to work out which trail they should follow, but they had had the advantage of numbers. Since there had been enough of them to take every intersection and to follow every path, they had found their way in the end.

The soldiers were beginning to swarm into the lower, deeper part of the cave, but they weren't yet in sight. Using the column as a spiral staircase, Yorsh first and Clover at the bottom, the small group began to climb.

Beach had taken off his armor, and this time he didn't get stuck. They came out among the ferns by the river. They were in the southern part of the city. The Dogon was swollen with water, and beyond its banks lay the judge's palace. The guards caught sight of them and aimed their bows, but Clover and Beach managed to give the impression that they had already arrested the two fugitives. It really did look as though they were escorting them.

They climbed up the bank and set off toward the palace: the boy and girl in the middle, hands behind their backs as though they were in chains, and the two soldiers by their sides. Robi pretended to stumble and picked up some stones. Yorsh was carrying his sword and bow. He tried to keep them hidden between the folds of his long tunic. He had his hands behind his back, and everything was fine until their potential enemies were standing near them.

When the first pursuers emerged behind them in the middle of the ferns on the riverbank, the fiction was revealed. A moment before the first arrows began to fly, Clover and Beach started running. They were unusually fast, even Beach, despite his barrel chest. Yorsh didn't see their flight as a betrayal, but actually as a liberation. He no longer had to worry about the two fugitives or their families, because they would make it on their own, somehow or other. He only had to deal with the eight soldiers ahead of him, the six on the roof of the palace, the unknown number they had behind them, and the four horsemen who were blocking their path. Then he had to get through the big gate and recover his still-unnamed horse, hoping that he would find it where he had left it. This time he couldn't use the river as an escape route, because Robi couldn't swim and she was too small and fragile to resist the cold of the water, but Yorsh knew that they would make it, somehow. He wasn't afraid. Not with his sword in his hand. He leaned over to Robi to tell her not to be scared, and saw that the girl was holding a slingshot and trying to take aim. She nodded firmly, still looking straight ahead.

An arrow nearly hit her. Yorsh gripped his sword. He was seized by fury at the sight of those soldiers weighed down with weapons and armor, aiming their bows at two poor wretches who hadn't hurt anyone and just wanted to get away. His fury became a storm. A fierce wind rose up against the soldiers. Blinded by the dust, they couldn't take aim, and the few arrows they managed to fire were blown away by furious gusts before they could reach their target. The horses reared up and unseated their riders. Yorsh managed to make contact with the mind of one of the animals, the big black mare closest to them. He talked to it of freedom and golden beans. In its head he created images of reins being removed. For a long time the mare was indecisive, then slowly it began to approach. A group of soldiers surrounded the two fugitives. There were three of them, young, tall, armed with swords—three normal, ordinary military swords made of good steel.

Yorsh's sword flashed brightly. When they clashed with his blade, the others splintered and shattered. Inside his head Yorsh felt the pain of the man whose shoulder he had wounded, the youngest of the three, but his hatred for anyone who wanted to kill Robi canceled it out. More soldiers came running, and yet more—a heap of helmets, shields, and swords in which Yorsh could no longer make out faces and expressions. He charged at them, one after another. With each sword that flew into pieces as it made contact with his own, he was filled with courage. An officer with many medals on his armor was about to attack him from behind, but a stone fired by Robi struck him full in the face.

Suddenly, the mare made her mind up and began running in their direction, sending the soldiers flying. Yorsh managed to stall her and put Robi in the saddle, almost holding her in his arms, and to do so he had to put down his sword. That was enough time for the tall soldier with the grayish beard, who had recently arrested him, to come close. A blow from his sword caught Yorsh's leg, and blood spurted from the gash. Then the man raised the sword to bring it down on Robi's head. Yorsh picked up his sword and fought back, and inside his head he felt the other man dying: he felt the memory of the man's childhood, his fear of the dark and the void, his sorrow for a woman he hadn't married. As horror and pain filled his head, Yorsh managed to climb onto the mare behind Robi. He took the bridle, held Robi tightly, and spurred the mare toward the big gate. They crossed the main square, where the two gallows had already been set up: the big one for him, the smaller one for Robi. The judge administrator, in his fit of rage, must have abandoned even the merest spark of decency that had made him want to avoid the public execution of a child. The sight of the gallows designed for Robi restored Yorsh's desire to fight at all costs, even if it meant wounding or killing. He had to bring her to safety immediately, before he was weakened by his injury. He had to win his battle, and quickly. The mare flew through the streets of Daligar. The gleaming Elfish sword was drawn and covered with blood, and its fierce flash was enough to cast terror into anyone who wanted to stop them.

They were at the big gate. The drawbridge was rising in front of them. There were two systems of pulleys, a fast one using ropes, and a slower one using chains. Yorsh handed Robi the bridle, took his bow from his shoulder along with one of the three arrows that he kept in a little quiver attached to his sleeve, and fired. He knew he had to see the target with the eyes of his mind, not his body. As soon as the arrow left his bow, he set fire to its tip. One of the big ropes supporting the bridge was struck right in the middle and partly cut, and began to burn. Then it was the turn of the second bow. Partly cut by the arrows, and burned by the flames, the two ropes broke.

The bridge fell in front of them with a crash that made the old boards splinter and throw up a cloud of reddish dust.

The mare galloped over it like the wind. The soldiers around the big gate fled rather than intervening. The dust cloud kept the archers from taking aim.

They were free! They had done it! They were free!

Yorsh had a wound in his leg, an Elfish sword in his hands, a horse, and a bow with a single arrow. And he had Robi with him. He had done it.

* * *

They passed through a clearing and a little forest of chestnut trees. The other horse was there. As he had promised, Yorsh hadn't tethered it, and the horse had stayed where it was. The sun was setting. The air was becoming colder. Yorsh became aware of a curious sensation at the top of his stomach that he hadn't felt for years, thirteen, to be precise, and which he identified as hunger. A terrible hunger. He climbed slowly down from the mare and leaned against her body. His wound didn't hurt too much, and his leg still supported him. He tore a strip from his tunic and bound his leg. He collected a few handfuls of chestnuts and shared them with Robi.

Yorsh wanted to say something. He wanted to say that they had made it. They had been successful. They were alive. They were together. They were free. He would have liked to say how happy he was because she was alive, because she was free, because she was with him.

For some reason that he couldn't understand, the thoughts of all the things he could have said tumbled about in his head and collided like argumentative magpies, and in the end, of all his thoughts, the only one that came out was the least important—the one that really didn't matter to him at all.

"We should have left him the crown. The king, I mean."

"But he was dead," Robi objected firmly. "He was really very dead."

Yorsh felt more and more embarrassed and stupid. How had he managed, of all the things he wanted to say, to get mixed up?

"It was written in the book," he explained. "'... *He who has the destiny of the warrior will have the sword. He who has the destiny of the ruler, the crown* ...'" he recited. "He was the king: we should have left him the crown, I think," he added uncertainly.

"Oh, so that's it," said Robi. "Then it's not all that serious! Look!"

She stuffed her hand into her big, filthy canvas bag, and the Elfish crown glittered as she brought it out.

Yorsh stared openmouthed at the crown.

"Did you take it?"

"No, Beach took it, the fat one. He climbed up ahead of me when we came out into the air, and it was easy to slip it out of his bag. He still had the rings for his children—there were loads of them, rings, I mean. I'm a good thief, you know. I can steal anything," she added with a little smile that was both shy and proud. "But if you say it's important, next time we pass by there we'll give it back to the king, so he'll be happier. Will he come back to life like the rat, or will he stay dead?"

"He'll stay dead."

Yorsh wished he could think of something more clever to say, but he consoled himself. There would be time. Soon. At that moment they didn't have any. A hunt was certainly being organized back there; they would have to get a move on.

The mare was called Patch—Yorsh had read that from its memory—but his own horse was still unnamed. It must have changed hands lots of times. There had been considerable confusion about its names, and none of them had stayed in its mind.

He had to give the horse a name. A name that was completely right for it, as Fido had been for the dog. He thought about something that would give an idea of both its speed and its beauty.

"I'll call you Lightning," he said out loud.

Robi thought that of all the names you could give a horse, that was the weirdest. You call a horse Patch or Hoof or Tail or simply, Horse. She thought that this one would probably be the first and last horse ever in the world to be called Lightning, because it was really a stupid name, but she said nothing.

The horse's mind replied with a nod of agreement.

Yorsh on Lightning and Robi on Patch, they headed for the House of Orphans, each of them munching on their handful of raw chestnuts, slowly, to make them last as long as possible.

During the first part of the journey, Yorsh became aware of his terrible exhaustion. Exhaustion so complete that it turned into pain, but then eased slightly. The sky opened up. A few stars shone.

Every now and again, he and Robi glanced at one another.

Yorsh felt the pain of having killed a man, an injury to his leg, and an army hot on his heels, but at the same time, of his whole life so far, a life that had included flight on a dragon, this was his happiest moment.

They reached the House of Orphans as dawn was

rising. A soft, cold mist rose from the ground. They were tired, happy, hungry, and free. As they passed through a vineyard that blazed with red and gold, two brigands appeared in front of them. They were masked, and armed with Phlesh and Slump's cudgels, and wearing the unmistakeable rags of the House of Orphans. They threatened horrible reprisals if the horses weren't given to them immediately. There was a moment of mutual puzzlement, then they all recognized each other. Their assailants were Falco and Fowlpest. They were cheerful and declared that the dragon, before the beer had sent it to sleep, had entrusted them with the task of rounding up as many horses as they could, to take everyone to the sea. Yorsh and Robi had been the first two riders to come that way.

Who was "everyone"? Everyone who had joined up with them, Falco and Fowlpest explained. When the rain had stopped and the smell of their roasting meat had spread around the area, settling on poor villages and farms where the rabbits were better fed than the humans, all the starving people had joined up with them. The ones who had nothing. The ones who had nobody. They had gathered up all the uprooted and the poverty-stricken, the ones who had lost their land and had dreamed of finding new land—and there were plenty of them.

Still on horseback, Yorsh and Robi reached the clearing where the House of Orphans stood. There were the remains of fires all over the place, some of them still smoking, and as the smoke rose, it mingled with the fog. On the ground, goose, chicken, and duck feathers mixed with autumn leaves. Three empty beer casks lay on their sides around the dragon, with people sleeping inside them. Others were inside Phlesh and Slump's cottage, and a few were in the farmyard. The House of Orphans was no longer standing. In its place, an unbelievable number of stones were piled up to form a small hill: it had been demolished.

With the help of Falco and Fowlpest, Robi got down from Patch's back, stopped to look at the House of Orphans, then bent down, picked up a stone, and hurled it at what was left of the north wall, close to where she had slept. She stood there motionlessly for a long time, gazing into the distance. Cala spotted her and ran toward her shouting. She had kept aside a real chicken thigh for her, valiantly defending it against everything and everyone. Chickens don't do that much thinking, and they taste better than rats, too.

The dragon was in a stinking mood, frankly, and had an unbearable headache. Yorsh furiously asked him how he could have thought of leading two innocents astray, transforming them into brigands and horse thieves. The dragon replied that the word "innocent" was clearly a matter of opinion, and that these two already possessed such natural talents for banditry that it would have been an act of cruelty not to allow them to express it. In any case, if Yorsh was so clever that he had a better way of gathering the people who had shown up and transporting them all the way to Arstrid, he was more than willing to listen to his advice. There were the orphans from the House of

Orphans, who ranged from little more than toddlers to teenagers—the older children could walk, but the little-more-than-toddlers couldn't, which meant that they had to be carried.

Then there was the group of strolling players who had appeared from nowhere all of a sudden. Well, not all of a sudden, exactly: they had arrived when the smell of roast fowl had begun to spread across the plain, and they had taken up position there, stoutly maintaining that one of the children in the House of Orphans was a distant rela-tive, which meant that they, too, were part of the company. The strolling players were two grandparents, six great-grandparents, seven parents, both fathers and mothers, and twenty-three children, ranging once again from little more than toddlers to young adults, with all the possibilities in between, and practically none of them capable of walking more than a few leagues. Then there were the old people who had escaped from the Northern Farm, which was a place where they put old people, apparently, the same way they put orphans in the House of Orphans. The people ate in proportion to the amount of work they were still able to do, and since the old people were pretty exhausted, given their old bones, they couldn't do enough work to eat more than a frog.

One of the sentries from the House of Orphans had come back and asked if he could stay. He was a big fellow with pimples and red hair, who had been given the honor, after being one of the inmates of the House, of becoming one of its guards. Roast geese aside, he had come back because he couldn't think of anywhere he could go, anyone else he could be with. He had neither the capacity nor the courage to go wandering on his own, and he couldn't work out why he should have, given the life he had always led. At least he was fit and healthy, and the same was true of the "voluntary" workers from the county of Daligar: two diggers armed with hoes and a carpenter-woodcutter equipped with an axe and a saw, who had escaped from the iron mine beyond the hill to the north. Yes, the smell from the spit had reached as far as that. That was the direction the wind blew, and one becomes very sensitive to scents one hasn't smelled in years. The three of them were in the most precarious position, so to speak, because they had brought their tools with them. They maintained that the tools had always belonged to them, and had been theirs long before the judge had assumed power and asserted that everything under the sun between the Dark Mountains and the high valley of the Dogon belonged to Daligar, when in fact, the woodcutter had inherited the axe directly from his father. But these objects had now been declared the property of the county of Daligar, so not only were they guilty of stealing geese, they were also responsible for the theft of tools, which meant they could be hanged twice rather than once.

Finally, as though all of that were not enough, the hospital to the east, beyond the ditch with the brambles, had been cleared. No infectious diseases, fortunately: just the halt, the lame, the scrofulous, and people so exhausted that they could barely stay upright, who had declared that they would rather die on the spot than go back where they had come from, and that was that.

No, they were not all well enough to escape. If the whole group had been in a fit state to walk for a whole day, there would have been no need to resort to banditry to get hold of the horses. The oldest, the sickest, and all the youngest children couldn't have walked all the way to the Dark Mountains, not in a single stretch, perhaps with the whole of the county's army hot on their heels, and there would have been little chance of snacks on the grass or picnics among the flowers.

No, the dragon couldn't flee, not before he'd drained the last of the beer and gotten over his hangover. In fact, had he been in a position to escape, he would already have gone back to the Black Mountains, because he was a dragon, the last of his tribe, the last of his species, and dragons had never mixed with anyone who wasn't a dragon, and he would soon have had enough of sniveling brats and moralistic elves, not to mention that terrible hangover of his. It was as though someone were hammering away at the inside of his head, and each bang was a spasm of pain, faint but deadly, between the fourth and the fifth parietal bones and, while they were on the subject, the pain in his back feet hadn't passed either, not to mention the pain in his back. Yorsh seemed to remember that dragons had a total of three parietal bones, but after the years spent with the brooding Erbrow the Elder, he had developed a remarkable sensitivity that told him when to keep his mouth shut.

The fog thinned out and showed the peaks of the hill

where half a dozen little scorched patches of earth interrupted the regular pattern of the vines. Yorsh stared at them
in puzzlement. Fowlpest explained that beer gave the
dragon hiccups.

CHAPTER THIRTY-THREE

SINCE THE passing of her father and mother, Robi hadn't had her hands on a chicken thigh. The meat melted deliciously between her teeth; it had the taste of a mother cooking, a father hunting. They'd even used some rosemary! She didn't know whether to gobble the meat down so that the hunger would pass more quickly, or eat slowly, one morsel at a time, to make it last a little longer.

There were people everywhere. They were all in rags. They looked tired. Some of them looked ill.

Yorsh was trying to gather them all together in a hurry. Sooner or later, and sooner rather than later, the cavalry would come from Daligar, and then everyone would long for the slavery of the farms as a happy age of gold, because what would happen next would be infinitely worse. Yorsh was injured, he was limping. He tried to assemble all the people, but the impression was that of a herd of sheep with a lame sheepdog. As soon as it seemed that they were all there and could get going, a few of them would start wandering off again, going to get something, heading in search of one last bunch of grapes, hoping for a final piece of bread or a mouthful of beer that might still have been lurking somewhere around.

Robi understood. They had been in a state of despair for such a long time that they couldn't even hope to escape. When you have years of hunger and weariness behind you, "tomorrow" becomes a difficult thought to keep. All that fills your head is the here and now. Be a bit less hungry now. Stay here because walking is an effort. If you've only ever taken orders and been whipped when you tried to do something you haven't been ordered to do, you find that you can't do anything you *haven't* been ordered to do, not even to save your life.

The fact was that they were so used to being fearful that the threat of a possible attack by the cavalry of Daligar didn't bother them. It didn't seem any worse than their own hopelessness, which had oppressed them all their lives. And then they reflected that slaves don't get killed, because you'd have to do their job yourself. That wasn't the case, however: if they didn't get away in a hurry, they faced the fate not of a slave, but of a corpse. A corpse without a name, without a grave, abandoned in the middle of the mud for the worms, the vultures, the crows, and the rats.

Besides, they didn't really believe that there was a chance of getting away, and it was clear that they couldn't do it. All they wanted was to scrape together a few more mouthfuls and then accept whatever life had in store for them. They had never grown used to being hungry, so that not losing even the tiniest grain of corn, the smallest grape, seemed more important than avoiding a clash with the cavalry.

Robi shut her eyes. Blue formed behind her eyelids. Now she could make out the waves; she even heard the sound they made, and saw white birds flying toward the horizon. She saw a beach, and recognized some figures: the little old woman who was playing with Cala, the slightly bent one with the stick, the hook-nosed man who was currently standing in the middle of the vines. On a fishing boat she recognized Falco and Fowlpest. They were destined to make it! Yorsh was clearly capable to guide them. He didn't know it, but there was something he must know how to do. Something he considered insignificant, or not useful at that very moment, something that was actually extremely important.

"What can you do?" Robi asked Yorsh bluntly as she joined him.

Yorsh was puzzled for a moment, then began to list the things he could do. The first thing that came to mind was his ability to bring midges back to life, and Robi had to summon all her faith lest she lose heart; and then the list was enriched with . . . lighting fires without tinder . . .

opening locks without keys. . . . He could raise a wind that confused his enemies, as he had done in Daligar, but that took a lot of effort. He had managed to do it just for a few moments, and then he had been unable to get his strength back for half a day. He could heal wounds . . . no, not his own, only other people's. . . . He could . . . bring midges back to life—had he mentioned that already? And rats . . . and chickens . . . once a rabbit. . . .

Over the past thirteen years he had mostly read. He was very good at reading; he could read seven different languages, not counting Elfish. . . . He had spent thirteen years in a library that had more or less everything . . . including books on military tactics, but they explained what to do when there were two armies, and now they had an army on one side and on the other a band . . . of . . . well, perhaps they should forget military tactics. He had read books of astronomy, alchemy, ballistics, biology, cartography, etymology, philology, philosophy . . . how to make grape jam . . . and then there were the stories. What stories? The ones he read to the dragon—no, not this one, the other one, the parent of this one, when it was brooding . . . dragons brood . . . Female? He didn't know, he had never quite worked out whether it was male or female . . . but when a dragon broods, its brain doesn't work all that well because brooding makes it very tired. . . . No, dragons don't have their brains in their bottoms, they have them in their heads like everyone else, but when they're brooding they don't work all that well . . . then you have to keep them company by telling them stories, like the story of the princess of the beans.

"What's the story of the princess of the beans?" Robi asked.

"Well, once upon a time there was a queen who couldn't have children, and she was terribly sad, because her life was draining away, month after month, season after season, and she had no one to cuddle. . . ."

The silence was almost complete. Even the ones who were munching on something had stopped. Robi had forgotten everything; she had even forgotten to finish gnawing on her little chicken bone, and only wanted to listen. She felt as though everything that was happening, including the impending arrival of the Daligar cavalry, was at that moment less important than the terrible sadness of that unfortunate queen, which filled her now.

Yorsh stopped talking and looked at her in puzzlement.

"Go on!" cried Robi.

"What happened next?" asked someone else.

"Come on, don't stop!"

"How does it end?"

The ones who had heard the story from the beginning told the others, who hadn't heard it and were coming quickly to listen.

Yorsh looked at them for a long time, more and more perplexed, and then started over again.

He raised his voice and, without breaking off, he looked about him: everyone had gathered around to hear his story. He started to count them, still without interrupting, even making his counting part of the story: at the point when the queen is in the field of beans and starts eating them, he counted them out one by one. They were all there. They could get going. Arstrid was less than a day's walk away. There was water along the road in the form of streams and waterfalls. Their bellies were full. They might be able to make it.

Still telling his interminable story, Yorsh woke Erbrow, who had started snoring again, put the two smallest children on Patch's back while he himself took Lightning, because his wound prevented him from walking, climbed on backward, facing the crowd, and set off. The dragon brought up the rear. Not for a moment did he stop complaining about how at every step his headache was a match for the pain in his back feet, not to mention his backache, but he did keep his voice low enough for Yorsh's story to be heard. The story was endless: each time it sounded like it was about to end, he started off again with a new discovery, a fresh abduction, a belated realization, another evil deed, another duel. . . . The sun rose. The layer of mud grew thinner. Legs began to tire. The desire to sit down for a while on the edge of the road increased step by step. The smallest children took turns on Patch's back, but the others had to walk. Yorsh's voice had grown hoarse, but he didn't stop.

The strolling players had taken out their flutes and started to underline the important points of the story with musical accompaniment: when the princess of the beans began to flee the ogres with her people, the music became louder and more piercing, and Yorsh had been able to break off to take a drink of water. When he started up again, the story he told had become curiously similar to theirs. There was a flow of refugees, and the only way they could save themselves was to go on marching.

Robi listened to their despair, their hopes, their fears, their courage, and felt within herself the fierce desire not to stop, to go on step after step, until the final stretch of the road they had dreamed of, the one that wouldn't stop until they reached the sea. She looked around: exhaustion had vanished from the faces of the others, too, drowned out by the story they were listening to, which warmed them from within like a fire. The only one who was completely exhausted was Yorsh. Not only was his voice getting hoarser and hoarser, but his hands had begun to tremble faintly. The sun began to sink toward the west: soon they would disappear into the Dark Mountains.

Just past the last bend, when the remains of what had once been the village of Arstrid became visible, everyone finally understood why the Daligar cavalry wasn't following them. They were right in front of them, massed in Arstrid, blocking the gorge.

CHAPTER THIRTY-FOUR

ORSH WAS filled with horror. He had dragged everyone, step after step, story after story, toward disaster.

He stood dumbstruck, staring at the last sunlight gleaming on the soldiers' armor. He had led them to the slaughter. Stronger than anything was his desire not to have to choose, not to have to decide what to do next.

Yorsh was silent. Everyone had stopped. The dragon ambled up along the column, bringing his headache and his footache with him, until he drew level with Lightning and Patch. The sun reached the peaks of the Dark Mountains, and long shadows were drawn on the ground, then the clouds swallowed everything.

"What's the plan now?" the dragon asked drily.

"Any ideas?" Yorsh asked hopefully.

"I go to the right and you go to the left and we encircle them?" the dragon suggested ironically.

"In the war on the trolls, a dragon set a field on fire to avoid a battle. It happened in the fourth century of the Second Runic Dynasty."

"The *fifth* century of the *Third*," corrected the dragon. "And it was in the summer. A torrid, dry summer: it only took a sneeze. It's the end of the autumn now. You see that brown stuff on the ground between one stem of grass and the next? That's called mud. M-U-D. Mud has numerous properties, including that of being uninflammable, which is the opposite of 'combustible.' It doesn't burn and it doesn't catch fire. If you like, I could make a few little disks of burned grass, as long as it doesn't rain, but I don't think you'd be terribly impressed."

Yorsh and Erbrow went on staring at each other. Night fell, and it began to rain softly.

Robi closed her eyes. Again, everything filled with blue. And again, against the glittering sea she saw a long series of little figures: Yorsh was there, and Cala, Falco and Fowlpest, that tall, crooked man, the little woman with the limp. . . . They were all there. They would make it. All of them.

Between the elf and the dragon, they could do it—they just didn't know how. And they had to hurry. Desperation was slithering through the crowd like a snake through mice.

And like a snake, it was swallowing up everything it found in its path. Wails alternated with shouts and curses. At any moment, people would start to run for it, scatter about the plain, easy and miserable prey for the armed horsemen, like a cluster of frogs fleeing vultures.

Robi intervened. "You can fly," she said to the dragon, "and spit fire. And Yorsh has an invincible sword. Of course you can do it."

"His sword isn't invincible. I don't wish to give the impression of being pedantic and fanatical about tiny and insignificant details, but neither of us is invulnerable. He's already injured, and my anteroinferior scales, the ones on my belly, well, they're . . . they're a bit *soft* for arrows. I spit fire from my igniferous glands, which are going to run out sooner or later. And now since I've got . . . a . . . a . . ."

". . . wretched hangover?" Robi inquired solicitously.

"Let's just say I'm not at my absolute best," the dragon said. "I can carbonize one or two horsemen for you, allowing that our warrior here will let me, but there will be enough of them left over to let us know that they weren't awfully amused."

"You could frighten them," Robi suggested. "They don't know that you're . . . that you're . . . empty?"

"Exhausted."

"Exhausted, exactly. They don't know that. Look, it's not impossible. You can distract them on this side, and we head toward the gorge. Some of them will attack us, but not many. Yorsh can deal with them."

"And what then?" the dragon asked. "I can't distract

them forever! They'll enter the gorge sooner or later. And what about the waterfall? The gorge leads to a steep waterfall, don't you remember? It's called the Dogon Ravine and it's impassable. The stairs leading to the library are blocked by a landslide. We saw it on the day of our first flight."

"The waterfall isn't impassable. The inhabitants of Arstrid got past it. And so will we," Robi insisted.

"Fine," said the dragon. "Then they'll get through, too. Rather than being massacred here, you'll be massacred on a beach."

There was a long silence. Robi became aware of a sensation in the upper part of her stomach, which wasn't hunger, but fear. She had learned to trust her visions, but she knew that they were incomplete. Perhaps they would all reach the blue water of the sea as she had seen. But what if the judge's soldiers got through as well? Then the blue would turn bright red, or very dark pink.

"We'll get through and they won't," she cried stoutly, "because we're intelligent and they're stupid. We're escaping to save ourselves, we're escaping to live, and they're just carrying out orders. Something will come to us, something that they don't know about. We'll do it. They have capes and armor—the rain will hinder them more than us. Their horses will slip in the mud more than our feet will. But we must act now!"

"Really?" said Cala, who was drenched to the bone and lying in the mud, having just slipped. "Will the rain bother them more than it bothers us? Are you sure? Does that mean we aren't really finished?"

"Now!" Robi yelled at the elf and the dragon. "We must move now!" Then she turned around and looked at her wretched band, which was dispersing beneath the rain. She had the idea of jumping onto Patch's back, but the three little children already sitting there were clinging on so tenaciously that it would have been impossible to dislodge them. She tried to gather the group together, because if they were united, they had a chance; scattered, they were lost.

She ran from one to the other, slipping in the mud.

"Once upon a time," called Yorsh with all the breath he could muster. "Once upon a time there was a band of heroes, who . . . who . . . had been slaves. Once upon a time there was a band of slaves, who . . . decided . . . to . . . go . . . to become free people, and to do that . . . to be free . . . I mean . . . they reached the sea. . . ."

Yorsh started to tell a long and magnificent story. He made up names, he described armies; he described the refugees one by one, and one by one, they all heard descriptions of themselves with different names and different stories. Their fear started to fade. Their exhaustion began to loosen the grip that it had on their tired legs and their weary minds.

The rain stopped. A mild wind rose up and opened the clouds. The light of the moon lit up the plain and the gorge of Arstrid, on the other side of which lay freedom and the sea. The ragged band began to pull together.

"Once upon a time there was a band of slaves that became a free people by crossing a great gorge. . . . Follow Robi: stay together and go toward the gorge. She knows the way, she used to live here. The dragon and I will protect the column. You stay together, follow Robi."

Robi needed to be as visible as possible in the faint moonlight. It was very dark, and lots of people confused her with Cala. She still had the king's crown in her pocket. She took it out and put it on her head. The moon lit it up, and the crown gleamed in the darkness.

At that moment, the cavalry moved. The charge began. Yorsh drew his sword. Lightning was exhausted, but now he regained his strength. He reared up. Robi saw Yorsh's sword shining in the moonlight, like her crown. For a moment, it was as though the moonlight had crystallized time, as though reality and dreams had fused in a motionless moment. Then everything shattered.

Erbrow had finally decided to intervene.

A terrifying roar rang out.

A terrible flame pierced the darkness.

The cavalry stopped, uncertain. The ragged army took heart. Between them and the lances of the soldiers of Daligar stood the bright sword of a warrior and the blazing flames of a dragon. Inside them was the story of a band of slaves who had crossed the world to become a free people, and that had turned them into a band of heroes. In front of them the little queen's crown glittered in the darkness like the warrior's sword.

Falco and Fowlpest, armed with their cudgels, rushed to Yorsh to protect his sides. The two men who had escaped from the mine where they had been "excavatory employees for the county of Daligar," bringing their shovels with them, clutched them now, ready to fight. And a woodcutter, previously a "tree-trunk operative," had brought his hatchet along, adding, like the others, the crime of "theft of working tools" to that of "abandonment of assigned post." He had decided to use that tool. All the men, the women without children, and the bigger boys gathered around Yorsh, who never stopped talking. He was telling of the heroic gestures of Pentrivore and Fearless, brigands who had become lieutenants; Garamir, who had come from the woods with his magic axes; the Courteous Hoemen, who had just awoken from a spell. . . .

A shower of arrows fell. But the dragon had taken up position between them and the cavalrymen, and the arrows bounced off the thick, hard scales of his back. The ragged army continued on toward the gorge.

"We'll manage," Robi cried happily.

"For how long?" the elf wondered aloud.

The sky cleared completely. The clouds melted away. It grew colder. The moonlight fell brightly on the skeletal remains of Arstrid, on the loop of the river, which glinted like silver in the darkness. Above the river, on one side, the rocky crag was so steep as to be almost sheer, and the other side wasn't much easier, consisting as it did of earth and a wood of enormous, ancient oaks, which, with their gigantic black roots, clutched at masses of white granite upon which the moon now cast its glow.

Protected by Yorsh, his little army of warriors, and by the threatening, mountainous back of the dragon, the refugees entered the gorge one by one. As Robi passed by what had once been her home, her eyes filled with tears. She brushed her hand along the charred walls and remembered when, two years previously, she had been dragged away from there. She had left a line of river pebbles, white, round, and identical, so that she would be able to find her way back again. Her dog, Fido, had tried to protect her, and had been lamed in the attempt. In all her dreams, when she returned to Arstrid, Fido came hobbling toward her. She looked around for him, in the hope that he might have stayed to guard the house and wait for her, but clearly that was a ridiculous hope, because no dog is faithful enough to wait year after year. Her eyes filled with tears, which didn't fall down her cheeks—as always, she held them back. They had to go on.

Robi looked behind her. The ragged army was safely through the gorge, with Yorsh and the others bringing up the rear. The dragon blocked the entrance to the gorge, protecting them from the cavalry. But for how long? The moment he moved, the cavalry would attack.

The ragged group was worn out. Some of them were starting to throw themselves wearily to the ground. No story could give them the strength to march on. The smaller children were whimpering with cold and hunger. Even Patch seemed unable to go on. Lightning had come to a standstill. Robi knew they were not safe for much longer. Soon, the cavalry would be upon them.

And just then, the dragon rose into the sky.

His wings opened. His magnificent green whirls stood out in the light of the moon.

He was magnificent.

MAGNIFICENT.

MAGNIFICENT.

MAGNIFICENT.

MAGNIFICENT.

He rose into the sky in a hail of arrows, and even in the faint light of the clear night sky, Robi could make out the red trails of blood running from the wounds that had opened up one after the other on the soft scales of his chest. As in a dream, Robi heard Yorsh's long "Noooooooooooooooooooo" fading away in the darkness like a useless supplication. One last huge flame filled the sky, lighting it brightly. A wave of deadly fire washed over the oaks, and although they were wet, they began to burn. The charred roots crumbled and lost their grip on the masses of granite, which began to slip down, dragged by the mud and the remains of the still blazing trunks. The dragon struck with all his might against the last rocks supporting the whole side of the hill, but he had to stay in the air to do so, his chest facing his assailants, and he was pierced by more arrows, and yet more, and yet more.

A huge flood of earth, stones, and fire formed. It plunged into the gorge with a terrifying roar and blocked it up. There were rocks and mud, and more rocks and mud, and then some more rocks and mud, and broken trees. The whole side of the mountain had fallen in, closing up the gorge of Arstrid for good.

The dragon's wings beat one last time, and then Erbrow fell and disappeared forever on the other side of the impassable wall of earth, stones, mud, and broken trees that now protected them.

Robi closed her eyes. Everything turned blue, and there they stood, outlined against the glittering sea.

How had she failed to notice before? There was no green anywhere.

The dragon had never been part of her vision.

They would all be saved because the dragon had died for them.

She had known the dragon for half a day. She had exchanged a few peevish words with him, but without him, their dream of freedom would have been mere lunacy.

For two years the image of the big green wings had brought her consolation in her despair.

Robi burst into tears, which melted together with Yorsh's lament.

CHAPTER THIRTY-FIVE

THE WORLD was flooded with light. A cool wind had come to freshen him up.

His headache was gone: Erbrow could fly again.

He could finally get going. A good vertical flight, with his back to the archers.

No point in waiting. Sooner or later, the entire ragged group of them would be slaughtered. Better sooner rather than later. It's irritating to wait; deferred executions are an act of cruelty.

He, who was a dragon, would reach the library, where, being a dragon, he would live for a few centuries, flying over the sea and gobbling down dolphins and gulls. When the moment came to brood, he, who was a dragon, would withdraw into his splendid library where golden beans, pink grapefruit, and an inexhaustible supply of storybooks would cheer him up until the birth of his descendant, who, being a dragon as well, would gobble down dolphins and gulls for centuries, and so on.

Because he was a dragon, and they were just a crowd of stinking wretches.

But to fly away with his back toward the archers, he would have to fly over Yorsh, Robi, and the others, and look at them for one last time as he abandoned them. Nonetheless, loneliness had always been a dragon's fate, and betrayal had always been a bearable necessity for his race. He who is a DRAGON owes fidelity to no one.

Erbrow remembered that no one would look after his baby.

No one would teach it to fly.

His child would be desperate and alone. Perhaps it would die in a fire that it had started itself with a sneeze or a whimper, or because it had got itself caught up in its own tail.

He recalled Yorsh teaching him to fly.

He couldn't do it. He could never go, leaving them on their own to face the cavalry. In his head, across his various memories, the disapproval of his ancestors echoed, because he, a dragon, dared to think of risking his life for such ordinary creatures, a crowd of stinking wretches.

He was a dragon. The last dragon. The lord of creation. And a dragon fights for nothing but himself, because there can be nothing in existence with a value equal to his. He had to go. He had to abandon them and save himself.

If he went now, he would go on living—a very long life in total solitude. A little dragon would be born and it, too, would live in solitude, allowing that it somehow managed to survive its own desolate, empty childhood. Even bleaker than being a phoenix.

He considered that there were no more dragons because loneliness had killed them off. He realized that you can't live century after century nurturing your own magnificence and your own loneliness.

He reflected that what is important is not things, but the meaning we give to things. Sooner or later death comes for everyone. More important than putting off death, is giving it a meaning.

In the darkness, beneath the moon, Yorsh's sword and Robi's crown glittered with a silvery light. Erbrow knew then that his legend would be passed down. For centuries and centuries the bards would sing of the last dragon, the one who had brought a great Elfish warrior and a little ragged queen toward their destiny—as founders of a place where people could be free.

The great dragon rose up into the sky, and his flight brought salvation, a great fall of mud that closed off the gorge with a vast, impassable wall. But in doing so, he bared his belly, his vulnerable part, where the arrows didn't bounce off like peas, but stuck deep in his flesh, while great floods of vivid blood stained the green of his scales. The dragon flew with his great wings spread in the moonlight, then there were too many arrows, and there was no blood left.

Erbrow, the last dragon, fell to the ground and spent his last moments there, in the muddy grass.

Right until the end he dreamed of not dying, of being able to live a little longer, even with his chest pierced with arrows and the mud around him drenched with his blood.

Then his mind was filled with a dream—the first dream he had ever dreamed in his life. He saw himself as a baby, a recently born puppy, with his head resting in the lap of his Elfish brother in an endless meadow of daisies.

He opened his eyes for the last time. A miracle—he was surrounded by thousands of tiny flowers, bright in the moonlight, beneath the feet of the soldiers who were cautiously approaching. Erbrow looked at the petals and felt happiness filling him, then he closed his eyes again, this time forever.

CHAPTER THIRTY-SIX

DAWN ROSE, cold, foggy, and pale. Yorsh shivered. It wasn't just the wound, the exhaustion, and the cold, which he no longer had enough energy to withstand.

Losing Erbrow weighed upon him like a boulder.

The dragon had been his family, his brother. Everyone he loved or who loved him seemed destined to die.

Everyone but Robi.

Robi was alive. He had to keep his thoughts fixed on Robi—on her breath, on her smile—and then the pall lifted enough to let him breathe.

After the massive landslide, the refugees had collapsed

in a heap, piled on top of one another to keep warm, amid the remains of the shacks of Arstrid. They had lit some fires to dispel the cold.

For Yorsh, the night had been a ceaseless drip of disappointment. He was constantly hoping to hear the flap of wings, to see the flames. It had to be a fiction, a trick, a kind of joke. It could only be a fiction, a trick, a kind of joke. Perhaps they had injured Erbrow, and captured him. They would take him in chains to Daligar and keep him prisoner. He, Yorsh, would go with his sword and free him; he would face off the whole garrison and then they would flee together, Erbrow with his big wings open and Yorsh on top.

And yet, at the same time, he knew. One part of him went on telling himself fairy stories, and the other part knew. Yorsh's mind had been capable of perceiving Erbrow's mind, just as his eyes could see him and his nostrils smell him. Yorsh knew that Erbrow was dead. Where the dragon's perception had been, there was now a black hole of frozen nonexistence. Yorsh knew that he was now in a world where dragons no longer existed, where Erbrow no longer lived.

Then a sudden realization froze him like a bucket of river water. He had a habit of thinking of the dragon as a kind of big brother, with a complicated play of multiple and hereditary memories that allowed him to speak in the first person about events that had happened years or centuries before. This habit had made him forget that Erbrow had actually lived for less than two months. He had been like a meteor. Yorsh remembered that in the ancient Elfish tongue Erbrow meant "comet."

Robi had sobbed for a long time. She too, like her mother when she was in despair, let liquid flow from her eyes. Her nose was filled with snot, her eyes were red, and her eyelids were swollen the way they are when you haven't slept for two days. On the one hand, Yorsh still found it extremely eccentric, unhygienic, and uncomfortable, while on the other, he wished with all his heart that he could have cried as well.

As though all that were not enough, there was also the horror of having to kill.

When dawn had lit the world, the problem of food had made its reappearance. Everyone was hungry. Everything that they had brought with them—the remains of the banquet in the clearing at the House of Orphans—had been finished some time ago. Arstrid's orchards and vines had been felled or burned. Nothing was left but trout. At that point, the Dogon was swarming with fish. Their silvery scales flashed in the water, and Yorsh had a bow with an Elfish arrow. No one had ever dared ask him, but at a certain point, he had found the hunger of all those poor people, especially the children, impossible to bear. Life and death are joined together, Erbrow had said.

The death of some was joined to the life of the others. Yorsh would never hear him say it again. Never again. Never again would he hear him snoring. Never again would he see him breathing. Never again. Whatever he did, the two words echoed inside him. Never again.

Yorsh put the arrow to the string of his bow and took aim. Never again would he hear his voice. As an elf, his aim was infallible because he aimed with the eyes of his mind, but each time, he was torn by the desire to miss, lest he feel the pain of the dying fish. He fired. Never again would he see Erbrow's wings in the sky. Yorsh saw the arrow hit the trout, and felt within him the trout's desolation over its own death. The same thing would happen another fifty times before the day was finished. He had to feed ninety-nine people, and one trout was enough for one adult or two children or three babies. The woodcutter threw himself into the water to recover the trout. He and one of the two farmers were the only ones who knew how to swim, and they had to take turns at the task of wading into the freezing water to recover the prey and the only arrow they had at their disposal.

Never again. Never again. Never again.

Yorsh started again. He caught another few trout, and after they had eaten, the river of people resumed its march. Walking, fishing, and resting in turn, they would reach the waterfall. Yorsh remembered when he had flown over it on Erbrow's back. Never again. Once more he wished he could cry.

They walked, they fished, somebody managed to find some berries. Before sunset, they set up camp. The woodcutter cut big branches of fir and pine, with which he formed a rough-and-ready shack. On four wood fires, trout lay roasting. They advanced day after day, with a curious sense that time and their lives were somehow suspended, in waiting.

Yorsh thought again of the first time he had traveled this way. He had been in a boat, lying on his back, with two marvelous people who had struggled not to eat their smoked trout in front of him. This time the journey was longer, rockier, and more tiring.

But they had to go on. Autumn had drawn to a close. Any day the first snow would come, and things would get much harder.

Sometimes the road was easy, and they could walk along the shores lined with little beaches, and other times they had to clamber over steep, slimy rocks, slipping in the moss or, if the banks were impassable, make lengthy detours through the woods, taking care never to stray far from the water lest they lose their bearings and stray from the path.

Suddenly, the waterfall appeared ahead of them. Not all that suddenly, in fact; its presence had been heralded by the roar of the cascading water, but the sight of it was dizzying. The water thundered down from an enormous height, making rainbows where the light fell on it. The sea lay down below. The horizon touched the sky in a long line interrupted by nothing but a tiny island on which a wild cherry was losing its last leaves. Among the rocks on their right, starting from a tiny beach that could be reached only from the tumultuous waters of the river, there rose the narrow flight of stairs to the very high rock upon which were inscribed the words HIC SUNT DRACOS. Part of these stairs had collapsed beyond repair, and the inscription was now a lie. Isolated from everything and everyone on the now inaccessible peak, the library guarded its useless treasures.

By focusing his attention on Robi, Yorsh kept his anguish at bay.

HIC SUNT DRACOS. Here be dragons.

Never again, to the end of time.

But Robi existed, the elf reminded himself. Robi was in the world, and so were the others. He knew them all now. All of them, one by one. It was a curious sensation after the life he had lived in solitude.

Robi existed and she was with him. He had to go on thinking that.

"How do we get past it?" asked Falco, astounded at this magnificent and steep waterfall.

"I don't know," Yorsh replied.

"We'll never do it!" Fowlpest added uneasily.

"Of course we'll do it," Robi serenely reassured him. "We can't not do it. The inhabitants of Arstrid have already passed this way. It must be possible!"

Yorsh felt braver. Erbrow mightn't have died in vain. They would do it. He just had to think a bit harder. He looked about him. The sea was blue. Around them, the last leaves were brilliant red and gold on the nearly bare branches of the trees, while the peaks of the Dark Mountains were white with snow. There must be a way.

Nothing came to mind.

* * *

"Well, it's not difficult. You've just got to dig!" muttered a voice. Two voices.

The two miners from Daligar county had christened themselves the Courteous Hoemen, after some characters from a curious and heroic story invented by Yorsh. After lives spent considering themselves as little more than beasts of burden, they had felt filled with a new light of dignity and importance. For the first time in lives spent muttering to each other, they dared to speak out loud, to say something in public. The two Courteous Hoemen had climbed onto the southern part of the ravine and discovered there wasn't just rock, there was earth as well. Using branches as props, they could dig a path, against the rock, beneath the waterfall. They needed a team of people to pass the dug earth from hand to hand, a few men to take over when their arms were tired, and some straight pieces of wood to support the excavation.

If everyone lent a hand, they could do it.

CHAPTER THIRTY-SEVEN

HALF A DAY wasn't enough. It took them three whole days. In the end, there wasn't a person left who didn't look like a statue of mud. They had carved their way first through earth, then through rock, using pointed stones in place of the picks they didn't possess. Their arms were so tired, it seemed impossible that they would ever not be.

It was a slow, strenuous, and magnificent descent. The sea opened up before them, the waterfall roared beside them with a mist of iridescent spray. The air smelled of salt and myrtle and the wild fennel that grew stubbornly in the cracks in the inhospitable rocks beaten by the wind, along with tiny wild orchids. As they climbed down, they had their first glimpse of the little freshwater lake formed at the bottom of the waterfall, among the maritime pines, before the long white beach that lined the bay beneath them. On one side, the bay continued on into a flat coastline, while on the other, it was sheltered and closed by a rough, green promontory, on which tiny lights would soon twinkle at night—the new houses of Arstrid!

Yorsh no longer had the strength or the ideas to go on telling stories, but the traveling players brought out their instruments, and the music gave those who were working the strength to go on. They clenched their teeth and kept at it. Hour after hour, span after span, they dug their path.

As they dug, they noticed pieces of burned rope dangling from the rocks and the lower branches of the big chestnut trees that jutted out toward the horizon. The former inhabitants of Arstrid must have gotten down by a system of rope ladders, which they had burned behind them after reaching safety.

Yorsh's wound had begun to close but hadn't fully healed, so he wasn't one of those clinging to the side of the mountain opening up the path. Instead, he stayed at the top, along with the older women, the smaller children, and the ones who were resting once their labors were over. When the Courteous Hoemen found a rock so hard that it was indestructible and impossible to move, they sent Cala to come and get him. Yorsh arrived and tried to come up with an idea. He remembered a book on mechanics in which he had read about levers, but there was no fulcrum here to move the rock. They might have split it in two with wedges, but there were no cracks to slip wedges into, and nothing to use as a wedge. A faint wind rose up, bringing with it the cries of gulls more clearly now. Exasperated by his weakness, Yorsh took out his sword and brought it down as hard as he could on the granite, which shattered beneath it. The blade was undamaged and even more brilliant than before, as though strengthened by the blow. Robi's serene smile spread further across her face, and everyone applauded.

Their descent was slow. One step at a time, all holding each other by the hand, like a single, long snake, to be sure that no one could fall.

When they reached the bottom, they were so exhausted and emotional that they stayed in silence for a long time, looking at the gentle motion of the waves as they flowed onto the beach. A few people knelt down and kissed the sand. Some of them went to touch the sea.

Yorsh had first smelled the scent of the sea while flying on Erbrow's back. It had been then that he had thought that touching the sea divides your life into before and after, because after you've done it, nothing is as it was before. Silence reigned for a long time. The children were the first to move. They swarmed onto the beach, fascinated by the motion of the waves. Yorsh, who had read six treatises on seashells, taught them to dig beneath the sand for edible creatures, and they began to collect them, noisily and cheerfully

Robi had also squatted down on the shore, plunging

her hands into the soft, damp sand that came away easily, revealing the smooth and elongated shells of the big pale-pink bivalves between her fingers.

"My father used to say that what's inside the shells is good to eat, even if it thinks and possibly even understands poetry," she said with a laugh, her big eyes gleaming like stars. Yorsh told himself that sooner or later he would have to tell her how the joke had first arisen.

They set up camp in the pine grove near the little lake beside the waterfall. It was a good spot, and there was plenty of water. The sound of the waterfall mingled with the sound of the waves like a voice singing a lullaby.

A sheer wall of pale rock hung over a clearing.

Yorsh took his sword and carved ERBROW into the wall, first in Elfish characters, and then in the current Runic ones. A small crowd of people watched him in fascination. Some of them came close enough to touch the letters with their fingers. They asked what it meant and Yorsh explained.

"Fine," said the woodcutter. "That was the name of the dragon, wasn't it? And it will be the name of our country. We will call it Erbrow."

Then one of the former "customs officials of the county of Daligar" said, "Then write: 'That which a person works from the land is his own, and no one can take it from him.'"

Yorsh wrote in clear and careful characters, not changing a syllable, because if you have fought for the chance to speak, you have the right for what you say to be left unchanged.

After he had finished, he added everything the others dictated to him:

> IF A PERSON DOESN'T LIKE IT, HE CAN LEAVE,
>   AND IF HE COMES BACK LATER, THAT'S ALL
>   RIGHT, TOO.
> NO ONE CAN HIT ANYBODY.
> THE HOE THAT YOU HAVE ALWAYS WORKED
>   WITH, WHICH BELONGED TO YOUR FATHER
>   BEFORE, BELONGS TO YOU.
> AND YOU CAN'T HANG PEOPLE, EITHER.
> YOU CAN TRY TO READ.
> AND WRITE.
> ALL THAT YOU TAKE FROM THE SEA IS YOURS,
>   AND YOU DON'T HAVE TO PAY ANYBODY
>   FOR IT.
> IF A FATHER AND A MOTHER DIE, THEIR BEST
>   FRIENDS BECOME THE FATHER AND MOTHER
>   OF THEIR CHILDREN.
> NO LITTLE CHILD MUST WORK.

There was a long silence.

"Everyone can try to be happy as best he can," a woman said.

Fowlpest's voice added: "It isn't forbidden to be an elf."

Yorsh wrote that down too. Robi and Cala had a long whispered tête-à-tête, punctuated by odd little giggles. Then Cala, blushing to the roots of her hair, with Robi hiding behind her, announced the final law: "A person can marry whoever he likes, whoever he really likes, even if the other person is a bit different, and no one can say anything."

When he had finished, Yorsh read the list, and everyone approved.

Then they all dispersed to sort out their first night in Erbrow, a country of free men, women, and children.

Cala and Falco stayed and looked at one another.

"Robi said someone would come and get me, and take me away from the House of Orphans," Cala said.

"An elf and a dragon came," Falco reminded her.

"Yes, I know, but they came for everyone. I thought someone would come just for me. It isn't the same thing."

Falco sat down on the sand. "I dreamed that for years, too. I dreamed that someone would come specially to get me from the House of Orphans. I still dream of it, really, even now that we're out of there."

Cala said nothing, then Falco went on: "So let's do it this way: I took you, and you took me, so we each have someone who came specially to get us."

Cala nodded and then she too sat down in the sand, close to him.

The sun set over the sea. A strip of pink and gold lit the horizon and the sky filled with light, while in the east, in the first darkness, the first stars shone. A gull flew toward them.

Robi and Yorsh walked toward the water, where the waves were beating.

"You know," Robi began, "my name—"

Yorsh interrupted her. "Your name is lovely, I really like it."

"You like Robi?"

"Yes, it's like the sound of a droplet falling, a stone skimming on water. It's a beautiful name."

Robi remained dubious and thoughtful, with the hint of a smile on her face. "And the prophecy?" she asked again. "Your destiny? The girl with the light of morning in her name?"

Yorsh shrugged and looked at her. He blushed fiercely and gave a vague wave of his hand.

"Our destiny is what we want it to be, not what has been carved in stone. It's our life, not someone else's dream."

Robi nodded. She bent over the water and put her little boat with the doll in it and watched it gently bobbing about. Those were the toys her parents had made for her, they were all that remained of them, apart from a slingshot, her name, and herself.

"My children will play with them," she said with great certainty. She knew. She had seen.

She wondered if she should tell Yorsh about her name, about the prophecy.

Again, a smile spread across her face.

They had their whole lives for that.